To Fawnia

A beautiful vivacious spirit who is simultaneously captivating and spellbound.

A dreamer, a muse, one who strolls in the fantastical and ventures beyond in the mind.

Lovely, creative, an inspiring mother and precious friend.

This one's for you...

Chapter One

The dim intermittent headlights barely cast a yellow hue into the cloudy dusk enough for anything to be seen but for a centimeter or two in front of them. The raindrops were thick and heavy, pushing against the windscreen of the rented car with the stoic older driver behind the wheel.

Glancing at him with an intentionally shallow breath, she wished she had put on a coat but didn't want to bring attention to herself and break the uncomfortable atmosphere between them by moving too much.

Whilst it had been a hot September, some of the evenings had been cooler of late and she shivered discretely with her hands firmly in the lap of her long red cotton dress.

The driver had barely spoken a word to her and had originated in the city where their meeting had been previously arranged.

He was in his sixties and held the deep etchings of sternness in his expression, a humorless man who had little interest in small talk or even hearty conversation. Whilst she often preferred solitude over the stimulation of gatherings, this was a long drive to be had with one who disliked conversation all together.

"Is this the village you spoke of?" she asked hesitatingly as she glanced at the long endless wooden fences that bordered the large farms and estates around them.

"It is the Hamlet of Wanderling," he confirmed neutrally.

He turned the steering wheel slightly so they ventured left, away from the main road of shops further up and approaching a low hill.

"Claremonde Hall is where you'll be received," he added. "We are near so best you be ready for it."

Not really knowing what to expect, her new employer had not detailed the house so much and had been vague in many respects. But when the driver said the name, it sounded official, like a landmark, a place that people would reference.

He hadn't explained in his letter that it would be a country estate house and yet by his tone, she got the definite impression that he lived alone, not in shared quarters whatsoever.

That is what drew her to the position. She liked to write and ponder and stroll and from what little he had detailed to her, this place would offer her the opportunity to be alone. Here she could distance herself from the harried increase of vehicles and advancements in the over stimulation of modern devices.

Mostly this was her opportunity to start afresh. But she was frightened. A new beginning could bring the clear taste of horizon whilst it could give one pause as to whether a wise decision had been made.

This was a risk and she was willing to take it but she was not sure how it would turn out. She wanted to embrace it, even if the consequences would be hers alone.

The daylight was nearly completely gone now and while it was early evening, it had been a long journey, nearly three hours and she wanted to rest.

So many possibilities had been swirling around in her mind but none had prepared her for this first turn. At the beginning of a long dirt road they looked up at a stone archway with the words, Claremonde Hall, across it.

It was an ancient engraving on centuries old stone. And the road ahead was not a drive for a cottage or a townhouse; it was a mysterious winding road through a tunnel of overhanging trees.

The rain was lessened by the shelter of the foliage and yet she couldn't see it at first, it was extremely dark on the road itself. It was only when they finally came out into a large clearing that the imposing building greeted them.

It was unlike any she had ever seen.

Perhaps a hundred or more rooms, wide and with at least three stories, large columns and side turrets of medieval era stone. But what was most striking and ominous was not the vastness of the estate, but the darkness of it.

There were no lights, just a pitch black icy cold picture of abandonment, the rain pelting down into the opened structure.

It was a ruin, at least a third of it burned and destroyed, charred and broken like an amputee statue, magnificent and startlingly sorrowful.

"My gosh," she said aloud in spite of herself. "What happened here?"

He paused there, stopping the car so she could see it, and perhaps he, even in his consistent state of detachment, was in awe of it. It was beautiful, strikingly imposing and covered in vines, grown over it in time.

"The fire," he stated simply. "It's rightly under his ownership but the master of the house said it's not his dwelling now."

As they drove by very slow, quietly in respect of an ancient grave, she wondered why it would be. Who had lived there and how many and why should they not have remained in the rest of the house that looked perfectly usable?

He was a driver, likely from the city where he met her so he wouldn't have been able to enlighten her, she could tell this was his first time being there. But it was a mysterious unsettling sight, and she felt watched, as if the grand structure had shadows that lurked about, gazing upon them curiously.

It was a foolish notion and she shook her head for the idea of it, and then looked at the back seat to check on her travel bags.

Her entire life had been packed inside of those bags; she left nothing behind. She knew that even if it didn't work out here, she would never look back, never return. It had robbed her of so much hope and spirit that she would rather be alone in a room the size of a box than in that house again.

Driving around the side of the commanding mansion, the wind picked up and there were three more roads, small and narrow, they led to various untold destinations. One she could see as they drew closer was a carriage house to the right where horses would have been kept, but she suspected none were there now.

The left road was darker, she couldn't tell what was down that way but the road in front of them finally had it so the car lights illuminated a large house.

It was likely the servant's quarters or a guest house once but it was quite large considering.

It too was old, perhaps fourteenth century, bricked with many windows, two storeys and perhaps thirty or so rooms of its own. Though she could not see it in great detail, she could make out large bay windows at each side of the double front door and it was not without ornamentation, a grand structure in its own right.

It also had a large paved clearing and this is where the car was readying itself to end its journey. Glancing back, she could see this servant's house faced the back of the stately country manor.

Unlike the mansion, it had no particular name but it did have lights on inside of the rooms and looked well kept and neatly maintained with large rose bushes and gardens around. Somewhere inside was her mysterious employer. He had contacted the agency that had gotten her, and many other women, work in clerical or nursing duties; in her case, both.

His name was given simply as, McKinley, but no Christian name or title other than that. All she knew was that he was a man of good means; he was seeking a childless amiable woman to help with light nursing care and secretarial responsibilities.

And he had paid handsomely for her to get there. Near three hours in a rented car could not have been a small sum.

Once the car came to a stop, she stretched out all of the aches in her lower back and the wind outside pushed against the door as she tried to open it.

It wasn't horribly cold but it was damp and inhospitable and the moon was barely making an appearance behind the rapidly moving rain clouds.

Shutting the door and waiting for the driver to open the back door for her, she remembered the promise she made. She said to herself that 1931 was going to be different, that it would be the beginning of something good rather than another ending or another non-occurrence.

She had no responsibility to this man or this place or to anything or anyone she came from. She was free and had a little income saved so that should she need to start again, she would. But she would see, she would give it some time and let it happen slowly before she made any definite decisions.

Reaching for her four over-filled suitcases, she made sure she went into this house consciously. It intrigued her immediately; the history, the beauty and the possible serenity at her disposal.

The driver offered to take her cases to the doorstep, which was wide and fortunately covered a little by a bricked overhang with a hanging lantern at its center. The doors had thick misted glass and black medieval style hinges. She knew inside would be impressive. It must have been the hub of activity once with maids and stable hands and cooks passing each other during long days.

"This is the key," the man said to her as he put it in her hand and left the suitcases close to the doors. He then reached into his pocket and took out a folded envelope with a letter inside. "He said for you to read this once you've gotten in."

It was a curious arrangement and she was a little frightened by it. It was all very cloak and dagger and the driver's lack of warmth didn't help things at all. Tipping his black cap at her, he straightened his black suit jacket as he approached the vehicle, quickly stretching his arms up and then his back before getting back into the car.

Quickly fumbling with the one key with a small red knotted twine attached to it, she immediately felt that this was the prior attendant's key. She only knew that it had been an older woman who had been with the family a long time and was not physically able to do the work any longer.

Glancing over her shoulder at the car which was already eagerly making its way down the road towards the pitch black mansion and then to the winding road, she put the skeleton key into the lock and turned it.

It immediately worked, much to her relief, but then came a quick flooding of insecurity and worry about what she would face inside. He said he lived alone, but with such a huge estate, she wondered who else might live there as far as workers.

Straightening her back and lifting her head as she had been taught, she got two of her smaller cases under her arms and held the handles of the other two as she quietly and gently pushed her way into the hall.

The floors were hardwood, the hall was long and narrow and one electrical sconce was lit on the wall. The hallway was longer than any she had seen and while she was sincerely glad that no one was there to greet her, she was also concerned about getting lost.

Closing the door behind her and promptly locking it, as was her habit in any residence she had been in, she quickly consulted the letter.

The envelope was sealed shut so she had to rip the top of it and take it out. It was hand written, somewhat shakily, but it was legible.

Miss Belmont,

I welcome you to my home and hope you are not anxious upon your arrival. I retire early due to my health and apologize for my poor etiquette not having greeted you.

There are 36 rooms in these quarters. I am certain you have observed Claremonde Hall and I understand you have not originated from this area so perhaps you will have questions.

In all due time.

For now your journey has been a long one so I ask that you begin your day tomorrow, early at 5:00am when it is my preferred time for breakfast. In the kitchen area you will find a list of tasks that I hope you will not find too daunting.

The kitchen is the second room on the left of the hall after you enter. My room is the last room on the left. Your room is opposite mine in the event I should call upon you with my bell. Infrequently I may require your assistance.

I have two housemaids, a driver, two gardeners, a groundskeeper and a steward. They reside in the adjoining rooms that are separated by a wall beyond this hall. You might sight them on occasion but I wished to explain to you that I am a man of solitude. I do not require them to wait on me hand and foot like they might have done with my predecessors.

My previous personal attendant, Miss Wilshire, will continue to visit. I do hope you find her affable and informative, though she has a tendency to fill the air with expression and hearsay but is a delight nonetheless.

Consider your room your own; there is an en suite for you also so that you should not need to leave your room in the night. Your prior overseer, Mrs. Marsh, had informed me that you do not possess great social interests. She has said that she outlined my few rules including no personal visitors, although you will be given ample free time to roam and visit the village.

The key that you possess will also lock your bedroom door.

Slumber well and until we meet tomorrow,

Mr. Noble McKinley.

Wanting to get out of the dark hall and away from the unsettling sensation of self consciousness, she lifted all of her suitcases and tread as quietly as possible. Unfortunately the creaky floor was not at all kind, but the sound of the wind and rain outside at least muffled some of her footsteps and broke the tension of tremendous silence.

She passed various doors that were closed and noticed the entrance to the kitchen but could not see well enough to capture any details. It felt like a long walk and her life suddenly seemed distinctly unsecured.

Not realizing how long the hallway was, she did see that there were no paintings or transom windows, the walls were unfinished stone, old and unadorned.

Slowing down, concerned she might drop her suitcases; she held her breath and listened as she drew closer to his bedroom door. His letter said his room was on the left. The door was closed and no light shone from beneath it but she could hear sniffing, perhaps a dog but it was hard to tell.

It was all very strange, knowing a complete stranger lay there beyond that door and she, an utter unknown to him, should be entering his home this evening. Her door was open, the one he said was opposite his and she leaned forward and peered into the darkness, hoping she was not about to walk in on an unsuspecting servant.

"Hello?" she called out in a whisper.

Listening, she did not sense anyone was in there but it was still disconcerting. Getting all four of her cases in, she then felt around along the wall until finally she found a pull chain on a wall sconce and tugged on it, bringing light into the room.

It was much larger than she had anticipated and someone had gone to the trouble to wire the light so the hanging lamp at the ceiling came to life at the same time as the sconce.

The first thing she noticed was that one of the bay windows was in her bedroom and that the curtains were open. Although it was unlikely anyone was standing outside at this time, especially in the rain as it was, she knew well enough that anyone could see in at her so she walked directly across and drew the thick damask blue curtains closed.

Then in haste, she tip toed back to her cases and nudged them aside with a shiver as she closed the door and fumbled for the key so she could lock it.

It was a thick sturdy old door and she imagined the servants of yesteryear likely never gave it much thought. They were known to have worked often times over fourteen hours a day, not leaving much but to sleep and toil.

Wanting to explore and yearning to sleep, she allowed herself a brief investigation but then she too wished to retire early.

While exhausted, she didn't trust she would sleep too well. Claremonde Hall seemed to be overshadowing this grand house and the mysterious Mr. McKinley seemed kind in the letter but he could just as easily turn out to be a tyrant or a bore or both.

There was no knowing, and her mind might go in all directions contemplating it at some point deeper into the dark night.

But for now the fatigue was holding her captive and hunger was just as insistent. Reaching for her smallest bag, a small brown one she had gotten at a charity shop, she unlatched the front and opened it up. A great many long cotton dresses had been pressed tightly into it, making the most of the small space, but there on top was her sandwich.

Unwrapping the brown paper, she took it out, it was squished but it was the best strawberry jam and butter sandwich she had ever eaten because she was so hungry for it.

Taking another bite and quickly opening a larger case, she reached for a thick coat and put it over her shoulders. There was a fireplace in the room but she was not sure if there was any way to light it, not seeing matches nearby.

Whilst chewing, she surveyed the room and noticed that the beige walls had no pictures on them. A Victorian dresser, ornate and with a curved mirror, had one crocheted doily, a slender blue and gold vase that went with the curtains, and a small picture frame.

There was no picture in it, leaving her to wonder if the prior occupant, Mrs. Wilshire, had left it there for her on purpose.

Other than that, the bed covers were cream colored, as were the pillow cases. There was a thick muted floral rug beside the bed and a small bedside table with drawers.

It was a substantially large room, perhaps it had once been two rooms or it was simply that maybe five or six had slept in centuries ago. But one thing it was not was warm. It was not warm in temperature and definitely not in décor'. It was bereft of personal touches, color and femininity.

Just the same, the double sized brass bed, its headboard pressed against the left wall, looked genuinely comfortable and it was a generous room to have to herself, clearly without too much hindrance of noise from neighboring occupants.

Wiping the crumbs from her hands, she was relieved to notice a decanter of water on the bedside table, as well as an upturned glass. But she wanted to look further into what was behind the other door, the one along the wall opposite the bed.

It was a narrow beige door, painted to match the neutral wall color and her new employer had mentioned in the letter that there was an en suite.

She had shared a bathroom with two other women once in a group home, but never one to herself.

Such luxury seemed well beyond the means of anyone she knew.

But perhaps this grand building had much to spare its few occupants. And this only deepened the mystery of the head of the house, Noble McKinley. *Noble.* What an unusual and yet brilliant name.

He could be many things and yet she had a picture of a weak unassuming perhaps broken man. He would have wrinkles and thick eyebrows and look like a librarian and speak like a solicitor.

Opening the door inward, she reconsidered her evaluation. It didn't matter how he appeared, he wrote eloquently and was hospitable in his language. She would not dismiss him so easily without first offering him ample opportunity to make a good impression.

It was she who had to make the effort to bond, he had taken her into his home, and she would repay him with hard work and kindness.

Not being able to find the light straight away, she could see enough that there was an old cast iron bath with a shower head as well. A deep sink against the wall was beside a solitary toilet.

Making use of it after such a long trip, she quickly found her nightgown and long socks and got into them while intermittently drinking some of the water on the bedside. This place had some true history, dripping of regality and it must have been astonishingly beautiful once. But this room had a hospice like atmosphere and she hoped this did not reflect the personality of her overseer.

Returning to the bay window, she peeked out from the side of the right curtain and there was a hint of moonlight casting its halo over the ruins of Claremonde.

She wanted to know more, it was beckoning her to ask the questions. What happened here? What happened to everyone who once lived here and why was this man not living in the other part of the mansion?

There might have been a simple explanation but staring up at one of the high windows; dark with no one inside, Genevieve Belmont experienced a strong sensation of awe.

There were discoveries to be made and not only would she learn all there was to know about Noble McKinley and Claremonde Hall and its ruins, but soon she would become part of its story.

Chapter Two

The loud ringing of the alarm clock echoed out into the bathroom, but it was too late to be effective as she was already fully awake and washing off with a cloth she had in a sink full of hot water.

Wiping her hands off on a bath towel that she had brought with her, she quickly slid the mechanism across on the top of the rounded clock and sighed.

She had set it for half past four and the sun was beginning to rise although she suspected the estate house in front of them was blocking some of it at this point. It was a cool morning but yesterday's rain had given into a cloudless late spring day and she felt if she was given the chance she would greatly enjoy a stroll outside later.

Shivering a little, she pressed her bare feet into the small thick rug on the floor in front of the deep sink affixed to the wall, and listened as the floor creaked out in the hall. He must have been an early riser like herself so she now knew it was best to set her alarm earlier so she had ample time to prepare breakfast before he entered the kitchen.

Quickly rummaging through her suitcases she found her perfume and squeezed the atomizer, ensuring that a nice floral fragrance would waft from her clothes on occasion. She rushed it over to the small back edge of the sink where it just fit and offered the small area a little pink hue.

Then with equal haste she sifted through her dresses and chose a demure gray slightly silky dress that crossed over the bodice, tied at the waist and had some light flare which flattered the curves of her waist and hips and bust. She kept her figure in check and ensured not too eat too much in the evenings, especially now she was nearly forty two, the body was less cooperative as time went on.

Thankfully she had packed a handheld mirror, a white one with cherubs in the handle, and she looked in it, reviewing her face as she applied some pink lipstick and rouge, she was pleased her face was still pretty even if it did show some wear from time. Her big blue eyes still shone and she was still noticed on the rare occasion she ventured out.

But she did not seek to turn heads now; romance was the dream of the young and the quest of the foolish, she could not allow herself to chase another rainbow. She had matured and now she would simply strive for a good healthy life of tranquility and kind exchanges.

For now she was eager to get into the kitchen and hopefully have enough time to work out what to do and have things ready in time for the master of the house to enter. Her heart was pounding with the anxiety of meeting him and performing well.

Mrs. Wilshire had been with his family since his childhood. Genevieve had a lot to live up to and anyone without patience might quickly tire of an inexperienced attendant.

Lifting her chin and checking her medium length brown hair that she had partially pinned back and lightly waved at the bottom, she was ready.

Having made her bed and pushing the suitcases under it, the plain room appeared orderly and she went for the door, unlocking it and putting the key into a small pocket on the upper left of the dress.

It was not appropriate to wear a hat or gloves but she did feel underdressed considering this being her only opportunity at a first impression. Walking down towards the end of the long narrow hall, she noticed the front door she had entered in and it appeared a lot less threatening now. Sunlight that filtered in through two rooms that had partially opened doors, illuminated the floorboards and she could see the last door on her right, knowing that it was going to be the kitchen.

Entering the doorway, the sun was strong and she couldn't see at first so she held her hand up to shield her eyes and was shocked at how large the kitchen was. It had obviously catered a whole group of people cooking and preparing together at one time. More than likely they had all been slaving over the stove and using the wooden tables for creating large meals for the main hall.

The floor throughout was hardwood and there were a couple of beige rugs at convenient places like in front of the stove and the cast iron wash sink. Thinking it over as her eyes adjusted and she looked at the window which allowed a beautiful view of tall trees and vivid red and yellow flowers; she realized this kitchen had once been utilized by the servants for their own matters.

Whoever lived in this house, someone had to prepare their meals too.

The many workers of Claremonde would have had to find time to cook for themselves although they probably did not eat as good as their masters.

Walking over to the wash sink, which thankfully had large taps for both hot and cold water, she saw a note. It was written by the same shaky hand and told her what was needed for breakfast and gave brief descriptions for some other light duties.

From the right of the room, her ears picked up an unusual sound, there was a consistent low hum and she noticed a strange short white cabinet, metal perhaps, with a cylinder on top. It seemed to be the cause of the noise, and hesitant, but not fearing a trick, she reached for the silver metal handle and pulled it.

Looking in she now realized it was a cooling refrigerator. She had seen them in catalogues before and had heard that Mrs. Marsh had considered saving money for one, but they were still relatively new and quite costly for most incomes.

Having seen milk and ham on the list of breakfast items, she reached in for the glass bottle. While looking over at the wooden table that had eggs, butter and strawberry jam on it, she felt as if she was being watched and slowly turned her head to look at the doorway.

Straightening her stance with milk and ham in hand, she gazed upon the fluffy friendly faced dog, black, medium in size and with an endearing smile. He didn't bark or look at her curiously, instead he was watching her and she walked over to the note, confirming that the dog needed to be let out.

"Hello *Simon,*" she said, crouching down and beckoning him over.

Unlike many dogs she had spent time with over the years, he was not overly concerned by this unfamiliar face, instead he appeared to know that hands had been changed and more importantly he needed to go outside.

He had happy eyes and a touch of auburn in the hair around his face and was more than willing to approach her to sniff and explore this new resident.

Bringing his nose into her hand and then burying his face into her side, she pat him and was immediately smitten with this kind greeter. She had never had a dog of her own and was so glad to discover she would now be able to see one every day.

"We are friends already, Sir Simon," she whispered, pressing her cheek against the top of his head. "I will give you ham and we will talk about the world in quiet times. But for now let me get you outside for we do not wish to give your master something to slip in."

As if he knew that her standing was the same as declaring his next intention, he rushed out of the door and she followed him out of the kitchen and towards the front door. Unlocking it, she was glad that the morning air was already warm and the sun had gotten high enough that it shone on them.

Simon seemed to know where he was going, his fluffy tail wagging as he visited a great many nicely trimmed bushes before sniffing ardently at an apparently favored tree.

While he ran around, enjoying the sunshine and then laying on his back and rubbing it into the ground joyfully, she stared at Claremonde Hall. Again she couldn't help but feel someone was watching her but the shadows behind the windows were too dark.

No lights were on but it was quite conceivable that the surviving part of the house, at least two thirds of it, might still be at least somewhat occupied. It could just as well be that someone was actually watching her now, curious about the new arrival to their estate.

Having achieved all he set out to do, Simon rushed up to her as if they were old friends and she pat him and smiled at him. "I suppose you will be looking for food," she said as she walked back to the house and opened the door for him, locking it behind her.

The floorboards creaked again and she assumed that with her unique situation she simply noticed because of the tension of waiting.

Returning to the kitchen and approaching the large, almost wall sized stove, she could see that the meal request was simple and something she could accomplish.

Soon enough she had eggs and ham with peas and mashed potato on two plates with two sausages cooking in a frying pan on the stove top.

The toast was ready and he had left instructions to make food for herself with whatever she wanted, but his looked so good she made the same but less of it. The percolator was plugged in and the sound of it was comforting on the wooden table beside the stove.

The white china cabinet had beautiful ornate plates on display behind their glass doors but the gilded floral china plates melded into the background of the white walled room.

Looking down, she knelt to search the lower sections of the china cabinet while Simon came up to see what she might have in store for him.

"What specifically are you searching for?" a male voice asked from the doorway.

Not immediately turning to look at him, her heart pounded wildly and she was frustrated with herself for caring at all what he might be like. "It is not important," she replied neutrally. "I had wondered if perhaps there was some breakfast cocoa but I know that is not a common ingredient."

"For the eggs?" he asked, perhaps with a lilt of jest.

Standing, with her hand on Simon's head, she smiled. "For the coffee actually," she said, before she turned to look at him.

Her smile faded immediately and in spite of herself she was staring at him. He wore a cream, well fitted collared knit shirt and some high-waisted pants with a neat belt against his healthy physique.

His expression showed surprise too and perhaps she was not what he expected either. For the briefest moment, they were both completely taken off guard; all expectations no longer alluded to.

Taller than she expected, his brown hair was waved and his eyes blue, he was leaning against the doorway where Simon went to greet him and she did make note of a cane in his left hand but had to tend to the eggs before they were burned.

He didn't speak immediately, and she wondered why, and worried he may have taken her staring as an offense. He was perhaps in his late forties or early fifties but he did not have the air of a librarian or professor or someone crotchety or grouchy as she had presumed.

Turning off the stove, she then started to spread the butter onto the toast and put the eggs on the sturdy white plates.

"Mrs. Wilshire kept a myriad of items for her cooking so I would imagine she had breakfast cocoa somewhere, perhaps in that older ice box in the left corner," he suggested.

Nodding, she went over to it, which took a short time even with the expansiveness of the room.

Close to the entrance of the room was a large dining table, not luxurious as one that might have been in the hall itself, but rather a long eating table that was probably used by the servants, so it was quite old.

He walked over to it and pulled a chair out. "My disfigurement upsets you," he remarked somewhat sympathetically. "I should have forewarned you."

Speaking of the burn scars down the right side of his face and down his right arm, she had been surprised by it but it didn't rob him of his appeal. It looked like he had been burned quite terribly and his right eye did not open all the way but she would never have stared upon a man for that reason.

Wanting to console him, to reassure him, she also insisted on being gently honest because she believed that one was found to be the most convincing when speaking in sincerity.

Turning to look at him, having found the tin of cocoa, she held it in her hands and suppressed a shallow breath. "I see the scars but they were not what surprised me," she stated in earnest. "When I came here, having made a prior judgment in my imagination, I had assumed you would be a much older man and not as pleasing or as charming."

A smile crept on the left side of his face which seemed to have more movement. He could tell she was honest in her statement and she could see that he was overdue to hear some flattery. "And what do you make of me now, Miss Belmont? Does it disappoint you that I am not feeble and elderly?"

Smiling slightly, she felt immediately that she could be herself and as hesitant as she was, she could only suppose to permit her tricklings of wit and garner his reaction without completely silencing her inclinations. "I had prepared myself for dull conversation," she replied straightly. "But now I am uncertain on how to proceed."

Leaning forward a little, he was silent for a second and then let out a loud appreciative laugh. Simon began to rush to him and bark, perhaps not entirely used to him being so loud.

"Indeed!" he said as she finished up with the food preparations, getting all of his food on one plate with the toast on a side plate. "I understand your assumption, but I *will* say, Mrs. Wilshire was quite beyond my years and yet she kept me thoroughly entertained by her stories and she had a great many of them."

Unplugging the handled percolator, she brought it to him and put it on a plate on the table and then poured him a coffee. "Then perhaps you should be the one concerned about boredom," she stated dryly. "My tales are not likely comparable to hers."

Returning to the sink, she reached for a tray that was tucked away in a corner on a shelf near the stove. She put her plate on it and then brought her cup over to pour some coffee into it.

"Why the tray?" he asked as he picked up his fork.

"I was going to take it to my room to eat my breakfast," she said, worried she had assumed wrong by making her own food.

"Were you not intending to join me?"

Although it wasn't what was taught in her courses of hospitality, she was relieved that he had said it. "I was not certain of your preferences but I would be glad to, should you wish it."

"I *do* wish it," he said with a smile. "This will be your home now, Miss Belmont. One should relish comfort in one's own dwelling. Not just that, but I would like for you to tell me about the breakfast cocoa."

Reaching for the small white creamer, she poured some milk into her coffee, taking the darkness out of it. Using a butter knife to bring the lid up on the tinned cocoa, she scooped some into her coffee and gave it a thorough stirring.

"I lived in a small women's school for a number of years," she explained. "That is where you wrote to my overseer, Mrs. Marsh who taught us both nursing and clerical responsibilities. She was also as fond of anything sweet as I was. Together, by some happenstance, we discovered that this enlivened coffee all the more."

Smiling, he glanced at her hand, absent of a ring, pale and slender as it placed the teaspoon down on the side of her small toast plate.

"I should like to try it," he stated with some curiosity.

Sitting gracefully and mindful to maintain poise and also conscious of him being her employer, she nodded. "I am not certain you should simply attempt that without prior experience."

Laughing again, she heard Simon finish up his plate of cooled egg and ham and then nudge himself under the wooden sitting table to place himself between their feet. "I am willing to take the risk, Miss Belmont."

Scooping a slightly smaller amount of cocoa onto the spoon, she leaned over and put it into his coffee and stirred it."

"May I enquire on your Christian name?" he asked, somewhat hesitant in case the question seemed too personal on their first meeting.

She too was a curious creature and enjoyed learning the intricacies of people's histories and was more than happy to divulge her own. "Genevieve," she replied, sipping her sweet milky coffee.

Openly studying her face as if she was a painting that he was trying to decipher, he subtly nodded as he thought on it. "How does your family address you? Is there a special name they bestowed on you in your youth?"

Having received a few abbreviated names in her time, she did find it was not the easiest name to shorten. "I am not in communication with them," she replied neutrally. "Although when I was small my mother called me Eve."

The musings in his mind were apparent in his gaze but he did not yet insist on further information. "What is your first question?" he asked.

"My *first* question?" she countered, somewhat confused.

Smiling, he finished his mouthful of egg and bit into his toast and jam, as he nodded. "When one becomes acquainted with another, they can only learn about each other through a concession of questions."

Sensing a kindred spirit, surprised and yet refreshed by her good fortune, she was willing to chance a witty retort. "I would much sooner indulge conjecture and simply make your story up than actually ask you the truth."

Laughing a little louder, he began to cough and she quickly came around the side of the table, genuinely concerned. Simon hastily approached them while she placed her hand on his back and studied him, rubbing his back slightly, trying to move things around.

He placed his hand up as he sipped his coffee and sputtered a little more before another sip. "I am well, I am well, Genevieve, thank you."

Returning to her chair opposite him, Simon also returned to his place between them at their feet. "I am sorry that I inflict you with my wit, it can be dangerous."

Smiling, his eyes lit up, genuinely amused. "I have not endured a better infliction if it is such," he said, sipping his coffee before gesturing to her that he was enjoying the added cocoa. "I would like this again," he stated, giving his review of it.

Making a note of it in her mind, she nodded before asking her first question. "Why *Noble*?"

Raising his eyebrows, his unharmed side more so, it was clearly an enjoyable subject for him. "My mother, bless her and her reckless abandon, she was quite the muse," he began, recalling her fondly. "It took some coercion but she had convinced our father that we should be named after virtues. I, being the second son, was blessed with, Noble."

"And what of your siblings?" she asked curiously.

"My brother, twelve years my senior, was their first child and christened, Valor, while my younger sister was given, Prudence."

Truly grateful for their breakfast, she realized the sausages were the best she had ever eaten. But more than the good food and the sweet hound at her feet, she was genuinely fascinated by this man and his far away world.

"Do you like it?"

"The sausages?" she asked.

Laughing, he shook his head. "My name."

"Oh!" she said, laughing as well. "Yes, yes I do enjoy it," she admitted. "I must confess if it is not too forward, that I believe it to be the most perfect name I have ever heard. It suits you well."

His smile faded somewhat and he sipped his coffee pensively as if coming out of a dream. "Perhaps once," he noted staidly. "Now I am alike to dear Claremonde, both of us broken and unsalvageable."

Sincerely wanting to sway him out of his melancholy, she was saddened he would make such a low professing of himself. "Of all things, there is nothing that can not be revived," she assured him.

Staring out of the window at the large trees outside, he sighed. "Perhaps the hall can be," he said quietly.

"Perhaps both of you," she asserted.

Looking at her, there was genuine surprise in his eyes as if hope might threaten to possess him against his will. "Do you believe you can perform miracles, Genevieve Belmont?"

Smiling at him as she sipped her coffee and cocoa, she nodded. "If I can make such an impressive breakfast, then with some practice, I may be able to achieve miracles too."

Chapter Three

Already in her new world for a week and Genevieve had bonded with the country house, the land and most of all, Noble and his dog, Simon. Over the years she had lived in various places and involved in a myriad of occupations, but after having been taught by Mrs. Marsh at the women's school, her life had formed direction.

Her youth was not a place she returned to often in her mind and her memories were not worth the reliving, but mostly she had meandered like a lost gypsy, a kite without wind and a heart without a home.

She had felt old, sincerely and bitterly, as if her skin was like wrinkled paper hiding a sad little girl inside, one who had lost dreams but held a brilliant mind. Essentially she felt she had been wasted. With so much to offer, why had she not been led to a place to utilize her brilliances?

But now as she walked back with Simon loyally at her side, the sun on her shoulders as the ends of her long yellow dress flowed at her calves, she felt alive. It was as if she almost believed that she was not close to the end, but instead ready for a new chapter.

Strongly fearful of being swept up only to position herself for a great fall, it was too late for her. She smiled; she smiled often and with her heart and her eyes as well as her lips. She was useful and appreciated and it was liberating.

And Noble; he was a man whose name was particularly apt to his nature; she so enjoyed his curious and intelligent mind and conversation. His sentences were like music, his words rhythmic and educated yet affable and genial.

Glancing over her shoulder, she knew that she would go there soon, entering the great hall of Claremonde. But for now it was too overwhelming. While it was not ominous, at least not in the daytime, she still felt as though it harbored secrets that she was not meant to discover.

Noble had said that no one lived there now, but it felt alive as if it had a heartbeat or a memory that would not die out with the embers of the past.

Grateful that he was a man of routine, she had quickly learned his preferences and habits and she had already written two letters for him to his cousins. He was impressed by her use of the typewriter and her suggestions in the use of language. There was not much in the way of nursing needed other than the occasional request for her to reach for things or bend to retrieve items and tend to Simon, although sometimes he did, if the happy dog was not in a hurry.

The mystery of his youth was all around and it was as if she knew not to speak of it, and yet he was an open book and she enjoyed that about him. But now, as her and Simon returned to the large open bricked area that fronted the grand servant quarters, she stopped.

Two people stood in front of the large double doors, the ones that she did not use too much, preferring the main side door. Noble was dressed nicely in tan dress trousers and vest over his white button shirt.

He mostly wore knit tops because buttons were difficult for him although achievable. From here she could only see his unharmed side, the left side of his handsome face and his cane in his right hand almost out of view. He was quite striking and standing straight, every bit the gentleman that he was raised to be.

Across from him was a beautiful woman, perhaps his age, in her early fifties, but lovely in both presentation and stature. She wore a long purple gabardine skirt suit with a mink collar, light for the warmer temperatures. Her pale skin barely blemished by time, she was tall with long pale red hair, cascading down her shoulders in goddess like waves.

What ceased Genevieve's step most was the fact that this woman was holding Noble's hand and he was nodding a little, his expression pained, aggrieved. She wanted to console and soothe him, a deep seated sadness in his blue eyes. The woman looked upon him tenderly and was speaking to him, likely in a soft lovely voice as she emanated grace as well as sophistication.

His eyes were set upon her intently and he was listening, thinking upon her words, not his usual self. There was something in the way they stood that indicated they had known each other a long time, perhaps intimately acquainted and Genevieve felt a pang in her heart. It was frustrating that she let herself feel that way, and she admonished herself for entertaining the idea that it should matter to her.

Simon strangely remained with her as if knowing she needed him to keep her discretion but suddenly they stopped talking and Noble turned to look at her. Stunned, she did not immediately move, embarrassed they should catch her staring, although it was merely because she was uncertain as to what to do, and now she had to think quickly.

Noble's sad eyes lit up and he beckoned her over, Simon quickly rushed ahead of her, now that she was in motion again. Attempting to appear confident and unaffected, Genevieve held her head up, her sunhat affixed to her waved hair and her gloves neatly set at her wrists. The sunshine had made her feel especially invigorated and pretty but looking upon this lady, she became more aware of her shortness and lesser dignity in poise.

Regardless, she would behave as she should. There was no rationale behind feeling inadequate, she was under his employ and she was best to remember her place and act accordingly. Offering a low gaze and polite smile in their direction, she approached them with clasped hands and waited for Noble to speak.

"Miss Belmont," he addressed her formerly. "I would like for you to meet, Miss Marjorie Atherton, she resides at the next property in Woodcrest Manor."

"Good morning," Genevieve said in response as the beautiful woman nodded at her with a genuine smile. "I am pleased to meet you."

Marjorie studied her openly, perhaps curious about her. "You have taken the role of Mrs. Wilshire, is that correct?"

Genevieve nodded, sensing Noble's eyes on her. "Yes, I am under the impression I have some high expectations to meet, so I can only hope some allowances will be made for the transition."

Marjorie smiled warmly at her and Genevieve's heart sunk, admittedly she was amiable and easy to like, she could not fault her in any way and despised any envy she might have. "How do you find, Noble?" she asked Genevieve. "Does he treat you well?"

She seemed genuinely nice and so in spite of wanting to be received as a proper obedient assistant; she could not help but remark as she would among friends. "Mr. McKinley has been difficult at times but has made some improvement."

Marjorie gasped before covering her mouth and laughing loud with Noble echoing her laughter in turn. "Undoubtedly," the statuesque neighbor said when she had caught her breath. Still smiling, she then must have remembered something and raised it with him. "*Is* Henny in communication with you? Has she recovered after her fall?"

"Would you like to join me?" Noble offered her.

Assuming that she was asking him about Mrs. Wilshire, Genevieve felt this was an opportune time to return to the house and discretely slink away, which she was able to do as he was occupied answering his companion. Simon decided to remain at his master's side so she went through the unlocked side door and did not lock it in case he intended to enter that way.

Having fulfilled all of her overseer's requests, she was permitted to do as she pleased unless he called for her and that was a fine arrangement for both of them. He was not demanding or tyrannical and he was genuinely appreciative of what she did for him.

And soon she had spent the entire afternoon alone in her room. Dinner was simple that evening and he had left instructions to make herself something and she could eat it in her room if it was more comfortable than sitting alone in the kitchen.

She suspected he had talked with Marjorie a long time, walking on the grounds. He couldn't get far but she had noticed his wheelchair was missing from the end of the hall and there were many paved areas that he could visit more easily than walking on the grass this way.

Trying to keep busy so she did not think too much on it, she brought out some of her crocheted doilies from her nearly empty suitcases, ones that she had toiled over having woven in pink and green floral centers.

These all added color to her room and she placed some sheer but feminine scarves over the curtains and the ornate but cream colored standing lamp. Feeling low, she pressed her hands on her face, warm, comforting; she was her only friend. Perhaps it was true and she knew it was because she often preferred her own company.

She was not shy but she was in need of much time to contemplate, to write and think and not be consumed with the gaiety of parties and the insincerity that came along with such things.

But this was not the cause of her loneliness. If no one crept into her heart she would not fear the loss of it but she couldn't stop it, she had grown fond of him. She had attached herself to the loving dog and the creaky floors and the shadows of the past.

And why? It had been a week, how could she have let it happen?

Shaking her head, she stopped the thoughts, the feelings and began to plump the pillows on the bed, considering her options. Perhaps she could purchase some yarn and some small pieces to adorn her small kingdom.

There was a small desk in the room, now it had an 18th century tea cup on it from when she had brought her coffee in earlier. Opening her personal diary, she sat at it, the desk on the right wall, and she brought her pen up in her right hand.

Staring at it, she sighed. Who would want to read it and what could she possibly write? Not in this state of mind, she could not possibly admit to the conflict inside of her. She had done well these past years, to mature and blend and retire into the quiet corners of the world.

How dare her heart beat when she had subdued its will?

Fatigued, she considered retiring early as well. Wearing a long silky pale blue nightgown with lace shoulders, it used to make her feel glamorous. She was still wearing her bra in the event she was called upon but Noble had been quiet and she only supposed he had taken Simon for his last outing for the night.

Walking across the room, she was glad for the touches she had added to it, and she pushed a small section of the curtain aside so she could look out at Claremonde. The moon was crisp this night and she noticed an angel carved into the outer frame on the side of one of the high windows. It was eerily quiet around it as if it was a sacred cemetery, a monument to a tragedy.

Suddenly she heard something in the house and turned to look at her locked bedroom door. Tip toeing, she got to the thick door and held her breath, pressing her ear against it. At first she thought it might just be creaking on the floor, the settling of a very old house, but then Simon was whimpering and it saddened her greatly. Uncertain as to if she should look in on him; it was then that she heard a voice.

"Genna!" he called out. She knew he was calling her but he sounded out of breath and her name was a mouthful for someone in distress.

Hurriedly putting on her light coral robe and tying it at the waist, she unlocked her door and rushed to his, and was glad to find it unlocked. She knocked and opened it partially before stepping in. "Are you modest?"

She thought she could almost hear him laugh a little. "Have you only assisted clothed patients?" he teased.

Peering in, she could see that he was wearing an old men's Victorian nightgown that he had mentioned was easier for him to get on than pajamas. "I was asking in the event that *you* would be concerned about it," she replied truthfully as she looked upon him partly lying on the floor with Simon sniffing at him.

She hadn't really seen his room before, only when he had the door opened as she walked by and it was a nicer one than the rest of the rooms, perhaps reminiscent of his days in Claremonde. It was more of an old fashioned gentleman's chambers with a burgundy bedspread and an ornate gold clock with horses at each side. There was a gold rug at his bedside and a high backed red Victorian armchair across from his lower ornate Eastlake bed.

"Did you fall?" she asked concerned as she walked over to him.

"That I can confirm," he said, studying the sympathy in her face. "Do you mind assisting me?"

"That is why I am here," she stated.

Patting Simon to calm his anxious pacing, she walked around behind Noble and crouched behind him, bringing her arms underneath his armpits and pulling him up the best she could. He was wobbly but was doing his best to assist her and she walked him over to the armchair, noticing the ceramic bell on his bedside table. "Perhaps we should put a bell around your neck," she only half jested. "I do not like that you fell without being able to so easily summon me."

"I assure you it wasn't my intention," he said with a light smile.

Bringing her hand up to his forehead, she tidied a stray hair and felt for bumps. Looking into his eyes briefly, she made sure he was not resistant to her touch as she gently touched his burned side. "Are you sore?"

"I am bruised but not broken," he assured her. "And whilst I have a voice; that should do well enough to call for you."

"What happened?" she asked quietly.

"Simon messed on the floor and I slipped in it," he replied neutrally.

Looking at the floor she could still see a small patch of urine and she worried it was her fault. "I should have taken him outside," she stated apologetically, looking around the room for a tea towel. "There is a small towel in my en suite," he said, as she noticed the door close to his bed and went towards it.

"He had walked with me," he called out to console her as she searched his bathroom. "He is anxious this day, much activity and it troubles him sometimes."

His bathroom was large and there was a chair beside his bath where he likely sat and washed himself with a cloth mostly. Old wallpaper was on the walls and still had many hints of antiquity inside. Finding a cloth on his sink, she came out again, relieved to hear she was not to blame. "I am sorry to hear that about him," she confessed sincerely.

Taking care of the mess quickly, she looked at him and then at the bed across the room. "Do you need help getting to the bed?"

"Place my cane here and I can do it well enough," he said, pointing to the side of the chair.

Quick to deliver it to him, she stepped back and moved closer to the door. "Is there anything else I can do for you?"

Appearing surprised at her leaving, he reached for Simon who placed his head under his master's hand. "What were you doing just now before I interrupted you?"

"I was in my room," she replied, clasping her hands together.

Discretely studying her in her flattering nightwear, he seemed a little melancholic but she found he looked handsome in his nightgown; he had clearly been a man of good health and activity prior to his injury. Smiling, he nodded as if he should have answered the question with less vagueness. "Were you reading? Is that your preferred leisure?"

"Oh," she said, walking back to him, enjoying the warmth of the fire that she noticed at the left of his chair. "I do not read a great deal but I do enjoy writing and crochet work. But in this particular instance I was arranging my room a little. I hope you do not mind."

"You were moving the furniture?" he asked curiously.

Laughing, she shook her head, only then realizing her long brown hair was down and unstyled. "I had some personal items that I thought would bring some color into the room, but I will put them back in my cases if you prefer I do not decorate at all."

His smile faded and he seemed a little shocked at the suggestion. "Genevieve, you are home. It is *your* room in which I would hope you adorn with your charm and color however you like. Do you find it comfortable?"

Smiling, she nodded. "Yes, thank you."

"There is a lack of warmth and color in it I suppose?" he mused, considering it. "It was not always this way," he added wistfully. "I myself enjoyed the rich color of decadence and age but I had lost interest at some point in time. Do you find the rest of the rooms similarly pale?"

Not certain how much she should say, she knew he could see her thinking on it.

"Speak earnestly, please. I always wish for you to tell me the truth of what you feel," he insisted.

Trying to keep polite while still sincere, she thought about the best way to explain it. "It appears in a temporary state," she said. "It is as if it is not lived in. It does not reflect a particular character and yes it does seem to lack color."

Listening, it was apparent he understood and more than likely he hadn't thought of it for a long time, Mrs. Wilshire must have been content with it. "Would you readily take on the task of enlivening the other rooms?"

"Yes, I would like that very much, if you are trusting of me."

Leaning back, she could see he was tired but he had a glint in his eyes, a spark of promise. "I will send for Clemens to take you into the village tomorrow if you are content to do so. You can gather together all that you wish to make it so these quarters appear lived in again."

Smiling, she couldn't hide her glee. "Will you write your requirements down? I would like to know your preferences."

"Not at all," he said as Simon groaned and lay at his feet now, closing his eyes. "I am looking forward to seeing what you do with it all."

"I appreciate your blind faith," she said with a smirk.

For a moment he was quiet and sometimes she felt as if there was an energy between them, something almost tangible that she could grasp like it was holding them together in a form of concentration. "Marjorie was quite impressed by you."

The mention of her name made her strangely self conscious. "Yes, she is truly amiable; such praise is high to come from one like her."

Smiling, a look of mischief came upon him. "Would you say, if *I* praised you, that it would be as impressive?"

Laughing, she sighed, relenting. She couldn't keep up her guard long around him; he had a way of bringing her natural self out in spite of her guardedness. "You above all others, Mr. McKinley," she replied honestly. "I would be particularly honored should you find it in yourself to praise me."

"I would prefer you call me Noble," he said with a smile. "And I would have no hesitance in applauding your many good traits. You walked today with Simon; did you step inside the hall?"

Shaking her head, she had wanted to investigate its dark shadows beneath the sunny sky. "I have thought about it," she admitted. "It fascinates me. I am as enamored with the ruins as I am with the history of it."

"You should go," he urged her with intrigue in his eyes. "I would like for you to see it. You should explore it; I know you must like to make discoveries."

Stepping closer to him, she felt the whole world was silent around them. "I will," she promised. "Did you live in it once? Have you been inside recently?"

"I did but I have not," he admitted, reaching up for her to help him. "Let us get this old ruin to bed shall we?"

His body stiff and rigid from sitting, she could feel his warmth as he leant against her, still using his good side so he did not fully depend on her. Walking to the back of the room together, he got into the bed and moved the covers aside, the fireplace flickering in the background.

Simon jumped up onto the bed and nudged in beside his master. "I haven't been there since the fire," he said, although he did not tell her when that was and she did not feel he was ready to get detailed about it. 'It was a long time ago," he added dismissively. "Tell me what you think of Claremonde, please do."

Bringing the blankets over him she turned off the main light making sure his side lamp was on.

Getting him a drink of water from the tap in the bathroom, she put it on his bedside table and tucked the blankets in over his chest.

"Good night, Genna," he said, trying out his new abbreviated name for her.

"Good night, Noble," she said, feeling it strange to say his name instead of just think it. "Sweet dreams," she added as she left the room and closed the door behind her.

A big draft met her in the dark hall and a whistling sound crept through as the wind echoed outside the old quarters.

Hastily getting into her room, she turned around and quickly locked her door, shivering and not knowing if it was fear or cold or both.

Using the bathroom, she was considerably tired so soon got into her bed and fell asleep shortly after.

Hours later, having experienced a heavier than usual slumber, she ached a little upon waking but then shot up into the darkness suddenly sensing something amiss.

A cold wind blew in, perhaps a draft from under the old door, and she heard creaking again, but it sounded like footsteps and then another set. Her heart was beating wildly. Had she heard a whisper?

Listening hard into the darkness, she was afraid to move and now nothing, no voices or footsteps and she wondered if she imagined it.

Turning the tall floor lamp on beside her, she grabbed her dressing gown and was surprised how chilled she was given it had been hot these past few days.

Checking that her door was locked, she then went to the window and carefully moved the curtain just enough to look out.

She couldn't believe her eyes, she was afraid to blink but the moon was on the building, illuminating it so brightly and no matter how she looked at Claremonde, it was complete.

The other side had a turret that matched the one on the left, it had a long hall with windows, the whole estate home was symmetrical, and right before her eyes it was all there, no charred bricks and exposed roof beams.

Afraid and confused, worried about her own state of mind, she wanted to call for Noble but what would he think of her? But he should see this; he would *want* to see this.

And then another sound interrupted her thoughts and this time it was shouting, a man's voice coming from a great distance, perhaps from the hall or outside of it. But she couldn't' see anyone and she didn't know what the voice was saying; only that she felt he might be calling for a person.

It was only once, she heard him call a name that she could not quite distinguish. Almost dizzy with fear, she turned to look back into her room and went for a blanket which was at the end of it.

Glancing once more outside, she opened the curtains fully and pressed her hands against the cold glass. The moon was now a crescent shape and barely had a glow and the silhouette of the imposing Claremonde Hall was partly destroyed, and she wondered if she had seen it complete at all.

Was it a glimpse into the past or a play of the mind or a story to be told?

She only knew as she returned to her bed, leaving the lamp light on, that she would not sleep well, not tonight or perhaps ever again.

Chapter Four

Fear had a way of robbing one of their slumber but fatigue won in the end, even if her dreams were wild and restless. The alarm hadn't gone off yet but the sun was unhindered and bright this morning and yet she was acutely aware of her surroundings.

Staring at the window, it was her intention to explore Claremonde and Noble had given her every encouragement to do so, but last night's vision frightened her. It was not at all alluring and she was not one to pretend something didn't happen. There was much in existence above her comprehension that could not be dismissed merely because she couldn't explain it.

Having a little time, she decided to run a bath and was pleased to find the water was quite hot. Getting in, she rested her aches into the deep tub and mused on everything that was said the prior night. Noble had a way of speaking that made her feel immediately comfortable but she had not seen him with others all that much. Perhaps it was simply his nature and no particular attention was being placed on her.

Closing her eyes, birds sang outside her window. While she was appreciative of her good fortune at being employed there, there was a definite sense of secret in the air, and it seemed inevitable that it would find her, and the night had become an ominous setting.

A noise alerted her to activity in the house and she sat forward, listening, hoping she could discern what it was, given that she was tucked away in the bathroom.

It sounded as if someone was walking around, perhaps Simon too. She wondered if he had another accident and his master decided to let him outside, but he was not an old dog and Noble could have called on her. Nevertheless, she was anxious to get dressed and get to the kitchen, and perhaps then she would learn what was happening.

Deciding on a figure flattering gold colored cotton dress with red roses, she brought her hair partially back and waved the bottom, putting a small velvet rose in her hair. Her purse was ready with gloves and lipstick in the event that she did go into the village, which was both exciting and intimidating. She was not sure what the people would be like and how she might be received or even if she would be acknowledged.

Tidying her bed, she parted her curtains to let the sun in and sprayed a little more perfume on her dress before leaving the room and walking quietly towards the kitchen. Stopping just before she entered, she could hear talking in there and realized it was Noble. Not wanting to be seen if he had company, she peered in only to find him looking directly at her.

Her eyes scanned the room and she realized he had been talking to Simon, who was quick to greet her with a wagging tail and a thorough sniffing. Glancing over at the wooden eating table, she noticed that it had been covered with a lace cloth. A clear drinking glass had been placed in the middle and had roses and daisies in it.

"I had Clemens pick some flowers," Noble stated proudly as he leaned back against one of the wooden counters near the sink.

Genevieve gestured that she would be right back and she went to her room and then returned with the small turquoise vase that had been on her dressing table. She then transferred the beautiful flowers into the vase and went to the sink to wash out the glass. "What is the occasion?" she asked him, showing that she was impressed.

Placing the upturned glass on the tea towel, she then thought that perhaps he was readying himself for a companion. "Oh," she said aloud. "Did you not want me to prepare your food? Are you expecting a friend?"

Surprise shone from his eyes. "Not at all, I would enjoy our breakfast greatly," he replied quickly. "Simon and myself thought it would better the kitchen if we gave it some color and have it ready for your approval."

"You did this to show *me*?" she asked, genuinely surprised as she noticed some folded table cloths and little ceramic statues placed aside on the table next to the electric refrigerator. "I am not sure what to say. I can not believe you rose early for this," she said with a laugh.

"Does it please you?"

Like a child needing to hear that he was appreciated, she was genuinely happy to tell him that he was. "I am truly delighted," she replied truthfully. "I have never smiled as much in a short time than I have in my entire life," she added somewhat sentimentally which was not her intention. "You have made me feel so welcome, Noble. Even if you cast me out this day I would be indebted to you for your kindness."

"I would not ask you to depart, Genna," he said, using his new name for her. "I hope that you will like it well enough to keep on with me, at least until I become intolerable. But Mrs. Wilshire was not repelled by me; therefore I come with *some* recommendation."

Smiling, she went for the frying pan and got some lard to put in it before getting the food from the cabinet and refrigerator. "I am not of your ilk, Noble," she admitted, not caring if it was a stigmatic subject to raise. "But I have met people from all walks of life and can easily identify a sincere person. You are abundantly good natured and I should think it would be difficult to find any fault in you."

His eyes lit up with her kind words and he knew that she was being genuine in relaying them to him. He was dressed in black dress trousers and a black vest over a tan short sleeved shirt, but his fitted vest buttons were askew, he had put the top button in the wrong hole. Noticing her gaze, he looked down slightly and grimaced. "Confounded thing," he sighed.

Walking over to him, she reached out but then made the request. "May I?"

"Please do," he asked.

She undid all of the buttons which had each been put in the next hole down and straightened them up, getting them in the right position. "I have done it myself at times," she said, making sure he did not feel he was inept in any way. "You have a keen eye for style," she added truthfully.

"It might be difficult to imagine, but I was considered quite a handsome man once," he said seriously as she got the last button done.

Close to him now, she could see the parts of the skin that had folded over and healed in thick areas of raised skin, pulling down at the bottom of his right eye a little. But she didn't notice it that much, it was obvious, but it seemed so irrelevant to his entirety. "It is not that hard to believe," she said, holding his gaze. "You are handsome now; it only stands to reason you were before."

For a brief moment he was without words and she drew away, not wanting to make him uncomfortable but he was touched by her words because he knew she was being truthful.

Simon suddenly rushed out of the room and heavy footsteps echoed out in the hall before a man, perhaps late twenties or early thirties entered the room. He was in a gray suit with matching vest and hat and a smile that radiated friendliness before he even spoke.

"Good heavens!" he declared as he removed his hat, showing a healthy head of dark brown hair to go with his cheerful hazel eyes. "I did not know *you* would be, Miss Belmont," he added, reaching out to shake her hand. "You do not look like Mrs. Wilshire at all."

Laughing, she liked him immediately. "Well, in spite of that, I do hope you will like me anyway," she said with a smile.

"I *know* I will," he said, looking at Noble and appearing a little surprised by his outfit. "You are dapper today," he noted. "Will you be coming along?"

"Not this day, Clemens, Miss Belmont will be riding at your side so you be certain to take good care of her," Noble insisted. "You will stay to eat with us now won't you?"

Clasping his hands together eagerly, he looked at Genevieve almost apologetically. "I will if Miss Belmont does not mind it?"

"I would enjoy it very much," she said, looking at the table beside the sink and relieved to see that they did have enough food for it. "I will get some more groceries today but we have enough to feed a tall young man like yourself."

Laughing, he removed his jacket, revealing a buttoned shirt beneath. He then placed it with his hat on a free table in the corner. "This cloth is nice on the table," he observed. "I haven't seen that one before."

"You will see a great deal more of these touches in the house, Clemens," Noble promised as he smiled at Genevieve. "Miss Belmont will acquire all that she pleases to bring this downtrodden dwelling into vibrancy again."

Clemens smile faded as he looked at her somewhat intrigued. "You will?" he asked. "Astonishing," he marveled, looking around. "Will you paint the walls?"

Noble laughed, as did she. "I hadn't considered it, but it might not be a bad idea. For now I will just decorate."

Before they knew it, breakfast was over, Simon was asleep at Clemens' feet and Genevieve had cleaned up the dishes. She was sorry that Noble would not be joining them but she suspected he didn't leave the house often because he was afraid of the judgment of others. She felt protective and knew all too well the cruelty of others. Where *they* saw deformity, she saw beauty.

Having prepared the engine and gotten the car ready, Clemens opened the door for her and they were soon making their way past Claremonde Hall.

He observed her staring at it and offered her a polite smile. "Beautiful isn't it?"

"I've never seen anything more lovely," she agreed.

"Have you been inside?" he asked, as he stared up at it.

"Not yet, but I had planned on going in today or perhaps tomorrow. I have a definite interest in history and it appears to be fifteenth century. Have you gone in there?"

Nodding he smiled with childlike glee. "It is like a royal palace, the seats are like thrones and the walls are rich and the, *everything*. All of it, you must see it."

Genuinely surprised, she had to question him further. "There is still furniture in it? Had they not emptied it out?"

Now he looked surprised and he looked at her before bringing the car to a stop as a group of swans wanted to cross in front of them at the clearing's edge. "One part of it is quite destroyed but the rest was not touched, they just stopped living in it."

"Oh, I assumed it had lost its stability," she said. But she ceased a further line of questioning, preferring him to give more away so if Noble asked him about her curiosities he would not be able to relay that she pried too much.

Just the same, she had to wonder why they did not continue to live in the remainder of the grand hall and now she wanted to see it even more, excited to know she had been given permission to adventure there.

Turning to study it as they drove around to the front and into the main drive, she noticed a man staring down from a third floor window. "Who is that?" she asked in spite of herself. "Is that the groundskeeper?"

"Martin is not here this week," he said. "None of the others go up there; they pretty much stay away from the hall." With his foot on the car brake, he glanced over his shoulder and squinted. "Where do you see him?"

"There on the third floor, the sixth window," she said, pointing.

He looked hard, not discounting her statement, but not seeing what she was. "Do you still see him?"

She could, but the glass in the window made it hard to capture details but she knew it was a man and she noticed him move.

Intrigued more than skeptical, she could feel Clemens looking at her. "What is he doing?"

"You must think me foolish," she sighed.

"No, no, please tell me," he urged her. "Is he moving?"

"A little," she said. "I can't see him well, but he appears to have dark hair and perhaps is in a shirt and trousers, his hair a little long but that is all I can see. He is-" she didn't want to say what she thought because once it was spoken aloud; it made it a solid belief of sorts. "I think he is looking at us but I am not certain," she confessed. "Perhaps it is merely a shadow from the way the sun is shining in."

Not satisfied it was her imagination, he clearly wanted to see what she could. "It is *not* a shadow, Miss Belmont," he said straightly before returning his attention to the road ahead and bringing the car back into motion. Not elaborating, he instead offered some light conversing so they could come to know one another. "Do you know this area well?"

Settling back into her seat, shifting over to avoid a metal spring in the leather bench seat, she replied. "I am from Chessmoor," she explained. "It is perhaps three hours in a car from here, and you?"

"I was around here but not close enough to see the manor houses," he said with a smile. "I've been with Lord McKinley for, well a good seven years or so now, and now I'm nearing thirty so he has kept me on a long time. He is the best of men."

"He is a *Lord*?" she asked, surprised. It shouldn't have been a shock but she hadn't expected it just the same.

"Oh yes, his family, the McKinley's, owned Claremonde right from the beginnings. I've met a few, and as far as Lords go, he is a real one. There is something about him that is–"

"Noble?"

Laughing, he nodded. "It is true, his name is his character."

Relaxing with the sun shining in, she studied the scenery anew, because she hadn't been able to ascertain much when she arrived on that dark night in the rain. There were no houses out here but occasionally you could make out the mysterious entrance to perhaps another large home hidden by tall trees. "He grew up in Claremonde?" she asked. "With his brother and sister?"

Shifting in his seat, he had an affable light way about him, eager to talk, willing to share. "The whole family," he confirmed. "Lady McKinley didn't have too many, just the three, but he was there with his brother, Valor, who is, I'm certain, a good twelve or so years older, and his sister, Prudence, as well as their father, for a time."

"Do *they* have any children?"

Giving it some thought, he nodded but was not certain of specifics. "Prudence had a daughter quite young and she is all grown now but I have only encountered her once, but Lady Prudence is pleasant. She is quiet but she is the courteous kind type of lady and she visits now and then but she is not around here nowadays. And I knew Lady McKinley well and she was the nicest lady, so motherly to all of us, everyone who worked here and she loved Noble like nothing else."

Saddened to hear him speak of her in past tense, she remembered that he said he had been with Noble for seven years so she must not have died that long ago. "Has she been gone long?"

"Nearly three years," he replied.

"The men didn't have any children?" she enquired as neutrally as possible.

"Valor was a real Romeo it is said," he relayed with a chuckle. "He had his pick of too many beauties to choose just one and Noble didn't marry."

"Why?" she asked, regretting her obvious interest.

Shaking his head, she could see he probably wondered the same thing. "I don't know why, Miss Belmont, but I believe, between you and me, that some bad things happened there when they were younger. I don't ask him, but I think he prefers to keep away from most people."

Genevieve understood completely. Her childhood and youth was marred by tragedy and a foreboding lack of trust in others. She, herself, had always been someone who preferred to be alone mostly, but everyone needed a close companion or two who they knew they could go to if needed.

Clemens suddenly pointed at a dirt drive leading somewhere down a long path. "That's where Lady Marjorie Atherton lives, but you can't see the house from here."

"I thought she was situated beside the Claremonde estate?" she mused.

Glancing at the drive as they passed, he nodded. "The houses are closer than the entrances," he explained. "But I wouldn't walk them without a day's notice."

Laughing, she had to agree. The size of land that these majestic homes stood on was almost beyond the horizon. Claremonde alone must have been in need of constant attending to with the gardens and fountains and brickwork. "I imagine it takes quite some time just to walk from one end of the hall to the other," she noted.

"It does," he confirmed. "I had estimated that whilst walking, it gives me enough time to eat lunch *and* a piece of cake to follow it before I could reach the other side."

Attempting to be perceived as neutral on the topic of Noble, she hoped her line of questioning would be received as casual so she did what she could to keep her tone light.

"I did actually encounter Miss Marjorie yesterday," she said with a smile. "Is she a love interest of Mr. McKinley?"

Complete bewilderment came upon his face. "*Noble* McKinley?"

"Yes," she replied curiously.

"No, not him," he explained, not having thought of such a scenario before. "She was the first love of Valor many years ago. They were quite caught up in each other."

"But she did not remain with him?"

Shaking his head, it was obvious that he knew a great deal but was missing some vital pieces of the puzzle. "No one knows why she left, but it was long before he died. Just the same, I think she kept a flame burning for him because she never married. She occasionally visits Noble to look in on him. More like a sister because Prudence really isn't near here at all."

Uncertain about how to raise the subject, she sensed that Clemens was pleased enough to discuss anything, but he may have been asked for discretion on certain matters. "Can you discuss the fire?" she finally addressed frankly.

With his eyebrows raised, surprised by the question, he smiled at her. "He didn't tell you about when or what happened?"

"No," she admitted gently, not wanting to sound disapproving of Noble in any way. "I can only suppose it is not a matter he enjoys talking about."

Clemens expression mellowed while he thought about it. "I don't know how it happened but it was in the papers at the time," he explained as he waved at a middle aged man at the side of the road, whose car had over heated she assumed.

"1917 I remember, it was the same year I met a girl named Peggy," he chuckled to himself. "I don't know her now but I remember that day, that year," he added with a sigh. "I still had a year or two of school left at the time, but everyone knew the McKinley's and they were a nice family, especially Lady McKinley."

"You knew her before you worked here?" Genevieve asked as she noticed they were driving into a main street with a large row of shops on each side.

"My mum did," he replied. "They both did work in the Red Cross and Lady McKinley helped out a lot but also gave a lot of money for the poor people around. No one could say a bad word about her and I saw Valor around the village because he went to Mr. Jones's photographic studio a lot of the time."

"Did people talk about the fire much?" she enquired curiously.

"For a long time." Clemens tipped his hat a little so he could see better. He then waited for another car to pull away from the side of the footpath so he could park there. "Everyone had their ideas about it but all the McKinley children were grown then and none lived there but they visited often. Noble would have been later thirties then I think."

"Oh yes they were grown at the time. His brother, Valor, he died a while ago?"

"Yes," he confirmed staidly.

Studying his face, she felt there was more to his response. "Was he alive when the fire happened? Did he know of it?"

Perhaps not expecting that she was not aware of this one particular fact, he walked around first to open her door, before telling her quietly what she wanted to know. "He was visiting the estate the day of the fire," he explained as she stood and stretched a little, closing the car door behind her. "He knew all too well about it," he whispered. "He died in it."

Chapter Five

While there were a great many rooms in the old servant quarters behind Claremonde, the sophisticated genial master of the house mostly utilized a handful of rooms in one side of the house. Not being able to get up stairs without a long process involved, he mostly enjoyed his bedroom, the kitchen and the gardens. The mid morning had him sitting in his favorite kitchen chair; it was slightly cushioned with a white crochet blanket for comfort.

Holding up a long but narrow floor rug, she watched his face as a smile came upon it. "It is a red and gold color and looks old fashioned," she explained. "I thought it would suit your room and perhaps you could put it in that area where you slipped recently. This way you might prevent another fall."

"I sent you to purchase items for the house and yet you think of me first," he stated in awe. "You are quite the exception, Genevieve."

Warmed by his flattery, she blushed as she reached for the boxes that Clemens had brought in for her. Knowing her later intentions, she had chosen to wear a long pale blue summer dress that tied at the waist and she completed the outfit with a simple blue velvet flower in her hair.

While this was the day she was going to Claremonde, she was happy to remain there in the kitchen, conversing until the sun went down if it were her choice. "Well I confess I got a lot for the house too but all with you mind."

Glee appeared in his eyes and it reminded her of a child waiting for a present. "I am surprisingly interested by this," he confessed with a laugh as he stroked Simon's head while the dog loyally guarded his side. "What else did you acquire? I am intrigued to know what will bring this old house to life."

Rummaging around in the first box, she wondered what she would show him first, equally as excited to share her finds after having spent a lot of time in Wanderling the prior day. Most people had been friendly and helpful at the many shops she had gone to, but being with Clemens, who everyone seemed to know and like, helped her immensely.

"I had wanted to explore the antique shop," she began.

"You should!" he declared enthusiastically.

"It was not open yesterday I'm afraid, but perhaps I can get you out with me," she offered lightly, not looking at him. She knew it was hard for him, just facing people in his condition, but he did not flinch like she assumed.

"You might tempt me to do just that," he stated with a mixture of hesitance and optimism. "Is that a plate?"

"I got four plates and bowls that have a floral design on them," she said, holding the large dinner plate up for him. "They were quite inexpensive but they were so pretty and I thought it might liven up our meals."

"I used to dine using fine china in my youth," he recollected wistfully. "Mother enjoyed the floral ones, and once father moved away we would use them often."

Nodding, she listened, sensing that their mother, one who named her children after virtues, was creative and delightful. "I imagine you have a lot of your mother in you," she noted, bringing the plate over for him to look at, pointing to the pink and green flowers adorning the borders.

His smile faded a little and he looked intrigued by her statement. "She was a unique endearing soul and should I mirror that in any way then I am honored for you to think of me like her."

Looking at the plate as she returned to the boxes, she was eager to pull out the paintings. "Clemens introduced me to an artist who recreates authentic paintings," she explained as she held the thick mildly sepia toned paper in her hand, rolled up like an old scroll. "This is my favorite," she explained, walking it over to him.

Unrolling it, he studied it, impressed by the artist's technique but then he looked up at her, something wonderful in his gaze. "Waterhouse," he said. "This is also one of *my* favorites; he has done quite a good likeness. The way she looks at the crystal ball, the way she ponders her destiny and what might unfold."

"You know it?" she asked, surprised. "It is beautiful," she agreed. "The colors are so rich, and her elegant medieval dress, I think it is just lovely to look at."

"I have the original," he said, sincerely enthralled by the synchronicity of her choice. "I acquired it perhaps ten years or so after it was painted. I have a few of his works in the gallery in Claremonde."

His wealth had not been at the forefront of her mind and she had forgotten that he could have acquired many things that were otherwise out of the realm of possibility for mere people as herself. "Oh, I suppose a re-creation would not do you much good then," she stated evenly.

Stunned, he shook his head and got to his feet, leaning forward a little to implore her. "On the contrary, Genevieve. You have resurrected my passion for the pre-Raphaelites and their romantic notions. This painting will have pride and place in this house, and it will be because you too see the beauty in it. It pleases me immensely."

"I was not able to find a frame for it that was a suitable size," she explained apologetically. "Do you know where I might find one?"

While he sat down again and thought it over, she began to unpack the food she had purchased, using the list Mrs. Wilshire had left as well as a few sweet items and extra breakfast cocoa for him to try.

"Is Clemens still on the grounds?" he asked as he looked inside the box and pulled out a pink and green silk shawl to drape over something and give it color.

"He said he would show me Claremonde," she replied, waiting to see what he thought about it.

"*Yes*," he enthused before looking further into the box as if it was Christmas time. "That is an exceptional idea. He would make for an apt guide for you. Please ask him to take you to the old study in the visitor's wing. We had left a lot of odds and ends in there and I do remember some frames that could be utilized for this. Please select the ones you like most, even if they have pictures in them."

Turning to look at him as she pulled on the refrigerator door, she was concerned that she was taking too much for granted. "Is there anything you would like me to do for you?" she asked seriously. "Do you have letters for me to write or any tasks you need taken care of?"

"I do have a letter I wish to dictate to you for an old tutor I have delayed a reply to," he considered aloud. "But it can certainly wait. Your adventure in discovery is mine also," he revealed. "You will see what I have lost in time and forgotten about and when you reveal it to me, I will relish the thought. I am glad for your inquisitive mind if you do not mind my utilizing it."

"No, I do not mind it whatsoever," she assured him with a smile as she placed the fresh cut bread in the bread box on the table beside the deep kitchen sink. "You employed me to be of use to you, I only hope that you can get the most benefit from me."

With his arms full of lace and rolled up paintings and velvet flowers, he studied her openly, thinking about her words. "Your prior overseer recommended your etiquette and skills but had mentioned that you were particular about people. She said that I would need to determine your suitability for here because you were restless."

Mrs. Marsh had always been helpful and fair in all ways and she was grateful for the time she had taken with her, teaching her every skill available to teach.

"I think she was warning you," she said genuinely. "I am not one to run away or disrespect my position, but if I feel unappreciated I can't help but question the permanency of my situation. I do hope I have not told you too much. I have been too long with people who have overlooked me or maintained me in discomfort and I have only this life and I can not endure more years in such a situation."

Not having foreseen such a divulgence he lowered the items in his arms and for a moment she felt that they were simply two people, speaking honestly, forgoing the rest of the world and all of their rules of exchange and roles of hierarchy. "I admire that in you, Genevieve," he stated sincerely as he looked upon her with his blue eyes and handsome partly disfigured face. "Tell me so that I know. Do you feel like a kite without wind being here? I appreciate you greatly."

"Oh no," she replied, approaching him with a small porcelain creamer in her hands. "I have never felt I belonged more, but I know Mrs. Wilshire was such a great part of your life, it would be foolish of me to think I can simply fill her shoes."

"You are not her," he agreed. "You are you and I would not, even now, wish to part with you. It has been a short time but you *do* belong here, and how will I see the house come to life if your magic is not the catalyst of the outcome?"

Reaching out to shake his hand, she knew in her heart she had to convince him that she would not abandon him. "You could find many others but I will stay as long as you will have me. I wouldn't want to be anywhere else. So let this henceforth be my promise and we will shake on it."

He reached up with his scarred hand and held her hand instead and she wanted to touch his brown waved hair, she wanted to hold him, to heal his insides. His smile was worth everything and she couldn't imagine wanting to look at another face.

"Miss Belmont!" Clemens called out as he opened the door and bounded in through the hallway. Simon rushed to meet up with him and Genevieve reluctantly released Noble's hand and stepped back subtly so it did not look scandalous in any way.

"The sun is shining in the ballroom and this is when the chandeliers shine most,' the young man declared excitedly.

Noble laughed at the younger man's enthusiasm. "Clemens, I understand you intend to be guide. Please take Miss Belmont to the study so she can look for some frames for her paintings."

"It would be my pleasure," he said, removing his hat and jacket and bringing them out with him.

Shortly after, he had rolled up the ends of his white shirt sleeves and put his jacket and hat in the car, ready for their walk in the warm sun.

A real excitement filled her as her low heeled cream shoes echoed lightly on the old brick pavement. Making the long journey at the side of the huge estate house, she shivered under the shadow until they arrived at the front of Claremonde and for the first time she saw it up close.

Clemens allowed her time to stop on the spot and take it all in. "Magnificent isn't it, Miss Belmont? Have you ever seen anything so grand?"

"I haven't," she agreed. "It is a shame that it's not being used now," she said quietly as if speaking of the dead. "On one side, I think of the history and how it should be preserved, but then I think of all those without homes and how this has so many rooms that no one lives in."

Studying her face, the pleasant young man considered what she had said. "There isn't a lot of fairness around in life," he lamented. "But I know Lady McKinley left here because she didn't want to remember."

"I understand," she said, and meant it. "It's hard to look the past in the face and make peace with it," she added as her eyes set upon an ornate, mostly burned, chair near a window area that was barely there anymore.

It was black and ruined from the many years of being left to the elements. And yet that one side was beautiful in its own way, the vines beginning their way into the charred remnants of yesteryear.

She could only ponder if that vision she had, was truly what this house had looked like in its first years.

Perhaps some nobleman entertained a hundred or so guests at once. What did they wear? What were their lives like then?

"Where is the study from here?" she asked, wondering if she could just come here an hour a day and stare at the majestic manor home.

"It is not far from this front entrance door on the right here," he explained, gesturing for her to come with him. "You look hesitant," he stated, with a slight smile but a little concern. "What are you worried about?"

Looking up at the doorway, she felt she might literally be stepping from one world to another, not a glimpse into the past, but becoming part of it. "I feel as soon as I enter I might be changed forever."

Gazing out into the sunny gardens and then in at the grand estate home, he offered her a genuine smile. "I assure you that you will be," he said, pushing the door further inward. "And what could be more thrilling than that?"

Chapter Six

At the right front of Claremonde was a large double door. It was taller than the entrance door to the servant's quarters and ornate with stained glass in upper panels. Beveled dark woodwork was intricately carved, framing the ancient doors that possessed an over sized iron handle on each side.

Clemens pushed one open and they stepped into an immediate coldness, a large dim greeting area and she was surprised that it wasn't locked up. "Couldn't anyone come in here and take something?" she asked, being well aware of the criminal ways of many in the city she had come from.

"We are too far from anywhere to make it worth the trip," he said with a laugh. "There are those big gates at the front too remember? It's pretty well locked up so trespassers aren't an issue."

"What about the other workers? Do they explore here?" Genevieve enquired curiously.

Pointing to a hole in the floorboard, given they were so close to the burned side, he sighed appreciatively, and she could tell he enjoyed it here. "Mrs. Wilshire was with the family since she was quite young and I think she didn't want to come too much in respect of Lady McKinley. I think one of the maids likes the garden around the other side but to be honest, I think they mostly get the creeps. They talk about it being haunted, old folks tales you know."

Shivering in the chill, she crossed her arms and noticed the large wooden columns and arch that led towards a wide set of wooden stairs. "I don't suppose you believe in that sort of thing?" she asked, mainly to gauge his response.

Drawing nearer as if he didn't want to disturb the silence, he nodded. "I know something is here, Miss Belmont. Even if you don't believe in that sort of thing, you have to when you're here long enough. I'm just not scared by it too much but it can get to you in these walls."

"Secrets?" she whispered.

Gravity formed in his eyes and he nodded again. "I leave well enough alone and I'm not too bothered by it but the steward wont step foot in here again. I think he saw something and he was spooked by it."

"I can only hope I don't upset anything," she noted lightly, but she believed his divulgence and she was frightened, especially after what she had seen the other night.

"A ghost that doesn't like you, is no friend of mine," he declared, placing his hand over his heart and smiling.

Laughing, she sighed, determined to enjoy the adventure and subdue her penchant to react to every sound or sensation. "I appreciate that Clemens. We are near the burned side, correct?"

"Yes, if you go back where that door is next to the stairs on the right, part of that room has come down and that's where you can look in and you can get through too but its not easy footing. I wouldn't recommend you go in through that way. The front is easier."

Smiling, she was interested in it like an old castle ruin, but she would rather explore it by popping her head in than endangering herself on crumbling woodwork. "I won't go without you," she promised.

"Oh, the study is back there beyond the other door I told you about," he said, pointing at it. "There is a great deal to rummage through. It is truly a treasure hunt. If you like history, some of the items are from centuries ago from right at the beginning of the McKinley's."

Enlivened by the possibilities, Genevieve made a promise to herself to appreciate everything she was about to see. It was so easy to forget the preciousness of history and how each item once affected one person in a special way. "Are you coming in?" she asked, seeing him look up the stairs.

"Do you like mice?" he asked obscurely.

Suddenly looking around on the floors, she grimaced. "I do my best not to meet up with any," she replied. "Did you see one?"

Getting closer, she was curious about him, there was something uniquely kind and likeable about him. She wondered if his home life as a child had been a good one or he had, like her, become empathetic through the experience of neglect or detachment.

"There is a family of mice in the chamber maid's room up on the second floor," he divulged. "I take some food in to them. I know I shouldn't because they'll probably invite their friends along, but I hate to see them go without, their little eyes look up at me and now they know I have the bread."

Her mouth hanging open, a light breeze from nowhere swept a clump of dust past them, but she was so touched in this moment. "I wish the world had more people like you in it, Clemens. We would all be better off for it."

Surprised, he then shrugged and lowered his gaze coyly. "Oh not so much. I eat some of the bread too, but if I have it to give, no reason it shouldn't be shared."

"I agree with you completely," she said, watching him step back so they could go towards the stairs. "Perhaps we should all help as many people or little mice families as we can. You have inspired me to better my usefulness. Is this the door here?" she asked, pointing at the last one on the right with just a narrow area between it and the stairs.

"Yes that's the one and it's no trouble getting into it. If anything startles you, call out to me, these walls echo well enough I should be down in a jiffy."

"Let's hope it doesn't come to that," she replied dryly as she placed her hand on the old door knob.

Drawing in a shallow breath, she entered in and could not see a thing. The little light filtering in from the hall allowed her to find an electrical light switch on the wall and she pressed it down, surprised that it was still active.

Being that fourteen years had passed, she realized that this must have been one of the rare houses of the time to be electrically fitted out here, so far from the city.

Her eyes adjusted and at first it looked like a room of boxes but then she realized it was much larger than she expected and there was so much to see she didn't know where to start. How could a treasure seeker have enough time to spend with each item of beauty and history, the glorious sense of discovery at their fingertips on every occasion?

The wallpaper was various shades of green with iridescent and velvet flowers in panels up to the tin ceiling. But the first things her eyes set upon, was the horse. At first she thought it was an old rocking horse, but moving aside an ornate eighteenth century piano bench, she saw that it was a carousel horse from a very old merry go round.

It must have been an exquisite sight in its day, the whole carousel with the many animals at a large Victorian show for children to ride on. The gloss was still there, the gilded ornamentation of antiquity; it had been a fine piece.

Who had wanted it? Someone over the history of Claremonde had purchased it for a display piece, had become instantly enamored with it like she was now. There were so many stories here, not just Noble's family but his grandparents and ancestors centuries back.

She wanted to catch up with Clemens, but knowing she would need to put a great deal of time aside to explore this room further, she wanted to look for frames first.

A small scratching sound came from a nearby wall, perhaps from the charred ruins on the other side of it. It was a mouse or a rat, but that wasn't what bothered her.

There was a strange sensation in the air and although she had heard the cliché about feeling like one was being watched, she genuinely felt it at this time.

She had never felt it stronger than in this particular room. She felt that if she turned her head, she was certain to see someone behind her, so she didn't. But she was ready to rummage through to get to the frames a little more hastily than before.

Even though the birds' singing outside was audible, it seemed distant as if Claremonde was its own world and the outside was a separate plain, and that was how she would sum it up being there. Here was a large world of history, grandeur and possibly tragedy and it embraced and coddled its kin inside but now it was empty, holding only its secrets.

Whilst enduring the overwhelming sensation of being watched, she concentrated on her goal. It was hard to see the woods for the trees; there were so many things there, sparkly and ornate, old and rare and she finally did see in the back left corner a handful of paintings leant up against each other.

Carefully navigating her way through the gilded chairs and small unopened jewelry boxes, she couldn't help but open one and noticed an ornate brooch, perhaps something military in its age. Beside it was a men's ring, gold and scrolled with a flat blue center and a coat of arms with griffons and a heart.

Looking around, she was startled by a dress hung up in the corner because she thought it was a person for a moment. With her heart pounding she delved through the piles to find a box that didn't have too much in it. Deciding to use it, she took out the paper bags of things so she could start putting some items together.

She almost regretted shopping now, for most certainly nothing would suit Noble more than to have the items of his ancestors interlaced with his current home. Thrilled at the idea, she didn't want to remain long simply because she wanted to see more of the hall, her master was sure to enquire upon her evaluations.

Putting the velvet box with the men's ring in it, she went for the frames. The first one, gold and bronze, beautifully decorated, contained a painting; a muted pale scene of a sailing ship on a foggy morning. It was probably a priceless painting and very old but it was rather dreary and seemed an apt size for the crystal ball painting and the frame was truly lovely.

She wondered where the gallery was and whether the original would be better, and yet it seemed a better start to have her version of it where they lived now, leaving Claremonde to retell its history as it was.

The next three paintings were portraits, painted perhaps sixteenth and seventeenth century and she stared at the men for a moment, standing proud with one foot forward, their tights accentuating their masculinity, their stern gazes imposing and intimidating.

She wanted to see Noble in their likenesses; she wanted to know how such important wealthy Lords became the remaining McKinleys. Prudence was the only one with a child, a daughter, but that was all of it. And she, or her children, would inherit this one day. All of these rooms for a small group of people when so many suffered out in the cold. It was hard to comprehend the imbalance in the world of good fortune and poverty.

Education and the lack of neglect alone could be the greatest of differences in man, so divided by this invisible force of who was superior and who was considered otherwise.

Lifting the heavy paintings and putting them in the box, she also went for the dress, which was so petite, a woman would have had to be pulled into a corset tight enough for a mop handle. But it was beautiful to look at and somehow she would include it as a showpiece instead of here in this dungy room of lost history.

"Miss Belmont? Do you want to see the main rooms?" Clemens called down to her.

"Yes, please, I would like that immensely. Would you be so good as to help me with a few things? I won't keep you long!" she called back.

"I'll be down shortly," he replied. "I wanted to find something for you."

She was glad because just when she thought her brief visit to this room was over with, she noticed something that she was eager to get to. Stepping on three boxes and a crate of empty jars, she reached for it; a leather bound book, flexible with many pages in it.

It was a journal, a boy's journal it appeared with small sketchings but nice penmanship. Flicking through the pages she could see it was quite full of writing, even down to the back inside page. It was an exciting find and she opened the first page, which indicated it was his first journal, and there the author of the writing was revealed.

Valor John McKinley, twelve in age, this first day of January, 1878.

Hearing Clemens descending the stairs, she quickly surveyed the room and was satisfied for now that she could get started on reviving their quarters. Turning to look in the box that the journal had been found in, she noticed ten others and quickly pulled them all out to put in her own box.

Sensing her young friend at the door, she smiled, knowing he must be curious. "I made some interesting finds, Clemens," she said, looking up and noticing his shadow but not seeing him.

"What did you say?" he called back, having stopped at the middle of the stairs.

Her heart stopped now as she knew that it had not been him standing there, but someone *had* been and it sent a shiver down her entire body. "I'm coming out now!" she called back, anxious to have him there with her.

He met up with her and she pointed to the box she had placed the items in and he carried it out for her. "Was someone else here just now?" she asked casually. It was only then her question seemed genuinely reasonable, after all there were others on the grounds that might have stepped in.

"I'm certain there wasn't," he assured her with a smile as she pointed to a couple of other things that he agreed were of great interest. "Did you hear someone?" he asked further as he went to the back of the room.

Shrugging, she wasn't sure how to respond. "I don't want to make a fuss about every little shadow but I thought you were standing here just now, I saw–, I don't know. You know that feeling when someone is waiting for you and you talk to them because you know they are there?"

Not at all surprised to hear her ask it, he nodded. "That happens a lot in here," he agreed. "I can only suppose if someone is roaming Claremonde for whatever reason, they are probably rather curious about us."

While it was a thought provoking subject, she had often thought about the possibility of hauntings, now more than ever. But the rational side of her questioned reason rather than accepting anything at mere hearsay. "Why would anyone be here, Clemens?" she asked seriously. "It is a romantic idea I'm certain, but realistically, I can't fathom why they wouldn't move on like anyone else."

Considering her words, he gazed at the room and held the box in his arms while he thought, truly wanting to give her a good answer. "I know I wouldn't want to stay even though it's nice enough here," he replied seriously. "I don't know why anyone would unless there was something keeping them here. But I know they're about, just not why."

"Do you know the time?" she asked, realizing they had been there a while.

"Noble gave me a watch last Christmas," he stated excitedly, taking it from his pocket. "It is nearing three."

Sighing, she pondered her options. "He said the steward is coming at half past and I should really have afternoon tea prepared but it won't take me long. Could we see a little before I return?"

"Yes, come on then," he encouraged. "There is a grand hall to the left up there that you will love."

Putting her acquirements aside for now, she followed him up the stairs eager to see what was up there, but it was too much for her eyes to behold all at once.

At the top of the stairs to the left was a large hallway, it was wider than the average room with beautiful pale blue and red wallpaper. Portraits hung intermittently on the walls with large vases of fake antique flowers and small French tables and chairs along both sides.

The floor was hardwood but looked almost untouched, still with a sheen to it even though the dust had settled long ago. The open doors of the rooms allowed the sun to shine across the hall as if heaven was trying to filter through in rays of light.

Clemens came to stand at her side and she could tell the sight had not lost its luster for him yet. "I never thought I would walk down a hall like this in my whole life," he said quietly. "It feels like home to me now. It doesn't belong to anyone so much, like an old photograph, but its part of me somehow."

Glancing at him, she understood completely. "It is as if the silence brings it to life. I feel like if I step any further I will enter the past."

Drawing in a deep breath, their stillness was somewhat obligatory in respect of all that had happened here. Genevieve glanced over her shoulder to the end of the hallway and there were large oval shaped burns in the wall where the fire had seeped through from the other side. "I am sad for them," she said.

Now more than ever she wanted to soothe Noble's woes but she didn't know what made her feel it so strongly. He emanated burden and at first she was curious about his past but now she felt that he needed to say it and he wouldn't heal until he did.

Clemens nodded but didn't speak but then he glanced down at his watch and apologetically walked away from her. "You don't have much time to return but I wanted to look again in the mother's room for something I know you will enjoy," he explained. "But you should at least see one room. Noble's is way further down but this first one here was the eldest of them; Valor slept in here as a child and he came here often to stay throughout his life."

She was eager to see anything, but now with his journals in her possession, she thought it might be an additional intrigue to the mystery of the older brother. "Yes I will go in here," she agreed as she watched him walk away and towards a room just pass a chandelier affixed in the gold painted ceiling.

The room was much larger than any bedroom she had seen, more like the size of a living room and perhaps, on initial inspection, it was used as a man's chambers where he would entertain his friends privately.

The sudden quietness as she stepped in was somewhat unsettling and a chill permeated the unattended room as if it had become a ghost when its predecessor passed on.

Plush burgundy rugs were beside the bed and in front of the fireplace. A deep burgundy leather armchair was close to the fire and for a second she imagined the sound of the flickering flames as he sat there. He had probably sat there often; there was still a slight indentation in the area where he would have been, reading or smoking a pipe.

He had died fourteen years prior but his spirit felt old, she couldn't place it, but there was a sensation of vividness in his absence. Perhaps that was the very essence of death, where once one departed, their existence became more poignant, their memory thoroughly investigated. Subconsciously we might have thought they could now tell us something.

The bed was a dark wood, curved with gilded details; it looked old, perhaps belonging to one of the earlier owners in another century. It was enough to hold a man and perhaps a lover, but not for a long sleep given the narrower width.

The covers with a rich red and gold damask design were slightly pulled back as if Valor had just gotten up and went to the bathroom for a short while. It was as if time had stopped and she was standing there waiting for him to return, to walk in and explain things to her.

There was another door to the right which she assumed linked to a bath perhaps, or even a room where he might change privately with a wash stand as they used to. But she really didn't want to let Noble down and could return here to explore at any time so for now she just wanted to take it all in, remember what she could.

The first thing that captured her eye was the long burl wood dresser. It was masculine but luxurious, French and curved with lion's feet and a curved wooden mirror on the wall above it. On the top of a green velvet runner was a photograph, an earlier style from the Victorian period, but a larger one than the small tintypes common for the time.

It was in a beautiful ivory frame, but the people in it were what truly caught her attention. Frozen to the spot, she carefully brought it up closer to her face to gaze at the faces of the last McKinley family; a father and a mother with two sons and a daughter.

By estimation and a little math, knowing that Valor was fifty one when he died fourteen years previously, he looked like he was in his mid twenties here. This was her first time seeing him and she understood why he had been popular with ladies.

He was handsome, nicely built with an elegant style, dress in a fitted suit with matching vest and cravat as well as a hat. He cast a dapper figure, but more so it was the confidence that he exuded with a smug, take on the world, kind of smirk that would likely have been both charming and intimidating. His hair was short and from what she could see, a little lighter than his brothers.

Noble appeared around eleven or twelve and she recognized him immediately. Struck by his complete unscarred face, she felt guilt for gazing at him here, but she was sincerely protective of him in a way that she had never felt for anyone before. He was a man of the world, he was still very much the master of his domain, but his cruel fate had forced the humility from him.

He had to have always been kind, she knew it was natural to him, but the fire may have scarred him in his heart also. Just the same, he was not smug like his brother, here, as a young man, he looked a little uncomfortable.

What she found remarkable, especially for this particularly stoic era, was that his mother, Lillianne, had her hand on his shoulder and he had his hand discretely over hers, openly affectionate for a good woman he spoke highly of.

She was beautiful as well as having a reputation for kindness, her hair was dark her eyes warm and her face pretty, the kind of mother one would ask for if it was in their power.

Noble's discomfort was likely the oppression of the imposing brooding figure that stood over them. The three youths were in the front, Valor in front of his stern father, with Prudence, who was close in age to Noble, beside him.

The young girl was particularly beautiful, her ringlets silky, her face perfection and her body already close to full bloom for her tender age.

The father, she had not learned his name, had anger etched in his brow, his side burns and his hat casting an ominous shadow on his subservient underlings. It would not be said aloud but she disliked him immediately and chastised herself for the unsubstantiated conclusion.

Glancing up from the photograph, she was ready to leave, but then when she glanced over at the mirror in front of her, she thought she saw movement. Spinning around, she wasn't sure, perhaps a trick of the light. But there, where she had seen it, something silver was peeking out from a gold velvet, footed stool.

Walking over to it, she could see the foot stool could be opened like a chest, and it was slightly held up by this silver object; a frame.

It was heavy and an oval shape with a blue velvet backing, but she was surprised by the person in the photograph. It was an early one also, of an unknown woman. The photograph had been color tinted which had then been a costly and rare acquisition at the time.

Unusually she was lying in water, perhaps in a shallow creek with smooth rocks at her sides beneath the partially clear water. Her hair, which had been lightly colored a tint of red, swirled around her in the water like a beautiful mermaid.

Her skin was particularly pale and her face with her reddened lips and blue tinted eyes, reminded Genevieve of a porcelain doll, she was almost unreal in her beauty. Perhaps in her twenties, she wore a thin blue dress, only thinly disguising her lack of undergarments in the sheerness of the creek.

She was looking at the photographer with intensity and a strange mysterious gaze. Genevieve had never seen a photograph like it, a fairytale almost, like she was a goddess.

Genuinely intrigued, she was going to bring it with her when she looked down and was shocked by what she saw. Five or six other identical frames were inside the foot stool. Quickly looking through them, she realized each of the women were similar and their hair and eyes the same tinted color, but each of them were different women.

Gathering them all up with the family photograph as well, she asked Valor aloud to forgive her for taking them and that she was going to take the family photograph to Noble.

But she didn't know what to say about the women in the frames, the mermaids of the past. For now she wanted to know more about who they were and who held the camera as they stared back up at them.

Chapter Seven

The grandfather clock in the hall struck three in the morning and bellowed out in the silent servant's quarters, chiming into the stillness of the slumbering world. Genevieve shivered but whilst tired, was excited to prepare a surprise for Noble.

He was an early riser like herself so she wanted to busy herself making sure that he was genuinely astonished to see all she accomplished. There was something wondrous about preparing a pleasant surprise; it was the giddy notion that soon enough ones mouth would hang open and their eyes would light up with genuine appreciation.

Noble was like that, he was one to express his observations openly and sincerely and he enjoyed all that was out of the ordinary or unanticipated. Hurrying, because she knew that Simon had heard her step into the hallway earlier, she had put on a nice knit tan cardigan that tied at the waist of her long pleated knit skirt.

The morning air, even in these warmer months, was not immediately inviting but she had gotten warm with the quiet coming and going from her room to the kitchen.

Soon enough another hour had passed and she could hear him stirring from his bedroom and she smiled and quickly surveyed her work, making sure she had not missed anything.

The table was set with a black and red rose embroidered piano shawl that she had personally owned. She had placed the turquoise vase at the center of the table with a fake red rose in it and each of the chairs had black velvet fabric draped down their sides to give some cushioning and for ornamental reasons.

She had opened the curtains and tied them with red and white lace and put little velvet pink rose buds in each tie. Pale red material with white lace table cloths adorned the three wooden tables that were most often used as counters around the walls of the overly large room.

Being that this side of the quarters did not have a designated lounge room, she had moved the large table over a little closer to the door and brought more space into the room. There she had managed to get in two smaller mauve armchairs from another unused guest room and set them up with a small table so people could sit there and talk.

The prior afternoon she had put the crystal ball painting and two others of a romanticized medieval nature in the frames and they now hung close to the sitting area.

Fearing that he might regret the creative freedom he gave her, she had hung up two paintings of stern ancestors but had carefully put little roses in their hands, ensuring not to damage them in any way.

And then at the back wall was the carousel horse, her favorite piece which did not necessarily fit in, but did not contradict the whimsy of the new décor.

Even the new table cloths had roses on them and she had gotten some nice cheerful floral plates as well. Having been frugal out of necessity in the past, she was determined that he trust her without concern, so she had the detailed sales ticket put aside for him and she was proud of her good affordable finds.

Putting her cream low heels on, now that they would not be heard over the silence, she checked her long brown waved hair in the partially open window and pressed her lips together to revive her pink lipstick.

Quickly getting over to the back left corner, she placed the Victrola needle on the thick record and low instrumental music played, bringing a new atmosphere to the room.

The door opened down the hall and his cane announced his pending arrival and she quickly turned away to turn on the stove, having prepared the breakfast food in advance.

With the sun not quite up properly, the electric light gave him a proper view of his new kitchen, and he stopped in the doorway to study it with great eagerness.

Not turning around, she tried to keep from smiling like a child, but she could hear that he was smiling and it made her happy knowing that she could do that for him. Simon finally walked over to her and pressed his head against her side, so she stroked his head and checked the percolator which was about done.

"There is a horse in the kitchen," Noble finally remarked with some amusement.

Turning, she looked at him and was caught off guard by his smile. There was something about him that she found uniquely lovely and having seen him as a youth in the photograph just made her appreciate him more. "I thought it better than putting it in the old stables," she replied with a smile.

Walking over to the table he liked to sit at, the one that was now a bit closer to the door and ornately covered with a piano shawl and vase, he sat in his favorite chair and smiled again.

"It is perhaps a little feminine but I can alter it however you please," she offered tentatively as she poured the coffees.

Glancing at the plate of food in her hand, he then looked at Simon who was smiling back at him in his own way. "You have done as you assured me, Genevieve. There is life here in the walls. It appears welcoming and elegant and the music makes me want to dance on my one good leg," he said in earnest as he studied her as well.

"And the horse?" she asked as she spooned some breakfast cocoa into his coffee because he had come to like it as much as she did.

Looking at it he laughed. "Somehow it feels suited to it all. I enjoy it tremendously. Even my predecessors there with their frowns," he continued. "You have aptly placed flowers in their hands, causing them to appear less threatening which amuses me to the point that I do believe I will laugh into the evening about it."

Putting his plate and coffee in front of him, she wondered if she should bring something up but perhaps she should wait until after.

Being the observant man he was, he noticed her expression right away and pressed her on it. "Did you enjoy Claremonde?"

"It was beautiful," she said as she got her own plate and coffee. "It was beyond that and more but I did not get to see much of it because I fritted too much time away in the study. I didn't know where to look first there was so much history in there."

Nodding with his mouth full, he appeared that he suspected it of her. "I must visit there again soon. I had forgotten how much I myself was captivated by what was there. I never appreciated it as a boy but as I became a man I realized the importance of it. So much to see and muse upon and preserve," he said.

She felt the same as he did. His ancestors may have not been particularly nice people, at least some of them, but the history was like bottled time, it was a story to tell, a fragment of turmoil to learn from. "Noble," she said as she gave Simon some of her toast crust. "I retrieved something from Valor's room, it was the only one I had seen so far but I wasn't sure if it would upset you. I will put it back if you wish."

Interest and worry formed in his expression but then he shook his head. "Do not be concerned that I will admonish you, Genna. I have encountered more people than I care to boast, and from it I can infer trust or deceit quickly. I know your intentions are genuine. I ask that you do not fear my reprisal. Tell me what you found."

His pale blue knit shirt flattered his blue eyes and she was relieved he could read her because she was worried that he might have issues with trusting her at first. Just the same she was hesitant to bring up the photos of the ladies in the creek. She couldn't be sure if he had taken them or Valor or if there was more to it.

Either way, she wanted to learn more and could not place why she held her tongue on that particular discovery. "There is a photograph that was in his room," she replied honestly. "It was of your family, when you were a boy, perhaps ten or eleven."

"*My* family? The four–,"

"Five," she corrected.

"Oh yes, of course at that age father was still with us," he nodded as he sipped his coffee. "I would like to see it; it *has* been a long time."

She had kept it aside tucked away on a small shelf behind the low refrigerator and brought it over to show him. Handing him the old frame, she sat and watched with interest as he studied it thoroughly. "Much longer ago than I realized," he mused quietly. "A curious boy I was, but now an old broken man."

Sipping her coffee and considering having another one, she was saddened when he spoke that way. He had convinced himself there was nothing left in him and she could see there was much more than he could ever realize. "What was said about your leg?" she asked straightly.

Staring up from the photograph he appeared surprised that she would bring that up in that moment. "It was suggested that it would heal but it would cause pain, there is arthritis in it," he explained curiously. "Why do you ask?"

Placing her fork on her emptied plate, she wasn't certain she could help but it was worth the attempt. "I had befriended a doctor who often talked about exercises to help with mobility in damaged or arthritic joints. He made great progress with his patients. I do not believe it healed them entirely but they could go through periods of walking unaided and their pain was eased."

Smiling, he had caught onto her thought process. "You raise this with me because I mentioned I was broken?"

Frowning a little, she nodded. "You don't need to be fixed, Noble. I think we can make things better. I know how you feel, and I don't bear the physical scars you do. But I don't see you that way. To me you are strong and striking and amazingly intelligent and charming and engaging. If I can do anything to bring your perception closer to mine, it would make me immensely happy to do so."

While his silence echoed reluctance to accept what she said, his eyes lit up and she thought he might be blushing a little. "How did anyone part with you, Genna?" he asked, looking directly at her.

Blushing herself now, she discretely sighed to counteract the effect it had on her. "No one was ever with me to begin with," she explained.

Intrigued, his eyes surveyed the room again and she could feel him giving in. "I suppose if you can lead a horse to the kitchen, you can lead this stubborn man to Claremonde."

Smiling, she looked across at the photograph in his hands, his breakfast already finished. "A handsome family," she noted earnestly.

Nodding, he could not take his gaze from it as he shook his head. "Even now I look at my father, brutish man he was. He wasted his entire life cowardly inflicting harm on the weak and reveling in his tyranny."

"Some people are born with anger inside of them," she said seriously as she collected their plates.

"You are right to say so," he agreed, glancing up at her. "Is your father a good man?"

"No," she said with a laugh at her abrupt response. "No, not at all, but I was fortunate to have not been influenced by him so I suppose that is something we have in common."

Suddenly Simon sprung to his feet and ran into the hall, barking, which is not something he did all too often. The front door closed which meant that someone had the key; she looked at Noble who smiled at her. "Is that you Henny dear?" he called out.

"It would not be a surprise if I told you!" she called back before appearing in the doorway of the kitchen, Simon sniffing her voraciously.

A heavy woman, buxom in a cotton sundress, striped with buttons in a lavender color with matching hat, she looked to be in her early seventies and had a cane with her also.

Genevieve turned and offered her a polite smile, feeling uncomfortable knowing that her much loved predecessor had returned and would certainly be critiquing her replacement.

"Ah, Noble, I see your ploy young man!" she declared loudly as she held her free hand to her ample bosom. "You intentionally caused my fall so you could replace me with this lovely girl. Shame on you!" she then finished with a raucous laugh before hobbling over to him, to kiss him on the top of his head.

Looking up at her, Genevieve could tell that he really cared about her. "Not at all," he insisted, reaching for her hand as she came to stand at his side. "If I had known how lovely Miss Belmont was, I would have allowed myself *two* nurses."

Clasping his hand in both of hers, she patted it as she smiled over at Genevieve, who was still holding a dirty plate in her hand. "Miss Belmont," she said, as if it was her way of getting acquainted with the name. "I had talked to your sweet Mrs. Marsh before we decided on you," she divulged a fact that she hadn't known. "You have been through the mill, haven't you dear? I hope you will feel at home here. This sweet boy will give you no trouble at all. He is the best of men."

A little shocked that Mrs. Marsh had told her anything about her past, she nevertheless understood that it was only her way of speaking highly of her, explaining how far she had come. "Mr. McKinley is not only very kind to me, but I find he is rather entertaining."

Noble let out a loud laugh and Henny was taken aback, not expecting humor on their first exchange but clearly pleased by it. "Indeed," she said, letting out a loud laugh that caused her whole body to jiggle. "He *is* entertaining, I do not dispute it," she agreed. "And my how this room has changed. What wonders," she added, giving it a thorough study with awe in her eyes.

"I thought it might bring a little color in here," Genevieve said carefully, not wanting to offend the older woman's tastes.

"Yes, my yes," she mused before looking at Noble. "Reminds me of your mother," she said. "Fanciful, witty," she added. "Oh! And the horse!" she noted with another laugh. "Dear me, it gave me a fright!"

Simon barked again and then turned a circle on the spot with excitement. Genevieve could imagine that Henny's laughter could bring life to any dark corner. "Lillianne's precious merry go round. Wherever did you find it?"

"In the old study," Noble replied for her. "Did you know it belongs to a larger piece?" he asked his new attendant.

Nodding, she recalled that just before they left Claremonde the prior day, Clemens gave her a key, one he had looked for in Lillianne's room. It was used to turn on the merry go round which was said to be located near the creek.

The horse that she had adored on sight was one of many and she looked forward to seeing it. "Yes Clemens told me," she replied. "I haven't seen it yet, but I am looking forward to it."

"Perhaps you will take me there," Noble suggested.

Smiling, Genevieve walked to the table to collect the remainder of their breakfast dishes. "Perhaps I will get you well enough you can walk there without my aid," she said more as a hope than an expectation.

Henny appeared genuinely surprised and before she spoke she walked around to face him so she could see him better. "You are looking well, Noble," she said seriously. "I wonder if this sweet girl will have you on your feet enough that you won't need a nurse any longer."

"I will still need a secretary," he countered with a smirk.

Laughing the woman nodded. "Yes I am certain that is true, dear boy." It was then that she noticed the frame in his hands. "Oh my," she reached for it and turned it around to study it in the light. "A lifetime ago," she noted gravely. "Your mother was so proud of you all, I miss her terribly."

"I do also," he said with moistened eyes. "She is with us still."

Nodding, she wiped a tear and smiled at him. "She watches over you and Simon," she stated cheerfully. "He was her fourth child that giddy pup."

Noble laughed but then Henny pointed at the photograph. "Do you remember what happened that day?" she asked him.

Mulling it over he shook his head but interest grew in his gaze. "With me?"

"Yes," she confirmed with a chuckle. "Your sister wanted her hair perfect and your mother had gotten busied with Valor and his suit so she asked you to help her."

"With her hair?" he asked surprised. "I suppose I have a vague recollection of it."

"You burnt a whole ringlet off and a portion of the back of her silk dress. Fortunately you had not burned *her* but she was not too happy about it. Just the same you all knew too well to keep silent about it so your father would not learn of it. But you had to help her for a fortnight with her hair so she was certain none of her scalp showed through."

Noble laughed and Genevieve finished washing off the dishes and placed them on a tea towel on the now decorated table beside the sink.

"I am so happy you are here, Henny," he stated sincerely. "But Miss Belmont has been a perfectly delightful attendant and I am blessed to know you both."

"I like you already," she said to her with a big smile.

Genevieve blushed but made sure she saw her appreciation. "If I can become half as treasured as you, Mrs. Wilshire, I will be a lucky girl," she said. "This room came to life when you entered it," she spoke her thoughts. "It is a rare person who can turn the lights on without electricity."

Noble laughed, as did Henny before she pulled a chair out to sit down close to him. "Please, do call me Henny. And your name is Genevieve?"

Nodding, she smiled. "Yes, and I would like for you to call me that also," she asked. "I am truly glad to meet you."

The older jovial woman's smile was genuine but then it faded as she placed the photograph down and stared at Noble. "I have news about Roger," she said.

"Your nephew? Is he well?"

Shaking her head, Genevieve sensed the beginnings of a sad conversation and excused herself explaining that she would write the letters that he had put aside for her.

Simon followed her as he was free to roam the house, and she was grateful for his company. Having a desk in her room allowed her time to type by the light of her open window. It was a nice morning full of hope and promise, sunshine and birds. Simon jumped up onto her already made bed, and hung his head over his paws looking at her.

Staring back at him, she sighed. The letters would not take her too long, provided she made no errors in typing and other things were calling for her attention.

Looking at a box beneath her bed, she thought of the pictures of the women in the water. Now that she had not mentioned it to Noble, it seemed an intentional secret, something she held back from him and she didn't like to feel that way. But how could she tell him that she took them? What would he think of her? But she was curious about them and their mysterious gazes.

For now though, it was the journals belonging to his brother that truly beckoned her and she pulled out the drawer of the small secretary desk and took out the first one, believing in starting at the beginning.

For twelve years old, his penmanship was quite impressive and his eloquence equally so. It was apparent immediately that he had a flare for the dramatic and an intelligent observant mind.

After the first paragraph, she looked over at Simon who was lying on his back and she wondered if it was invasive or inappropriate for her to read this man's personal thoughts. But on the other side, he was dead now and likely had much better things to think about, not just that, but she felt his writing echoed his need to be heard.

I am told I am now a young man, and for whatever reason, one day has made it so. This is my birthday, the day my mother gave birth to me with Henny Wilshire as her midwife.

I thought it best to make note of it so that you would be aware of these specifics. Mother says that to look into ones soul all they need do is watch their eyes as they speak. When father leaves she will tell me all of those that she believes to be insincere. They express one notion while their actions contradict it.

I have deceived, often really, she is likely to know. I love her, dear woman she is, but she is weak. She should fight. She should retaliate.

She tells me I am just a boy. I do not know all that is involved. But I know father and he is s a simpleton. Henny dislikes him and mother does her best to appease him but when he returns from his travels she avoids him mostly.

He has been with us again for near four months and Claremonde has been quiet, even the birds fear him and stay in the trees. Most days he will hunt but before then he will hit mother and yell at her and belittle her and she cries and whimpers like a wounded animal.

From my room I hear her on the floor, when he pushes her she falls and sounds like a sack of potatoes being suddenly dropped.

The screaming and cries never end and he is vile and I hate him. He does not call me by my name, he calls me 'boy' and tells me to get out of his sight and to excel at all I do for

I will take his place and I best be ready for it when I'm grown.

I will not be like him. I will silence this noise. There will be peace when he is dead and I will bring it.

I no longer wish to speak of him, let me rejoice for I am a year older and Henny has knit me a blanket for the draft in my room. Mother and the maids made me plum pudding and strawberry tarts.

Mother has taken me to the merry go round and we had sweet buns with Henny and the steward and we laughed and I tried to stand on one of the carousel horses but I could not do it long.

It was a day of rejoicing and father was hunting on another property so he did not know of our escapade and we are glad for it. I will say, however, that there is great change here and I am not certain how I should consider it.

Mother is with child and father said if it is a daughter he will have her locked away for women are of no use to him until he can marry them off. Mother says she believes it is a boy because he gives her strength inside of her.

Another boy and I am just twelve this day, he will not have much to say to me for years yet if he is a boy or if she is a girl. Mother says a babe can perish inside sometimes. But I will welcome a sibling, perhaps someone who understands what I endure, he will know, I will show him my hiding places.

He was writing about Noble. And how had it ended for them? She had not learned of how they got along, for certainly there was a great difference in their ages. Closing the journal, intent on typing his letters, she opened the curtains further and stared up at the great hall.

There was something amiss and she couldn't quite place it. Staring and getting lost in a day dream, her eyes suddenly caught movement on the second floor. A shadow in the window and just for a moment it looked like it was someone standing there.

It could have been a play of the light, the way the sun shone on the back of the hall, but her heart beat fast and betrayed her true feeling on it. She had not been sleeping well and was trying not to admit the fear to herself but she wondered if something lurked closer to these quarters too.

Frantically scanning the building, searching for a glimpse of what she had seen, she was glad not to find it, and perhaps Clemens was about, she could ask him later, he might be there himself like an adventurer, dreaming of yesteryear like she had done.

Whatever the case, she would not let it deter her. Fear of the unknown should never be an obstacle to hope or contentment. This was her home now and nowhere else would suffice no matter the ghosts that echoed around them.

Chapter Eight

A private journal could delve into the heart of someone and allow access to thoughts and feelings they would never otherwise express out loud. Just the same they could be boastful and on occasion self deceiving.

But Valor McKinley, who had written six journals in his youth after he began his first one at twelve, appeared to be sincere in what he relayed. While he did come across as smug and brash, he was not one to deny his shortcomings and would express them as freely as he would his own praises.

An avid writer, he observed much and left nothing to the imagination, but there was something Genevieve couldn't quite put her finger on that gave his halo darkened edges.

This particular morning had passed uneventfully and she and Simon had ventured into Claremonde, a place she had gotten to know better. She had spent hours at a time there and felt as though she hadn't even skimmed the surface of what there was to see and know.

Centuries of history were contained within these ancient walls and while the McKinley Lords of yesteryear were intriguing, Noble's direct family had mysteries of their own.

Two months had passed and the summer mornings were comfortable but the afternoons were a time to find a shady spot and drink cool cordial from the refrigerator. Genevieve had spent a lot of time with Noble and Simon as well as Clemens and had even become better acquainted with Henny.

Clemens had showed her where Lillianne's carousel was down by the creek. It had been built upon a large stone circular base and had gathered a lot of dust and some rust but Noble had made sure it was well tended to and it still looked new.

It was mostly horses with a mermaid and a unicorn and a Pegasus and a small rowing boat and Clemens had given her the key so in the warmth of the sun she could sit on it and read as the music played and it carried her slowly around.

But this day she was in Noble's boyhood bedroom at the end of the hall of the first wing in Claremonde. Like the other rooms it was large, expansive enough that he could entertain an entire room of people in there, but from what Valor had said in his journals, Noble liked to keep to himself.

All of the children did in their own ways but they loved their mother and each other and would delight in Henny's excursions to the seaside or the shops in Wanderling.

Things for her had been wonderful but strange. She had been dreaming of the red haired pale skinned women in the photographs, just seeing blurred images of them speaking or laughing. It was like in some moments she could hear them, not knowing what they were saying but they had been on these grounds, with Claremonde as their backdrop.

The creek had been such a peaceful place and the carousel down there was a special kind of magic, but lately she had sensed the same set of eyes watching her. The hauntings were moving or perhaps there was more than one and there was a stubborn unease at times that she tried to push aside, but it occasionally frightened her.

Having read of Valor's dalliances, she was well aware that he had been the photographer of the pale porcelain women with flowing red hair. But now she did not know how to raise it with Noble. She had spoken of photography in a casual aside and he had appeared distant on the subject, not wanting to discuss it and she didn't understand why.

Staring at the fireplace along the right wall where a low red chair was situated in front of it, she felt closer to Noble here. Having gotten to know him she knew how alike they were and how they both needed their solitude. It was partly because of a lack of trust of many but also because time was so precious and it was hard to spend it in trivial conversation.

There was peace in being alone, but now that she had met him, she greatly enjoyed being alone with him at the same time. She never tired of him.

Sitting against his pillows, ones he had used over fourteen years ago before the fire and before he left to live with his mother in the servants' quarters, she read a later journal of Valor's.

Having gotten through his early adult years where he documented a lot of his romantic and drunken liaisons, he now returned to a more pensive serious side.

This journal was begun in 1892 when he was twenty six, his brother was fourteen and his sister was eleven. He was still living there but was making references to where he intended to live next. He was also pondering whether his father would give him an allowance sizeable enough for him to reside where he wished.

Mother lost a tooth today, it was one from the back and she said it wouldn't affect her smile. She has little to smile about and yet she does. It had been dislodged through the force of a fist, perhaps this day or over time.

I am not sure if I pity her or admire her, but she would take a candlestick to him if she had any sense.

I have heard her attempts to suppress her cries, she now brings a blanket up so her screams are muffled when he deals the blows. His strength has hardly dwindled. It is a brute of a man that decides on a graceful wraith like her as an unmatched opponent.

I care not what he has or has not said to me in my time here. His name is Randolph Wallace McKinley, I tell you this for it is all that it means to me, a simple name on a page. He has not questioned me on my state of health or my intentions or my wishes and I do believe he is unaware of my accomplishments.

He is a figurehead, a dark ominous figure that looms and lurks, enforces and commands. Obedience and silence are his expectations and the sound of his hard shoes upon Claremonde's floors, instill fear and loathing and dread.

Remember him dear history, poor Randolph the tyrant, for he is the one that brings terror upon us and the shrill screams will be rolled up in his death shroud.

Young Prudence, she was behaving like a child should months ago but now she has hastily grown morose and skittish. She seeks him out so she can know where he is to avoid him. I have missed her laughter and her quaint observations. She was mother's doll but the shadow has cast over her. I should take her with me but mother would break into pieces and scatter in the gardens should I do it.

I would salvage them both but they must have the will to be rescued and they are imprisoned by the falsehood of his authority.

And my brother? Noble will rise above all of us and I see him now, a young man of fourteen, as he gracefully and skillfully duels with his fencing master in the gardens outside.

I look down at him now from my window, this second floor a great distance from the reality of the world of others, and I love him.

He is what I should have been for he looks away from the dark and solicits us all to the light. Noble is like an old man in a young one and he speaks with eloquence and more so conviction and much to my chagrin I can not dislike him. He makes me laugh, he amuses us with his subtly delivered remarks and he is wise beyond his years.

I tell him my thoughts in the night when the candles are few and the servants have departed. I go into his room and tell him stories and tales and he is bewitched, but he sees in me the truth, one I will not give credence to here. Young Noble summons me to quell those inklings, but I am me and he can not alter this.

Perhaps, in some happenstance irony, I have some of father in me and yet, I would extinguish any part of him if it were that uncomplicated.

But life is complex dear history, as are we all.

Fixing the clear button on the fitted waist of her knee length pale blue dress, she studied the pink flower buds on the pattern of it. Valor's words had given her a lot to think about, mostly about Noble but also about himself and the rest of the family.

Their mother, Lillianne, had died three years ago but what of the father? She believes it was mentioned that he had left, but where had he gone and had he returned there at any time?

The tall window in Noble's bedroom, alike to the others, was on the wall opposite the door and was close to the side of his headboard. Gazing out at the door and fireplace as the sun shimmered, dancing in the rays of light that were cast across the wooden floor, she pondered their mother.

Lillianne by all accounts was subservient to her husband and yet whimsical and joyful and creative. More than likely because they were lords and ladies, they lived in a world that dictated they mingle only amongst themselves.

Genevieve could only assume that Lillianne had been forced into an arrangement of marriage by their parents. Certainly Claremonde could not get into the wrong hands or be lost to a less than suitable descendent.

She pitied her, not only was she beaten and tormented but she was without love. Romance was like sugar, nothing tasted right without it. Someone like Noble's dream-filled mother would certainly have a head full of hopes and secret wishes.

Reluctantly getting off of Noble's bed, she stretched and placed a piece of velvet ribbon on the page she was reading and then closed the journal. Looking at a small round leather top table, she had come to love the framed pictures. They were sketches done by Noble himself of his childhood dogs. They were realistic and he had a true talent and he had worked hard on the pictures and had clearly loved his canine companions.

Noble had encouraged her to slowly bring him pieces of his childhood from his room but she decided against taking one of those pictures, feeling they should remain together. Instead, this day she brought him a black and red cross like medallion. It had been in the bottom of one of his large linen presses on top of a shirt from when he was a smaller boy, which she brought along as well.

Putting the folded shirt on his old with Valor's journal, she crossed her arms against a sudden chill and walked out of the room and into the long and wide hall of the first wing.

Stopping, seized by the feeling of being watched, she knew that Clemens was in Wanderling this day and would not return until later in the week. Holding her breath she listened intently. The sun was shining in a cloudless sky outside, it all seemed like a perfect day and the wallpaper shone as if someone had polished the walls.

Claremonde had accepted her, allowed her in without protest as she studied it eagerly and unobtrusively, but she was not alone. Footsteps above her, on the floor overhead that she had not yet visited, were audibly faint but discernable.

The father had lived up there from what she gathered. Valor had not gotten into details but the father would visit with his wife when it pleased him in her room or he would take a mistress if he so desired. But they had their own rooms. She could only assume the children were glad their father was not on the same floor as them when they were growing up.

Just the same, while the sound could be dismissed as the creaking and weathering of time and expanding of wood, footsteps had their own distinct sound. Thankfully she didn't hear them now. Everything that was unsettling was brief in nature, heard or seen or felt just enough to frighten but not enough to be certain it was experienced.

Drawing in a quiet shallow breath, she walked to the second to last bedroom on the right, the elegant and decadent bedroom of Lady Lillianne McKinley.

Even now the fragrance of a myriad of floral and delectable perfumes filled the air as if she had just sprayed it around this very moment.

The heavy mauve curtains hung from the ceiling to the floor over the wider window and sheer gold fabric was draped around it, bordering it like a scalloped romantic frame.

The atmosphere was regal and yet comforting, likely an apt description of Lillianne herself from what Noble had described. The bed was large and tall and likely very old with an ornate French provincial head board and bed cover that matched the curtains with gold silk pillows and cushions.

An empty domed bird cage hung from its marbled stand, empty from another time when a canary used to sing in it. Genevieve wondered how often Randolph visited his wife here and what remarks he would have made about her beauty and that of her room.

After the fire Lillianne had moved into another part of the servant's quarters leaving Noble to have the side he was in now. He said they had been happier after then, less overseen and freer to be themselves. She had died happy and loved but Genevieve wondered if she had pined for romantic love.

Walking over to the long French table neatly covered in gilded trays with perfumes and powder as well as brushes and handkerchiefs, she touched the top of the old celluloid glove box with a picture of happy children playing in snow on top of it. A framed photo was next to it of her and Prudence alone.

Prudence was a young lady in a beautiful ornate lace Edwardian dress and her hair partly back with ringlets. She was beautiful like her mother, both striking in features, lovely faces, beautiful eyes; they would have captured hearts and gazes wherever they went.

Lillianne's hair was dark and her smile modest. It was a lovely photo and likely one that she had favored.

Genevieve carefully leaned against the long dresser, studying the room. She had visited it a few times over the months and enjoyed it in there but worried that she was intruding on a lady's privacy. But Claremonde was a time capsule, left as it was after the fire, part of it destroyed and most of it still very much intact.

This room had two smaller ones adjoining it, one with a deep cast iron bath and a wash stand with a curved eighteenth century pitcher atop it. The other room was for her dresses and a multitude of under garments including corsets, bloomers, petticoats and stockings. She had likely taken a lot of them when she moved into the servant's quarters but some of these dresses were from her youth in the 1800s and they were museum quality like none she had ever seen.

Touching the silk, the beaded flowers, the grand bustles, she noticed something she had not seen on prior visits, a small set of hidden drawers blended into the wall. Opening the bottom one, with words of apology for the prying, she noticed it was filled with ornate shoes, likely from the sixteen hundreds. They were petite and Lillianne had probably kept them for historical preservation rather than use.

The top drawer had cotton corset covers and lace handkerchiefs but the drawer seemed to be slightly tilted, and out of curiosity, she pulled the garments back to see if the back of the drawer was broken, but a thin line was there and it was slightly raised, barely noticeable.

Trying to lift it, it didn't budge so then she pressed on it and it popped open; revealing a secret compartment.

Pulling open the secret door she peered in to see a small child's trunk, perhaps from the early Victorian era, It was a type of metal but was pristine and it was on its own, a secret for whatever reason. Pulling both drawers out of the wall she was able to work out how to open the whole section so she could reach in and retrieve the trunk.

With some hesitation, she brought it out and gently placed it on Lillianne's grand bed, sitting beside it and considering if she should open it or not. It might have been empty or it might have been something Lillianne would never wish anyone to see, hence the secrecy, and yet, once one had died, did it matter?

Genevieve did not believe herself any wiser than the next person and certainly didn't have the answers, but she honestly believed that once a person died, they were more content and less strained. If she had a secret, would she care if someone found out after death, or would she perhaps hope they would?

It was hard to say given that it might be hurtful to someone, so if she thought Noble might be upset, she would then have the burden of keeping it secret or being the harmer.

Hearing another creak above her, she decided to open it, for it would only be on her mind until she did. She would just have to consider her options once she knew what she was facing.

Reaching for the center latch dangling down, she lifted it up and the sound of the metal hinge echoed out and creaked as she slowly opened it all the way. The first thing she saw was a pink silk blanket or it could have been a pillow case. It was wrapped around something.

On top of it was a letter, folded once and it had clearly been read often. Drawing in a shallow breath she opened it and read, not quite understanding at first but then it dawned on her what had occurred. Lillianne had kept a secret and just as she assumed, she had been a romantic.

Lil, I can not remain any longer for I will endanger you. I will go to my brother and take Richard with me, he will be grown soon and he is a strapping young man of good nature who will benefit from the care of his uncle.

There is one amongst us who has been in communication with your husband. It is certain he is not aware but there is suspicion.

My love for you is infinite and until my demise I must wait again to embrace you and gaze upon your face. They must never know, it must never be spoken of.

I will in years return to my estate but I will not visit, I will be pained at the thought of you near and yet with the greatest divide between us.

I have cried for her, the one who had been the bond of our union. Dear Temperance. She will await us, my love. She will greet us when we once again meet.

Subdue your heart and fancies and know that I seek no other. Circumstance is our torment but our destiny is free. Be still Lillianne my dearest, be still and remember me.

Giles.

Reluctant to search further, Genevieve was trying to piece it together. Lillianne had been in love with a man named, Giles, and her husband had gotten someone to spy on them, so Giles stopped seeing her to keep her safe.

Who had he cried for? Who was he, this man who loved her so deeply?

But then it was clear by the small note written on the bottom by another hand. On the paper, by Lillianne herself, she had written;

Her first breath was taken in Heaven. Temperance Atherton.

Her mind was hurried, the name was familiar. Atherton, it was a name she had heard, it was *Marjorie's* name. Giles Atherton must have been her father.

And then the last piece was right there in front of her. Unwrapping the old fabric, she had not been prepared for what she saw. They were small bones, a skeleton of a tiny infant.

Lillianne had kept her all this time, the little girl who had died when she was born, the one who was the bond of love for Noble's mother and her true love, Giles.

He had been unaware of the sister born before him, the first she named of the virtues, little Temperance.

Chapter Nine

Two more weeks passed when something in the darkness of the night broke their time of tranquility and had Genevieve sitting up in panic. It was yelling, screaming for help and with her heart pounding she wasn't sure where it came from at first. Suddenly Simon was barking across the hall and the voice came again, it was Noble and he sounded terrified.

Throwing off her light blanket, moist from her summer night's perspiration, she looked around her room and then at her window where the curtains were closed, as if someone might be standing there. Rescue was not something she was experienced in, but no matter what, she had to get to him. Surveying the room in blind panic, she rushed over to the fireplace and grabbed a fire poker and rushed to unlock her door.

In seconds she was in his room, his light was off and she turned it on, standing in the doorway with her poker ready for defense if need be. But he was asleep and having a nightmare and the light had not woken him.

Simon rushed to her and kept turning to his master worriedly. Noble's blankets were wrapped around his legs; he was sweating profusely and yelling out. "No! No!"

His screams were from the stomach, sheer terror emanating from him as tears fell from his closed eyes. "No!" he sobbed as he reached out but then his hands went to his right side and he groaned in pain, curling up like a small child she realized he was remembering the fire.

Kneeling at his bedside she shook him a little and then harder before he slowly unclenched his fists and moaned as if the injuries were fresh. When his eyes finally opened, he appeared startled but then she reached up tenderly and stroked his forehead. "You were in a nightmare," she explained.

"The fire," he said; his voice hoarse.

Reaching for a glass of water on his bedside table, she gave it to him to sip and he did before nodding and falling back onto his pillow, exhausted.

Simon jumped onto the bed and sniffed him and then lay at his side, licking his hand. Genevieve went into his adjoining bathroom and took out one of the folded face washers and ran it under water, bringing it over to him.

He was only in a pair of white and blue silk pajama pants and his chest was bare revealing some deep scars and yet a healthy physique. Kneeling again she wiped the tears from his face and cooled his forehead off, before sitting at his side. "It haunts you still," she finally said quietly.

Gazing at her, he seemed comforted by her at his side but then he noticed the fire poker leaning at her feet. "Were you willing to risk your life to protect mine?"

Smiling, she did not want to overstate her heroism. "I am not foreign to being cowardly. I will admit I was hoping you had the trespasser subdued so I could simply hit him on the head with it, but I would have wrestled him if it was necessary."

Laughing, he reached out with his scarred hand and placed it on hers. "I suppose chivalry is open to us all now, Genna. I am glad you woke me but I am sorry that I troubled you."

"That is why I'm here," she reminded him. "That is my purpose here."

Strangely, he appeared saddened by her statement. "The concern of a nurse," he said quietly.

"No," she insisted. "A nurse tends to wounds *not* intruders. I am here because I wish for you to be safe because I would be most unhappy if you weren't. Now that I have met you I don't know how I could continue my life without you being a part of it."

Looking into his eyes, she felt she should look away but she couldn't.

Instead there was warmth there, an attraction there she couldn't push aside and his hand on hers only caused her to hope against her intent to remain neutral. But it was difficult not to get caught up in him, he was every bit the gentleman and they were so alike in moments they were two halves of the same person.

"The fire haunts me, yes," he confirmed, responding to her prior statement. "I am a weak man because I can not will it away. It gnaws on my memories like the flames that seared my skin."

Standing now, she walked towards his linen press and sifted through two drawers before finding new sheets.

Taking off the blankets, pulling them out from underneath Simon's body, she shook out the white cotton sheet and placed it over him and then brought up the top blanket which was not moistened from his perspiration. "You are a tower in the rubble because here you are and you face the ruins," she said.

"I can not forget it."

"You don't have to," she said. "You can make new memories. Even if it is tomorrow, even if you can only look forward one day, you can look to the future instead of stepping back into the past. Eventually you will not visit the past in your mind because your heart will be too busy with the future."

Turning on the lamp in the corner of the room, she brought his side table closer with the water and made sure his bell was within reach and then went to turn off his main light, stopping in front of the door in case there was something else he needed.

Staring at her, taking in her words, he glanced at Simon and there was a look of hope and inspiration in his gaze. "I wish for you not to leave," he said seriously.

Smiling, she was flattered he would say it. "I won't," she assured him.

"No," he said, apparently wishing to rephrase his prior request. "It is not that I wish for you *not* to leave, I am asking for you to *stay*."

"I will," she promised.

Studying her face with a sense of contemplation, he got that look of inquisitiveness in his expression again. "And what if you were not my nurse?" he asked curiously. "What if you were not under my employ and I did not pay you to be here?"

Laughing, she knew he did not mean for her to believe he was suddenly going to rob her of her income, but he asked questions like that and she was happy to indulge him. "Would I stay if you did not pay me?" she reiterated. "As long as you continued to feed me I suppose it wouldn't be such a poor arrangement."

He too laughed and glee was in his eyes as he stroked Simon's head. "Tomorrow we will go."

"Where will we go?" she asked curiously.

"To Claremonde," he said. "It is time for me to return home. You give me courage and I look forward to it."

Proud of him and hoping it would go well, she knew he had not returned since the fire and so it was going to cause him some anxiety no matter what he said now. "I look forward to it too, Noble. Sleep well," she said, opening the door and closing it behind her.

Breakfast the next morning was a quick affair because the master and his attendant were eager to begin their quest.

Noble, in his pale blue knit shirt and tan trousers, was strong enough to attempt something he had been talking about soon after she had arrived; he was returning home.

Now they were standing in front of Claremonde, Genevieve was wearing a cheery yellow and red rose dress and was feeling happy with Simon sitting between them, gazing up in equal appreciation.

"Are you in pain?" she asked him. Even though they had been walking in the mornings and afternoons and strengthening his muscles through exercises, she worried for him.

Enjoying her attention he smiled down at her. "If I am, I am not aware of it when you are with me, Genna," he stated lightly before returning his gaze to his childhood home. But then his smile faded as he looked at the remains of the right side of the building.

"What was on that side?" she asked him, not having given it much thought before.

"Have you not looked in there?" he asked surprised.

Shaking her head, she didn't necessarily want to tell him that she was frightened by it, but there was a practical reason. "I thought it might be dangerous to walk around in the debris," she relayed truthfully.

Studying her face anew as if the sunlight offered him more details of her, he stared at Claremonde again and she could tell that he was trying to remember it in its entirety. "The servants and townsfolk had removed most of it because they thought we would wish to rebuild," he explained. "The floor is solid enough at least the first level. Do you wish to explore it?"

"Not alone," she replied straightly.

Laughing, he placed his left hand on her shoulder and smiled. "Then we will venture in the three of us," he assured her.

Gesturing for them to proceed, he made his way slowly but with less uneven pace than in the past, and they strolled by many columns and smaller entrances to get to the third entrance door.

While the last third of the building was ruined, there was still large parts of it charred but intact, the double door being one thing that had held up.

Like the others it was unlocked, and opening it, a strange musty smell escaped while some black soot crumbled down in front of them. Simon sniffed it immediately, while Noble investigated the floor with his cane.

It wasn't like the entrance where the study was or the wide staircase leading to their bedrooms in the center wing. This first room was a ballroom and there were many doors leading off of it.

There were ornate gold columns with painted green leaves winding up them and the doors were arched with scattered ornate antique chairs and small tables around the edges.

The ceiling was black, the center especially like an explosion of flames had plumed upwards and hit it and spread out, dark and destructive. And yet a chandelier precariously hung at the center, a small part of it lilting where the ceiling was bent.

"Your ancestors liked to entertain," she observed aloud, noticing that the furniture and details were unique and yet likely late seventeenth century or even earlier.

Closing the door behind them but gesturing for Simon to remain close to him, Noble smiled in a mischievous way and a story formed in his eyes. "My great great *great* grandmother was a scandalous woman let us just say," he stated quietly but with some dramatic flare as if he was performing a play.

"She had the ballroom built?"

Nodding, he then shrugged a little as Genevieve tried to imagine it when it was not dank and damaged. "Lady *Amelia* McKinley was somewhat wild and impossible to tame but her ailing father insisted that their court indulge her every whim until she could produce an heir."

Simon walked in front of them and they carefully followed, watching him closely and checking the floor for weak boards, but it looked strong apart from the debris and dust. "Was there something wrong with her?" she asked quietly as if his predecessors were listening for any slight on their behalf.

Swapping his cane so it was in his left hand, he placed his right hand on her back and it caused her to stop, enjoying his touch. "She enjoyed dancing and laughing and performing on the stage in the next room which is destroyed. But those were not acceptable qualities of a lady at the time," he whispered.

"That is *all*? She was creative?"

Smiling, he was enjoying being there, he was reveling in having someone to talk to about the past because he too enjoyed history and was glad to have his ancestors be a truly fascinating group of people. "She was a lover of men," he said with raised eyebrows.

Looking out at the ballroom she was trying to ascertain how the structure of the building reflected what he was telling her. "More than one?"

"More than many," he confirmed.

"Was she not married?"

Nodding, he laughed. "Yes indeed, my great great great grandfather was a man of wealth and status and came from a family of equal standing. Having said that, he was weak in countenance and assertiveness and she had often remarked in her letters that he would drape his limp body over a chair like a piece of wet linen and lacked so much in personality that his character was indeterminable."

"An arranged marriage?"

Nodding, he shivered a little. "Fortunately mother was against such cruel practices and most certainly none of us three would oblige such a harsh tradition. However, Amelia was content for it as long as she was allowed her dalliances."

Walking in, Genevieve imagined it in glimpses almost like she could hear the faint sound of piano music in the background. Claremonde was truly magical. "Sometimes when I come here I feel if I simply take one more step I might enter the past and the lanterns will alight and they will all be here again.'

He did not laugh at her remark whatsoever; in fact he surprised her by appearing pensive at it. "I do believe the past is here captured someway and perhaps we can view it in moments, Genevieve. But we would not wish for it to remain. Certainly the gaiety and intrigue would have us enthralled but they suffered, they all did as we do in our own lives."

"Noble," she said quietly, feeling she did not want to disrupt any potential ghosts in their midst. "Can they be certain her husband was your ancestor? Could it have been one of her other companions?"

Smiling, he shook his head. "I had questioned that myself but there was much written at the time about it, a great deal by Amelia's own hand and in spite of her allowances, she was not unsupervised. There were limitations as to what was permitted for the very reason of the assurances of purity in inheritance."

"They supervised?" she asked, blushing at the divulgence. "And the ballroom was to entertain her guests?"

Suddenly stopping, he pointed at a dead mouse with his cane and gently pushed it aside with a warning to Simon to leave it alone. "She would have lavish balls and the upstairs rooms were at the time used for her many guests. She was a popular host and well loved for her generosity in gifts and spirit."

"What happened to her?" Genevieve asked, enthralled.

"She gave birth to a son she named Charles. He was healthy and a happy boy but her father soon regulated his behavior and kept him under strict observation so he did not become restless or rebellious like his mother."

"What did she do about it?"

Noble pointed upwards at a grand painted mural of romantic medieval lovers in the sky on the ceiling. "Her father who was still alive sent her to a convent across the ocean and she was not heard of after then. There was some conjecture that she had not survived the journey but there was also talk that she was able to seduce a sailor and have him rescue her, not ever returning to Claremonde."

"Were there any more balls after that?"

"No," he replied knowingly. "Mother held a handful of dances but father put an end to it when he returned from his travels. I do not believe she cared much for them anyway because she mistrusted the sincerity of others and felt it better to keep to herself and to us. But Prudence and I would play here often and she would like to dress up while I did my drawings here."

"The dogs, the dogs in your bedroom," she remembered. "Noble, they were so lifelike, you are quite talented. Do you still draw?"

"I loved them dearly," he said, glancing at Simon who had fallen asleep beside a piano at the back wall. "My right hand has not held still and I have not considered pursuing any of my passions since the fire."

"I wish you would," she said truthfully. "Perhaps you will need to have more patience with it, but a gift is not ended because it is harder to utilize, only sometimes you have to alter how you disperse it."

Gazing into her eyes, he kept his hand on her back and she realized how much she liked this room and how she pitied poor romantic Amelia. "I will try, Genna. Let us see what life I have left in me. Only you can bring it out of me."

Smiling, she wanted to kiss him in that moment, but she feared him sending her away and she did not want to misconstrue his kind words. "Upstairs is mostly gone?"

"Yes," he confirmed sadly. "Yes the second floor is gone, I had watched it–," but then he stopped talking so abruptly that he coughed. "And then there is below us, a floor that should mostly be stable and untouched apart from having been aged," he quickly added.

"There is a level beneath the ground?" she asked, genuinely surprised. But then she looked at his legs and he noticed it straight away.

"If you have the patience to get me there I would like to take you," he said, enthusiasm in his gaze.

She enjoyed watching his revival since she met him. When she was hired she thought she would be bathing and assisting an invalid man. Never did she anticipate how much she would care about him, how much she would adore his character, his intellect and most of all his willingness to return to life.

He just needed a little encouragement. He was not at all ready to be put out to pasture, he had so much life in him but he had forgotten himself and now he was remembering.

"I would love that," she stated sincerely. "What is down there?"

Smiling he pointed at the third door, it was way back in the right corner near a broken wall sconce. The fire had engulfed parts of the walls and doors and the ceiling but had left enough to be able to easily imagine what it was like in its heyday.

She kept close to his side as they walked across the ballroom floor when she suddenly smiled and he heard her because he looked at her curiously. "What are you thinking about, Miss Genevieve?"

Embarrassed he had caught her, she shook her head. "I was just imagining us dancing here," she said. "Just a fleeting thought I suppose."

Instead of laughing, he looked around and nodded. "Clemens excels at the piano and Henny is known to be quite the dancer, so I can not see good reason we shouldn't have a little gathering of our own. Would you like to organize it? Perhaps we can invite the maids and steward and gardener, hold a small affair with the estate workers."

Nodding, it seemed a wonderful idea and she pondered the possibilities as they drew closer to the door and he reached out to turn the knob. She glanced back and wondered if she was in that category. "I would dance with Clemens I suppose," she thought aloud.

A little shocked, he immediately dismissed the idea. "I would hope then that you save the first five for me, Genna."

Relieved that he would offer it, she smiled. "If you wish to dance I will be happy to accompany you as often as you wish it. Do you dance well?" she asked as Simon got in front of them and was happy to rush down in search of more wonders and possible rodents to chase.

"My siblings and I were taught by instructors a number of years in our youth," he explained. With his left hand on her shoulder, he stood behind her slightly as she guided him down a dark set of narrow wooden stairs. "But if you do not find me sufficiently up to the task then I can at least blame my wounds," he said.

Laughing, she was careful not to go too fast and noticed that the stairway wound around and it was quiet downstairs as if they were truly leaving an active dance and entering a quieter place.

When they arrived at the bottom, she instinctively took his hand and made sure he took the last step steadily.

She had not expected to see what she did, and having imagined the whole right side of Claremonde burned to cinders, here was a ballroom and below it a large room where an empty swimming pool once was. The room was untouched but the water had long dried up.

The pool was rectangular and deep with stairs going down each end of it. The floor around it was white tile and the walls were a cream color with white Roman columns rising from floor to ceiling. Plain wooden chairs were scattered around with towels and she noticed an old pair of ladies' Edwardian full body swimming trunks draped on one of the chairs.

"When was this built?" she asked, astonished to find it here.

Surveying the room with his blue eyes as he took in all of his childhood memories, he thought about her question. "Perhaps my grandmother had it built, I thought mother had said. My grandmother had thought the cold water extinguished her ailments and she swam in it daily."

Standing back with the door close to her, she wanted to see the room in its entirety, trying to capture it in her memory. Looking up she noticed a concession of long narrow windows that were likely hidden by bushes outside but allowed enough light in, casting symmetrical rays in the room. It must have looked magical when the water was there. "Was the water cold when *you* used it?" she asked curiously.

"Yes, it was not heated at any time so mostly Prudence and I would come down here with mother in the summer," he replied wistfully.

Simon sniffed the room thoroughly, this being his first adventure here and his tail was wagging enthusiastically with the myriad of scents. "I moved away quite a distance from here at twenty three, but I was close enough to visit mother and Henny every fortnight," he said. "Sometimes Mary accompanied me but she would tire of it here preferring to attend concerts and dances."

"Who is Mary?" she asked, not having heard the name before.

Glancing at her, he almost seemed to regret having mentioned her. "She was my fiancée'," he replied staidly.

She remembered him mentioning her once, but had not realized they had been engaged. "The one who left you after the fire?"

Nodding, he did not seem saddened by it, but it bothered Genevieve that anyone could have done that to him. Just the same, love was not something one could emulate. It was either felt or it was merely a form of compassion rather than adoration. "Did your mother like her?" she asked, trying not to sound too curious about it.

"She often said that father would have approved because she was of good breeding and a suitable match in our society," he said with a smile. "Mother found her pleasant enough although I could see they did not converse well. She found Mary to be too invested in social standing and less interested in the plights of the needy or even me. But mostly mother disapproved because she said that love could not be spoken from the lips if it did not shine from the eyes and she knew I did not love her."

Surprised by his frank admission, she glanced at him but did not stare. "Did you not ever love?" she furthered carefully.

Looking at her, he kept his gaze on her and she opened her mouth to speak but was stunned in the moment by the look in his eyes. "I never did," he replied straightly. "I was enamored on occasion, swept up at times but not like–, no. No I didn't, not truly."

With his heart so open and her courage near the surface, she considered asking him if that had changed. If perhaps the way he looked at her was a smoldering fire of a memory or the reality of how he felt now.

"Simon!" he called. "He is always scavenging," he stated exasperated as he used his cane to walk around and search for his dog behind columns and another open door near a basket of towels.

Genevieve was deep in thought as she watched him enter an adjoining room but then she heard something she had not expected.

It was the sound of water, not running water but the same sound that someone would make in a pool or a river when they were splashing around or swimming in it.

Noble had made good progress and had gone into the small adjoining room far off to the right of the pool area and was probably reminiscing in there while he retrieved his dog. But she was struck by a fear that she was trying valiantly to fight inside of herself.

Doubting all of her senses she slowly raised her gaze, her eyes first looking at the tile in front of her and then further out. That was the first time something really caught her off guard and she could see the rays of sun were temporarily blocked as if someone was waving, or a shadow was occasionally intercepting them.

With her heart pounding she lost the ability to speak or call out and yet she had to look, she had to see if her imagination was simply tricking her or it was a misunderstanding.

And yet the sounds of water splashing echoed in her ears, loud enough that it was no longer faint or even mistakable. Clasping her hands together and ensuring the wall was behind her, she drew in a shallow breath and looked into the pool.

It was full of water, cold mostly clear water, full as if it was about to be used.

She tried to call out, Noble had to see it, but then maybe it had already been full, maybe she did not realize it when she first entered the room, she got distracted so easily sometimes.

That must be it, she reasoned, it was there all along and she was not going to let Claremonde frighten her away. It was a magic mysterious place and it took you in its warm embrace while holding you at arms length simultaneously, but she understood what Clemens had meant now. He had become part of it and now so had she.

Whatever the sensations of the past in this moment were, they were definitely not the warm invitings of yesteryear. They were dark and foreboding and her instinct was to flee but she would never abandon Noble and Simon.

The vast downstairs pool area became silent and she understood now the feeling she had in the upstairs bedrooms. Sometimes it would grow still and that must be when something or someone was around. The sound, the feelings of current time were all seized and drawn away from the room filling her with a deep trepidation.

Nevertheless she approached the side of the pool taking slow steps and glancing only very briefly at the side door to see if Noble had come out. But she feared interrupting what he too might witness.

Calming her nerves, breathing lightly through her mouth, she crouched down to extend her fingers out to touch the water.

She could still hear the movement as if someone was in it but she didn't see anything and wanted to verify it was cold. Only seconds away from touching it, suddenly someone jumped up in front of her.

Screaming she fell back and only caught the glimpse of a woman.

She had long red hair and pale skin and she was gasping for breath, looking at her with terror in her eyes.

But Genevieve couldn't stop screaming and she became faint, not truly understanding what was going on.

Suddenly someone clutched her shoulders and she spun around to see Noble there. It was hard for him to crouch down but he was kneeling beside her in spite of his pain and she wrapped her arms around him, utterly petrified.

"Genna, what is it? Please tell me, what is it? What did you see?"

Simon sniffed and pawed at her, worried for her, worried for his master too who was not often on the ground.

Looking at the pool it *was* empty; it had been the whole time. Shaking her head, she wasn't sure if she should tell him but it was time she was honest. "If you want me to leave I understand," she said into his chest.

Pulling back so he could look at her, he appeared upset that she said it. "Why would you think I would want you to leave?"

Looking at the empty pool again she sighed. "The day I found the frames for the paintings I also found some photographs and I don't know why, but I held onto them," she confessed. "I didn't know at first if you had taken them but I also found Valor's journals and I have been reading them. I wanted to tell you earlier but the longer I didn't tell you the longer I felt I had done wrong."

Studying her face she could see that he was not upset with her but she felt terrible because her curiosity had put her in a poor light. And then he smiled a little, relieved. "Genevieve, if I found someone's journals I would read them too and my brother is sure to have had a lot of interesting things to say, he was hard to silence on many occasions. He led an adventurous life."

"I wanted to tell you and talk to you about it, I'm sorry I didn't," she said, happy to stay in his embrace for a minute longer.

"Reading his words, do you find yourself enamored like his many lady friends?" he asked semi jesting yet genuinely curious.

Shaking her head, she could easily say she wasn't. "He is interesting as you say but I much prefer his brother who is less wild and considerably more dashing."

Glee formed in his blue eyes and it was if she handed him the greatest gift in the world, like the weight lifted from his entire burdened body and she could feel it relax. "What were the photographs of?" he asked quietly, not taking his gaze from her.

But she looked again at the pool which was thankfully empty. "There were women with pale skin and long red hair, like Marjorie, but they were all young and I believe he had taken them," she explained.

"Were they in the pool?" he asked. "Valor eventually lived on this side when he stayed over in his adulthood. The ballroom and the pool were places he enjoyed bringing his friends, those ladies that you speak of. In the last part of the century, photography had become a unique passion of his. He enjoyed coloring them and of course he enjoyed his models."

"They were not in the pool,' she replied. "In the photographs they appeared to be in the creek like near where the carousel is," she said.

Staring at her, she thought she could feel his heart beat and he opened his mouth but didn't speak at first. Simon calmed beside them and the room became quiet and she could hear the birds singing outside again. "Were they alive?" he asked with great hesitation.

Glancing at him she could tell that he was fearful to ask such a question, not just because of what her answer might be but because he had now shown there was some doubt about his brother and his capabilities.

"Yes," she confirmed and made sure he did not see her flinch or look judgmental. "In the photographs they were."

He tried to stand and she helped him and together they were able to slowly straighten as he stared over at the pool now. His face so close to hers as he looked down at her, seizing her shoulders both for his stability and her comfort. "What did you see Genna?"

Lowering her gaze, she sighed. "I saw one of them, at least she looked like one of them and it was so sudden, it was only a second, but she looked afraid. The pool was full of water and she was gasping, that is all. The water was there for as long as you were in that room. I saw it and now I doubt myself as I say it to you. I can not rationalize it, Noble. I do not know what you think of me now."

Waiting for her to look at him, he did not look like he doubted her at all; in fact he appeared a little afraid. "Do not doubt what you see or hear or even feel here, Genevieve. Trust that these things are around us and know I will let no harm come to you. The past is visiting us. I do not know why, but I suspect it will not fade until its whim is resolved."

Chapter Ten

A haunting was a unique unsettlement; the dread that at any given time something might lurch out from nowhere and seize you. They could be behind or in front unseen until the unsuspecting person stood at just the right angle that they might capture a glimpse of those beside them.

It was fascinating, it was bewildering and frightening but when someone had to live with it day to day it was exhausting and added a tension where there wasn't any before.

But she would not leave, and Noble and Clemens and Simon and the other workers there had gotten used to it well enough, so should she. Not that she knew the others had experienced too much if they had not gone into Claremonde but they would have felt something, it hung in the sky above them and in the grass below them.

Too much had happened now and even though she was afraid, she wanted to find the answers. She wasn't even certain of the questions, only that something had occurred there, perhaps a great many things had, but someone watched them and she needed to understand it.

A part of her was worried she would never properly sleep again. A locked door did little to cease the wanderings of the transparent world. Nevertheless, there was a chance that if she could piece it together then maybe the past would not impose so much on them; perhaps true peace would be had by both the living and the dead.

The afternoon breeze was warm and pleasant as Genevieve stared at the old merry go round not far from the creek. This had been Lillianne's favorite place and she understood why. Willow trees hung over the bubbling brook, taller trees in the area shaded the grass and the carousel was a whimsical addition of magic.

The birds seemed to favor these trees and some swooped down taking turns at searching the shallow water as they sung a unified melody. Taking in a deep breath, she loved it here and had come here more often than going into Claremonde since the day she saw the woman in the pool.

Simon had come for the walk and was rolling around in the thicker parts of the grass close to the water. The carousel had pinks and greens with gold tints and it was clearly made with quality and intricate detail and ornamentation with gold heads and angels, cherubs and mermaids.

It was particularly beautiful and only had a handful of pieces on it, the horse having been replaced but exactly the same as the one she had brought into the kitchen from the study that day.

Looking back up at Claremonde she could not see the servant's quarters from here but sometimes got this strange sensation that she was incomplete when she wasn't there.

For now she walked over to the piece that looked like a small row boat and she sat on the seat inside of it. She did have the key to turn it all on but the serenity around them, the sounds of the brook and the birds and the scents of flowers and grass was too wonderful to interrupt with the music.

Valor's next journal was in her hand and instead of reading it out of curiosity alone, as a peek into the past; she now wondered if he had known something. Would he mention those women and had one drowned or would he say if something had occurred at all?

Opening the first page, this particular journal had a harder cover and the writing was slightly more erratic as though he changed his mind about what he wanted to write a lot as he got older.

He was now twenty eight and has moved out, but he mentioned at the beginning as a side note that he returned three days a week because his mother has trouble handling the transition.

Just the same, as she read through a little further, it was apparent that he liked to bring his lady friends there to take photographs and they of course were his lovers. He had not divulged too many intimate details but he was not one to commit his heart to one girl for long.

By the sixth journal he had gotten used to detailing the ages of his family members and the *'regular characters'* as he called them like Henny. At this time Noble was sixteen and studying art with a tutor and Prudence was thirteen.

There is much to tell and while I am not one to play into the hands of standard fare, what I write here is on the surface of things. I can not relay to you, dear future, what it is like now in this explicit moment. It contains an energy of uncertainty and yet I am experiencing a knowing.

Father is gone again. That alone might be a statement that you would easily skim over but it is different, this one time it is not the same as the other times. He travels often but I was here the night he departed.

Three months have idled by but ask me now and I will tell you that he will not return. He will not ever return.

Have you ever known something and not spoken it because there is nothing to validate it? Mark my words that I had said it, note that I believed it, tell me I am a liar because I tell you now, he will not return.

Mother too, she has not spoken the words but she walks up the stairs which she never does and searches his room for answers. What does she seek? She does not tell me but she never in the past ventured up there for fear of him, for the lack of want to be in the presence of his belongings, his essence.

She looks at me at times and it is a stare I can not properly detail for you, but she had not done it before. I will tell you this; secretively I express it in my head, a whisper to you, dear future. She looks at me with terror and relief, both at once and I do believe she wishes to ask me. For most surely she wants to know if I feel it too, the cusp of freedom.

While I pray inside of myself that he never return; I also believe outwardly and express it thus, that it is already true.

The night he last left, he had beat mother but then he retreated and it is not known where he went, we all kept from him and silenced ourselves so he would not retaliate. I fear something was afoot, unspeakable, but later I saw him.

It was two in the morning, long before dawn and it was not unusual for his carriage to arrive at this time but the driver was absent.

My room, as for all of us, was at the front of Claremonde so I could look down but a small stone overhang kept me from seeing who he spoke to. He was angry, not a surprise for any of us. Asleep was when he was not bitter or brutish, but this time he almost growled at this person. He was alive with rage and in the moonlight I tell you even then there was blood red in his cheeks at the fury within him.

And then he stepped forward inside. I listened with my ear pressed against the window pane and heard nothing. I waited. I was fatigued from my day but I was curious as it unfolded and so I forced my eyes to gaze into the clearing.

The driver did not return while I watched, nor did my father leave Claremonde. In the least of course he may have gone in another carriage from a different direction but that is pure speculation and the logic of a man in denial.

My father has yet to return but I wonder if he departed to begin with. He could have run out into the dew filled grasses and marshes around us to a secret person in wait of him.

Randolph is not a lover like I. My gaze is my mother's own, my own wild fantasies, like hers, wedged beneath my skin. I have gotten my wiles and my wants from her and he, poor Randolph, he wishes to own his kin. He is power and tyranny and prestige.

Why should he then leave Claremonde?

But then...it has been three months, perhaps future, you will prove me wrong and my ponderings are unsubstantiated.

It is doubtful, and yet...

And now I will shock you and I do enjoy to inflict some astonishment, nevertheless, this is not news I wish to relay but for historical reasoning I will tell you, Prudence has given birth to a child. Indeed you have seen that I mentioned the details of my beloved kin and I confirm she is but thirteen.

The identity of the father of this babe is unknown, but mother has fired the second stable hand although I believe him innocent. Prudence had taken an innocent interest in him, but I will not tell you my suspicions, for now I remain quiet on the subject.

She is bedridden for now, her young body will soon recover the violence of labor but she adores her daughter. In respect of my mother she has continued the strange practice of naming children after virtues and the tiny child is Patience Lilly.

Henny is decidedly smitten and mother has new life in her. With father's absence uncertainly indefinite and the birth of the small miracle, Claremonde is alive again and I am here more often than not; the betterment is undeniable.

I am an uncle, it is a strange statement to be made and stranger still for this child to see me as such, but she will be loved.

Speaking of that turmoil filled emotion, love has sought me out. For now, yes, we know that I can not embrace it long, but she is everything, the one that epitomizes all that her emulations strive for. And who is this fortunate object of my affection? No other than Marjorie Atherton, the daughter of the next estate on from us. I had met her twice in my youth but her family is as mysterious as ours and they are rarely seen.

Her father, Giles Atherton, is famously amiable and known for his love of privacy and abundance in philanthropy. I see this in her, she speaks quietly but has wit that parallels my own and I am rarely at a loss for words. Both her beauty and sharp words are enough to render me momentarily stunned into silence.

A goddess with her flowing red hair, her porcelain skin, her statuesque silhouette, she is perfection, an artists dream to both paint and sculpture her and she is mine. I will say it, she belongs to me, my beautiful doll and none other can compare, I am aware of this.

Know this, dear future, it has been said by man throughout the years, but invest your heart fully and know that it can be lost utterly. Love is a trap, an instability in its very foundations. If you relent and give your all to one, you risk complete destruction, but what a joyous gamble!

I will keep you abreast of further developments. Until then I will stroll with my goddess to the creek, eat and be merry. Valor McKinley.

Genevieve closed the journal as was her habit to do when he had completed a thought. It seemed appropriate to allow time between readings given that time was spent in between his writings. He *was* interesting, an intelligent vibrant man in his own right.

But Noble's family were each a mysterious enigmatic person, their own stories, their own unique tales that bore investigation and digging, layers beneath the superficial. She felt privileged to be privy to their private lives and be a part of Noble's life. There was an honor in it, and she felt honored to know him, to share her meals with him, to have him genuinely interested in her thoughts.

Contemplating now on all that she had seen and been through, she wanted desperately to clear the air and divulge everything to him. She wasn't sure whether it was the right thing but she wanted to allow him to decide what he wanted to know and what was best left in the past.

She had little interest in revisiting her own past; it had been a place her mind rarely wandered, but his present and past were entwined here as if his soul was planted in the soil.

Closing her eyes, she enjoyed the feeling of Simon against her leg. He enjoyed walking around the merry go round when it was not moving but always seemed to prefer remaining close to her or Noble or even Clemens, when he was around.

Her knee length pink sundress allowed the warm air to circulate around her and the day was perfect. But then something changed and she couldn't quite put her finger on it straight away. The birds quietened and a cooler air slowly wafted up from the creek towards them.

Opening her eyes, she could barely move as she looked down at Simon whose head shot up and his ears pricked up, listening for something indeterminable. Her heart began to pound; she knew the warning signs of an ominous presence. Remaining still, she did lean forward and touch Simon, hoping he would stay with her and then they heard splashing, this time from the creek.

No matter how brave she had been practicing to be, it took so much more to actually raise her eyes and look over at it. Not seeing anything, she was relieved and realized that it must have been a bird that had dove into it.

Standing up and collecting the journal, holding it in her arms, she smiled down at Simon who did not look so convinced.

She wanted to lightly say something to calm him but she couldn't, and a very low growl emanated from him. But what frightened her most was the fact that he was looking at her shoulder, just above it and all the hairs on the back of her neck stood up.

With the world around them eerily quiet she heard a voice, a male voice and it said something she couldn't understand but it was right into her ear.

Not waiting around, she did see the creek as she ran back up to Claremonde, and she did see a flash of red, maybe hair, maybe nothing, but she didn't turn around again. For all the money and treasure in the world she wouldn't turn around again, some mysteries were meant to stay that way and she had never in her life run so fast.

Simon was close behind, barking at the creek and then catching up to her, barking at her out of worry. "Run, Simon!" she ordered, and fortunately he did.

Not looking at Claremonde as she passed it, she immediately went for the servant's quarters and without warning, Clemens saw them and intercepted. "What is the matter, Miss Belmont?"

Latching onto his arms, she realized he had been picking flowers, probably something that Noble had asked him to do. Glancing back, she could no longer see the creek but the fear gripped her still.

"Did you see something?" he asked quietly as Simon sniffed him and jumped up.

Catching her breath, she shook her head. "Yes, no, I can't be certain," she said, feeling foolish. "I feel I heard a voice but I don't know."

"Where were you?"

"Down at the carousel."

"The creek," he said, unsurprised. "A man?"

Staring at him, she was astonished for him to say so. "Why do you ask me, Clemens?"

He nodded. "I've heard it twice down there but I don't know what it says, it is close to the water but I suppose it's a memory like the grass took a photograph of a moment or the like."

It wasn't such a strange theory, rather than a ghost; it could have been an unusual phenomenon where the past had been overlapping the present in a recollection. "The man's voice was close to my ear," she said and noticed that he seemed surprised. "I don't know what it said either," she stated dejectedly. "Is Noble in the kitchen?"

Nodding, she excused herself knowing he would soon be behind. Simon followed her in through the front and she quickly made her way down the hall and into the kitchen. "I feel I should leave," she said the minute she saw him sitting there at the table with a coffee and a book. "I can not bear it any longer."

Chapter Eleven

Noble, in his favored chair at the table in the kitchen, glanced up at her; he appeared shocked by her statement that she wanted to leave. "Has something occurred?" he asked worriedly.

Sighing loudly, she looked behind her at the window. "Much has occurred," she replied exasperated. "I question my ability to decipher truth from conjecture. I can not trust my imagination to not intrude on my reality."

Placing his book down, he stared at her and pat Simon, considering her words. "I understand your confusion, Genevieve but you mustn't doubt yourself. If you do wish to leave I will of course accommodate your requests. Is that truly what you wish?"

Hoping that he had offered up a protest, she pulled a chair out and sat on it, staring at him. "Yes," she said, regretting the upset in his expression. "At times the fear is overwhelming. But I can not leave," she sighed.

"Why?" he asked gently. "Do you wish to stay or is it simply you feel you have nowhere to go?"

Shaking her head, she had not even thought about going anywhere else, it wasn't that at all. "I can not leave because I can't take it all with me," she said truthfully.

"And if you go, will you then pack me in your luggage?" he asked, seeking answers in her eyes.

Smiling slightly she relented. "I have a case your size," she confirmed. "You would be the first thing I pack, and Simon would be the second."

Smiling wide he reached out for her hand and held it in his. "If you leave I ask that you take me with you."

Even though she was certain he did not expect her to go, she did believe he might just follow her if she tried. Their strange world had bonded them and held them together as if they always knew each other but simply hadn't met yet. "Do you believe something bad happened here?" she asked frankly.

Nodding, he sipped his coffee, keeping his hand on hers. "Of that I am certain," he replied straightly. "I am sorry these haunts have caused you grief, Genna. They left Mrs. Wilshire well enough alone; I do not know why they are so free with you. I want very much for you to stay."

"I will," she said. "I may not sleep again, but I will remain here just the same."

Leaning back into his chair, his smile faded and there was a sense of change in the air, a decision made, a question asked that he resisted before. "Did you see something?"

Glancing again over her shoulder at the window, the sun made everything seem so benevolent but now it was harder to relax, more happened since when she first arrived. "I wonder if my looking through things has dug up the soil where I shouldn't be digging," she mused aloud.

Nodding, he did not contest it straight away. "Yes you have brought it to the surface, perhaps Clemens too on his curious treasure hunts, but I do believe they want to be heard, or there is something someone wants us to know."

Studying him, she realized he had had a wash and gotten out of his dressing gown and put on a tight tan knit shirt and his hair was done. More often than not she didn't even notice his scars now. "I heard a voice," she said.

Simon suddenly got to his feet and rushed to meet Clemens in the doorway of the kitchen. The affable young man in white shirt and dress pants bent to pat him as he smiled at them both. "She heard the same one I did those times," he explained, having caught the tail end of their exchange.

Noble looked at her and she realized that this sort of thing had been going on for some time, and her employer was more than aware of it. "A man's voice?" he asked her.

Nodding, she looked at Clemens. "I don't know what it said."

"Did it come from near the creek?" he furthered curiously.

"No," she replied with a sigh. "It was right beside my ear and I did not stay long enough to ask him to repeat what he said."

They both let out a loud laugh and Noble beamed at her and then smiled at Clemens. "It does cause me to think that perhaps we should begin to investigate these happenings," he stated gravely. "I do not like the disturbance to you and I have seen that more is occurring now."

"Did you hear or see things here when you were younger?" she asked with hesitation.

Shaking his head, he looked towards Claremonde although it couldn't be seen from there. "There were times when I could sense things around. My ancestors have held this land for a long time, certainly there was some unrest but more so in these past years," he said, but she could tell he didn't want to think on that too much. "Clemens, where do you believe we should start?"

His friendly driver, a willing accomplice in any adventure, smiled given the opportunity to begin a mission of sorts. "The burned side," he quickly replied. "I think what is left over might have some clues for us."

Noble nodded, suddenly alive with ideas himself. "Splendid, Clemens. When will you go?"

"Now!" he replied with a laugh. "Here are the flowers," he added, placing a variety of them into the vase on the table that Genevieve had put there in the past. "I do not know what I am searching for but I will return with something!" he declared as he bowed a little and left the room.

Laughing, Noble, placed his tea cup aside and Genevieve took it over to the percolator and filled it up again. Bringing it back to the table, she poured some milk into it and passed him the sugar bowl. "I wish to ask you a question but I must confess I do not know how to ask it. Even asking you is offering information that you might not want."

Not concerned, he was always curious and she enjoyed that about him, but this was more serious. "Do you believe it would upset me, Genna?"

He often posed questions to discover what her perceptions of him were. "I believe it could," she replied truthfully. "It might alter how you feel about your family, but I had found something in your mother's room that I doubt you are aware of. I know you said I could look through anything but perhaps some things are better left in the past. Do you think it should be? Perhaps it is something she would not want you to know but then maybe now time has passed she would."

Now genuinely fascinated, he stirred two scoops of sugar into his coffee and sipped it. "About my mother?"

"Yes," she replied, returning to the sink counter to get a coffee for herself.

Usually a man of quick decisive responses, he did not commit to an answer straight away. She poured her coffee and brought it to the table and watched him think as she poured her own milk and sugar. "It is hard to know how to respond without comprehending the context of the question," he replied.

"I know," she said. "That is why I was reluctant to raise it. But I feel it important for me to tell you anything I find because you are not so easily able to go there for yourself."

Staring at her, he was clearly conflicted and then he gazed around the kitchen where his mother had probably been with him only three years prior. "Yes, tell me," he stated emphatically. "I will die, we all will and if not now, she will tell me herself," he added. "By then I will not take it as a surprise, for *now* you will bear the brunt of my astonishment."

Grimacing, she sipped her coffee. "That is hardly motivation for me to divulge anything," she said dryly.

He smiled. "I like how you tell me things, Genna. You have a way about you."

"I can not deny it," she smiled and then sighed. "Very well, but please know that I am sincerely sorry for any upset it causes you and also for the act of my original prying, I had not realized what I would discover."

"Duly noted," he said, placing his cup down and drawing in a breath to brace himself.

"I noticed a secret drawer in your mother's clothing room and when I pulled it out there were very old shoes perhaps from the earliest days of Claremonde," she began.

He appeared perplexed. "Shoes?"

Waving her hand around dismissively, she then shook her head. "That is not the concern," she quickly interjected. "The second drawer contained a letter and beneath a satin sheet or cloth–," she hesitated, uncertain on how to say it without it being alarming. "Inside of the sheet was something I believed she cherished and they were a set of infant's bones."

Staring at her, he did not move. He had not been prepared for such a revelation and his mouth hung open, uncharacteristically stunned. "Bones? A *skeleton*?"

"Yes."

"What had occurred?"

"I believe the little girl had died during childbirth, no intentional harm," she explained.

"A girl? What makes you say so?"

Amused by his sudden animation, she was swept up by his enthusiasm. "The letter gave details of her, including her name; she was your mother's child before you were born; a daughter."

"*My* sister? I have another?" he asked, suddenly joyful and confused. "I had another sister?"

"Yes."

"What was her name?"

"Temperance," she said with a smile.

Laughing, he clapped his hands together and Simon jumped onto his lap so he scruffed him playfully, kissing the top of his head. "The poor child did not take a breath I suppose. I wish mother had told us, I would have thought of her, I would have wondered about her. Temperance and she would be older than I."

Smiling, she was glad she had told him and was beginning to settle down after her encounter at the creek, however there was more to be said and she wanted it to unfold naturally.

"I look upon you now, Genna, are you still accosted by what happened this morning?"

Sipping her coffee, she wished she could keep the smile on his face, but he could read her so easily.

Before she could speak, he leaned forward and frowned as if he could derive it from her gaze. "And what of the letter? It said her name? Had mother written it?"

Shaking her head, she tried to hide the worry from her eyes. "The father did," she stated carefully.

"The father of Temperance?"

"Yes."

"And so *my* father–," he said but then frowned at her again. "But *her* father, it is my own?"

Shaking her head, she showed she was sympathetic. "No."

"Then mother–?"

"Yes."

Suddenly he appeared shaken. "Was she willing, Genna?"

"Yes, oh my, yes, she was not forced."

Relieved, he now crossed his arms and then looked out into the room again. Undoubtedly he wished he could talk to her because they had been so close and she had kept this from him. "It was a great burden she carried so long," he despaired. "Did she love him?"

Nodding, she felt a pang in her heart thinking about the sadness Lillianne must have felt so often thinking of the man she could never be with. "They were deeply in love," she confirmed.

Thankfully he did not appear distressed upon hearing it. He loved his mother and her happiness was important to him rather than the particulars of the scandal. "Who was he, do you know?"

Getting up and taking their cups to the basin, she did not turn around to look at him straight away. "I don't know if I should tell you, Noble. It might be better that you don't know."

"Is he alive?"

Turning around she clasped her hands together. "I don't know. I wouldn't think so but I am not certain."

"Please tell me," he begged. "I will not confront him; I simply want to know who made her happy. I want to know who she grieved for."

Drawing in a discrete breath, she approached the table. "Giles Atherton."

The name was in his mind, he was mulling it over, trying to recollect the familiarity and then she could see it form in his eyes. "Marjorie's father?"

"Yes."

"Then she too has a sister, she is the sister of Temperance also."

"I had not thought of that but yes that is true."

"Astonishing," he said. "I was never aware of it, mother had not given an inkling towards it, she must have suffered, as did he. I had only met him a handful of times and he was a pleasant man, a man noted for his good character and generosities."

"Do you wish that I did not tell you?"

"No," he insisted quickly. "I wish for you to tell me everything," he said seriously. "You cast no judgment or disapproval of me or my life. You belong here, Genevieve, please speak when you wish and what you wish."

"I am happy here," she said sincerely. "I am glad you want me to stay."

He reached out for her hand again and it was the warmest hand with the most beautiful heart behind it. "What you must think of my father," he said with a fading smile. "Had Valor mentioned my father?"

Nodding, they didn't need to say it out loud; he could tell she knew enough. "And *your* father, Genna? Will you tell me? You said he was also not a good man."

Holding his hand, squeezing it a little so it was a true reciprocation, she was content enough to tell him. "Only my aunt and Mrs. Marsh know," she explained. "I am not ashamed for his actions and I had only withheld it for concern that you might be a little horrified by it but I realize now your father and mine might have gotten along."

Leaning forward even more, like they were two secretive children, he laughed. "It makes me wonder how they bore such kind children," he said seriously.

In complete agreement she was actually relieved to tell him, she wanted to tell him everything. "My mother died when I was ten and my father went away not long after. I was raised by my mother's sister, my aunt, and I lived with her and my four cousins."

"Was she cruel to you?" he asked curiously.

"No, not particularly," she replied honestly. "My aunt was a well occupied woman and was not overly affectionate with her own children. I did my best to keep in the background so I did not become a burden to her but she did not pay much attention to me. I write to her on occasion and perhaps once a year I will hear from her and she will tell me what she is doing and she does not really ask about me."

"This saddens you?" he asked, sincerely sympathetic.

"It used to," she responded, thinking it over. "But I now see it for what it was. She did not have to take me in, I could have gone to an orphanage and she did not abuse me. My cousins and I clashed on occasion but were otherwise all in the same way about it. I matured and left it behind."

"And your mother was ill?" he prodded, trying to derive the full story.

Frowning at him, she was wondering why he thought it but then she was so young when she died, he must have come to that conclusion. "Oh no, that is not how she died."

With so many questions it was apparent that he had a new quest in discovering more about her. "Why did your father leave you? When she died, did he abandon you? Is this why you have distaste for him?"

Smiling a little, she was not doing so because she was happy, there was some strange irony in it all, an absurdity in her past circumstances and perhaps in his. "Well the police forced him to leave me," she explained. "He was later hung for beating her to death."

With widened eyes, he pulled back a little, sincerely shocked. His father had beaten his mother and Valor had said in his journals that she had come close to dying once. He knew what it was like, he understood the tension and the fear and the walking on eggshells. He didn't say anything but now seized her hands in both of his. "My mirror," he said, reaching up to touch her face. "I wish I could have taken you from there."

Shaking her head, she felt sad for her mother but Noble had endured the same. "It was so long ago, Noble. I wouldn't change any of it. I am here now because of every obstacle I crossed to get here. It is all part of me, it is all part of you and you are a brilliant compassionate man. Your father did you all a great injustice but you are truly the best of men because you knew not to be like him. You learned from him what you didn't want to be."

A gleam of sincere care was in his blue eyes as he looked into hers and he smiled at her and she breathed the air in between them. "Wise wise girl, Genna. You make me remember that who I was is who I am. I will not have you abandoned again."

Placing her hand on his as it was still warm against her face, she wanted him to have the same assurances. "And while I am here you will never be left alone." A thought suddenly occurred to her and she smiled a little hoping he didn't notice but he did.

"What is it?" he asked, mischief returning to his gaze as he sat back and tilted his head at her.

Shrugging, she didn't really want to ask but now was the only opportune time. "The first morning I was here, what if Mrs. Marsh had sent a sensible, hard working, but terribly un-charming attendant for you?"

Laughing he nodded. "You wonder if I would have treated her the same as I did you?"

Nodding she laughed too. "You do not seem the kind of man to trifle with lackluster exchange."

"Indeed," he agreed; glee in his eyes. "You are right to say so, Genevieve Belmont. Should she have sent such a woman, I would have allowed that dull but hard working woman to take her tray of breakfast to her room instead of sitting with me at the table."

Genevieve laughed and she knew he was being truthful. And she had never been so happy, no ghost or disembodied voice would compel her to run from there. "I suppose you are a lucky man after all."

Chapter Twelve

Claremonde Hall was a world of its own and walking up the grand staircase up to the first wing bedrooms, Genevieve felt as if she was revisiting the scene of an untold incident.

Having last been there when she saw the woman in the pool, she was surprised at how reluctant she was to set foot in the area again. However, part of it strangely felt like home and perhaps it was the calming influence of Lillianne or the care she had for Noble, but being there was bittersweet.

Stopping at the top, she turned back when Clemens called for her. "They're not after you, Miss Belmont! Whoever is around has long been in the dust here before you came. Try and push it out of your mind and we'll get Lord McKinley some answers!"

Smiling at him, she appreciated his rational approach. It calmed her to hear the reminder that she was not, in fact, an interest to whatever hung in the air here. Even though she was certain to be frightened no matter what, she had to remember she would not be harmed. "Do you think that if we discover anything, we can give them some peace?"

He thought it over before replying and removed his gray hat so he could run a hand through his thick brown hair. "I don't know that they will ever leave, maybe they are not even here, just some of their memories are in the walls. But I think it will help, somehow it will. But it's hard to say what will happen."

Sighing, she agreed. If they were only partially in the hall or only moments of time were captured, then what could be done about it? Yet it did seem as if they might be aware of them, that they knew Noble and Clemens and herself, even in a way that they were aware of their presence. "I just hope we can bring some harmony to Noble's life," she said truthfully.

"He likes you, you know," he said with a sheepish grin.

Laughing, she blushed more than she wanted to. "He seems the kind of man to like most people, Clemens; I would not put too much stock in that."

Approaching the bottom stairs, looking up at her, as he glanced at his wrist watch, his smile faded a little. "No, he likes you above anyone else that he knows, I am certain of it," he insisted. "Since you arrived, he looks happier and moves easier and yesterday I heard him singing in the garden."

"He sings?" she asked, surprised. "Does he sing well?" she asked curiously.

Chuckling, he nodded. "He does everything well," he replied.

Smiling, she believed him. "Yes he is hard to find a fault in," she agreed.

"But that is not all," he added, placing his hand out to gesture that he wanted to relay more. "He told me last week, when I drove him to the village, that he can almost walk freely now. He said it's because of you that he can, because ever since you arrived he feels like he has somewhere to go."

"He said that?" she asked, stunned.

"Yes," he confirmed, nodding for emphasis. "He had all but given up and you made him want to be him again."

"Thank you, Clemens," she said, truly grateful for his kind words. "In many ways he has brought me to life too and with friends like you, I have never been happier."

Coy, he hung his head and waved her comment away. "You're pretty wonderful, Miss Belmont. Just keep your wits up there and let me know if you find anything."

"I will," she promised. "If only I knew what I was looking for."

Smiling, he waved and started to walk away. "I'm going to the burned side," he called back. "Let us see who finds something first!"

Watching him leave, she looked down the hall at the bedrooms. Although Prudence was still alive, it was said she rarely visited and in many ways it felt like Noble was the only survivor of the family.

Listening carefully, already feeling that eyes were on her, she went directly to the first room on the right, the one belonging to Valor. He was rarely without words but she felt he still had more to tell.

Standing in the doorway looking in, noticing a crease from where she had sat on his bed last, she wondered about Noble too. She didn't want to admit it to herself, but she felt he might know something more also.

He was above reproach but there was a lingering secrecy around him and perhaps he was ashamed, or it was simply something he didn't want to discuss. Eventually she would have to ask him what he was omitting, but deep inside she hoped he would tell her first.

For now, as she gazed into Valor's room, never to be slept in by him again, she felt it fitting that he died at 51 because he would have wanted to be remembered as a young man. His death had made him ageless in the mind of all that knew him.

Walking in, wondering where she should search, she thought of his last journal and how it mentioned Marjorie abandoning him. For a man who spoke about everything, that was all he had said about it. Much had been written about his infatuation with her, his love, his lust, his perfect beloved. But one sentence suddenly ended it all.

She abandoned him, he didn't say why or how or how he felt about it. It was more so written for the purpose of historical documentation, to time stamp an event rather than discuss the content of what had occurred and it only made her more curious.

What *had* happened? She wished she could ask Marjorie but she barely knew her and she probably wouldn't want to discuss such a private matter anyway. She wasn't sure if asking Noble would be a good idea or not, he sometimes became sensitive when the topic of his brother was raised.

But Marjorie had left him, and had Genevieve blinked and missed the sentence, she would have been hard pressed in working out why he had moved on so suddenly.

He had written that he was romancing another, but this time *love* was not mentioned, she suspected it wouldn't be again. The slightly younger girl he spoke of was more impressionable, the type to yield to him, to look up at him. She was not an equal but a copy of Marjorie, less charming and wise but more willing and starry eyed.

Looking now at the window, the curtains open, the sun beaming in, she realized his words, his life, had taken a turn after Marjorie's departure.

He had gone from a romantic chivalrous lover to someone who valued outer beauty over any relationship with essence. Instead of finding a cherished match, he surrounded himself with admirers.

That could only lead to a type of desolation Genevieve concluded. Perhaps that was the feeling in this room, his dissatisfaction and his constant searching to reclaim what he once had.

Suddenly the atmosphere changed.

Calming herself, she tried to ascertain what seemed different, but then it became apparent it was the stillness again and bringing her gray shawl over her long gray dress, she pressed it against her neck against the sudden chill.

The sound became different as if past and present were overlapping and nothing was working. She was certain none of the clocks in Claremonde kept proper time because they stopped on occasion. She kept forgetting, but she wanted to ask Clemens if he had observed it or not.

Standing still, her heart pounded in spite of her intent to be brave. The floors in the hall creaked and then something that never happened before startled her beyond belief.

A huge gust of wind came through the window and pushed the curtain inward, lifting up like a ghostly silhouette and scattering dust across the old wooden floor. Unsure of what to do, she pushed through her fear and rushed to the window only to find it was closed. Sensing someone behind her, she spun around but no one was there. That was when she noticed something she had never seen during the other times she had visited this room.

The otherworldly wind had disrupted things from under the bed and right beside the end of the bed where the quilt hung down, was a piece of paper.

Reluctant to move, she glanced at the doorway. Never had she felt stronger that someone was there in that moment, staring back at her. It could have been Valor because it was his room, but it could have just as easily been one of the McKinley ancestors, a sixteenth century Lord with an axe to grind.

Either way she was eager to leave, but at the same time she really wanted to find something. Holding her head up high, gritting her teeth and clenching her shaking hands, she slowly walked over to the paper and picked it up, realizing it was inside of something.

Crouching down, she moved the quilt aside and saw that the one page was in a pile of papers, a small pile inside of a book of sketches, most of them loose pages.

Bringing it out, she flicked through it and looked up at the doorway again, wondering if someone was playing a trick on her because the pictures were hand drawn in pencil, they were done well and they were of the women in the photographs.

More notable was that they were mostly unclad with their hair colored in red and their eyes colored in blue, their eyes were open but their gaze seemed deadened and she couldn't be certain if it was intentional or not.

In spite of the drawings, which showed that Valor had a talent equal to his brothers, the paper she originally noticed sticking out was of immediate interest to her.

On first review it looked like random squiggles, but he was not a random man, even now in his journals he was still methodical. These appeared to be symbols, something self created perhaps and personal to him. Holding it up, forgetting the strange air around her, she stared, realizing that she had seen at least one of them before.

Wanting to verify her suspicions before getting Clemens' attention, she listened again, the familiar pressure and stifled atmosphere of the unknown was still around her but she wanted to get to the bottom of things. Testing Noble's theory that no harm would come to them by these unknown forces, she drew in a deep breath and rushed out.

She held the papers to her chest as she used the wall on the left side to guide herself down the grand staircase without tripping on her enthusiasm.

Rushing to get out into the sunshine, she pushed the heavy hinged door and hastened her step through the gardens until she arrived back at the servant's quarters.

Opening the door quietly, she heard Noble talking to Simon in his bedroom so she went into her bedroom and pulled down the top door of her secretary desk. Parting her curtains for better light she took out the first framed photograph and stared at it. In the bottom right hand corner was something written, it looked like one of the symbols but the frame partially obscured it.

Gently removing the back of the frame, she turned it over, dust marks and impressions made by the glass on top of it. Laying the frame pieces and the photograph on the bed, she poured over the symbols until she found one. It matched completely. But there was no explanation so she brought out the photographs of the other women and matched two others, each photograph having its own unique symbol.

Going through the loose pages, she got quite a bit through and worried there would be nothing further to enlighten her but finally there was one thicker piece of paper and taking it out the symbols were written on it in order, drawn nicely with neat handwriting beside each.

Each symbol represented one goddess woman and each symbol had a name beside it, that of the woman herself. The fourth symbol coincided with the youngest appearing of all of them, likely his first model and she recognized the name because it had been mentioned in his writing; Adela Williams.

She was the one he had said was naive and enamored with him. It made her wonder if these women had met anyone else in the McKinley family. Perhaps in his early days of photography and tinting, and after he had met Marjorie placing him in his early thirties, he was left to his own devices on the other side of Claremonde, the side that was burned.

Just the same, Genevieve felt that even if they couldn't work out the source of the ominous encounters at Claremonde, this would at least be one mystery worth looking into.

Maybe it was not a mystery at all, simply stories of the romantic encounters of a wealthy Romeo. These ladies may have gone on to marry and have families and would be older now; as Valor would have been had he lived. But she would need to find one to know, to know if there was something more to these images.

"What have you found, Genna?" Noble's voice said from behind her.

Spinning around, startled because she hadn't heard him coming, she didn't realize she had left her door open. He stood in the doorway, leaning on it, his blue eyes alive with curiosity, a subtle smile on his lips.

He was rubbing his hip, the one on his left side that was not burned. Having compensated his gait by over using his better side, the pain had set in some days more than others. "I would like to attend to that," she said before she replied to him.

Glancing at her bed, he left her door open and Simon wandered in behind him, wagging his tail. "May I?" he asked.

"Certainly, please do," she said, as she moved the pictures aside and helped him get set up against her pillows. Simon was quick to get up beside him and she handed him the photograph she was just studying, pointing to the fact she hadn't returned it to its frame yet.

Pushing him on his side a little, she began to use the bottom of her hand to rub the side of his hip as hard as she could in attempts to relax the area around the bone. "Do you know this woman?" she asked.

Studying it, he appeared more curious at her questioning, intrigued by her investigation, her interest in it all.

"I never knew them," he replied, reaching out so she could give him another framed photograph. "At times I would see them and they would politely acknowledge me, but they were spellbound by him. My brother was hypnotic, he would tell you that himself," he said with a smile. "He called them his porcelain dolls; there were a number of them after Marjorie."

"What happened with her?" she asked, feeling he was eager to tell her anything she wanted to know. "His journals said she abandoned him and then he never mentioned her again."

Shaking his head, he looked at the photograph, his mind wandering to the past. "He was more than willing to blame another should one be at fault, but he would not tell me so I can only assume he had upset her. She loved him that was apparent, but he never spoke of it. I often wondered but I would not venture to ask her."

"I agree," she sighed, massaging around the top of his leg to soothe it. "I feel she might have a piece to the puzzle but what if she didn't?"

"About the presence in Claremonde?"

Shrugging, she didn't know what she thought; it was too difficult to determine what was going on. "I believe that with so many people having lived here over hundreds of years, I could just as easily be looking in the wrong direction all together. But Valor–,"

"What about him?" he asked, interested. "Do you believe my brother is walking the halls?" he added with light amusement but not mockery.

Not wanting to show him the papers she just found, she didn't want to hide anything from him either. "I feel, oh you might think it foolish, it is just that I have been reading his journals and these photographs of his lady dolls and then today a gust of wind unearthed more."

"Outside?"

"No," she sighed. "I was in his room and a gust of wind came through the window but when I went to it, it was closed," she said, cringing a little at him thinking she might be somewhat mad. "I didn't imagine it, I assure you, but regardless, it lifted up some papers, some rather detailed sketches of his lady friends along with some symbols that match their names and photographs. I just wonder if he might be around and wants us to work something out."

"Or someone else wants us to know something about *him*," he said, not dismissing her thoughts at all. "May I see the papers?"

"No," she said quickly, standing and gesturing that she was done helping his leg.

"No?!" he asked with a loud laugh, causing Simon to sit up and look at them both for the cause of excitement. "Do you not wish me to help in your investigations?"

Smiling, she then frowned. "I do not think it necessary that you look at his artwork. He was an apt artist like yourself and I do not think the ladies would enjoy you seeing them that way."

Raising his eyebrows, he could see in her eyes that this was not the reason for her objection at all. "Perhaps you are jealous of my interest?" he ventured playfully but carefully.

"Certainly not!" she objected. "My hair is just as lovely as theirs but it is simply not as red."

Laughing, he sighed as he looked at her. "I was hoping to see the symbols you spoke of," he explained.

"Oh," she said, getting it for him as she blushed embarrassed at her open assumptions.

Turning the paper over to look at it the right way up while Simon sniffed it, he watched as she took a seat at her desk close by. "I did not have a collection like my brother but I caught the eye of a young lady or two in my youth, surprising as it is."

"I am not surprised," she said hastily and truthfully. "I imagine you would have had your pick of them."

Smiling, he did not deny it, instead changing the subject. "Did you ever marry, Genevieve?"

"No," she replied, looking at his face to see how he reacted to it. "I was not too wise in my youth. I would quickly seize a handsome face and then come to know them and discover they were either dull or immature."

"Perhaps you had too many to choose from?"

Shaking her head, she remembered some long relationships but it was never quite the right feeling, one or the other was not as invested; the whole thing had been daunting. "I think my expectations were too high," she confessed. "In my eyes there were not enough *viable* ones to choose from."

"Do you still carry that belief?" he asked seriously.

"Miss Belmont! Lord McKinley!" Clemens' voice bellowed out from the hall.

"In here!" she called back, the bedroom door still open where Simon jumped off to greet the young man. "I had forgotten I was going to tell him if I discovered anything," she quickly explained to Noble.

Clemens stopped in the doorway and immediately cast his eyes downward as if he had walked in on something he shouldn't have.

"Do not be concerned, Clemens," Noble said with a laugh. "Miss Belmont had been soothing my hip and then we were talking."

Clemens didn't look up immediately but simply nodded. "Did you give up the search?" he asked her finally.

Smiling, she then laughed at Noble. "No, actually I was matching some of Valor's symbols to these photographs. I'm not sure if it is significant or not but I was not certain what I should be looking for so I started with that."

"There were symbols?" he asked, suddenly animated.

"Yes, he had hand written names coinciding with symbols on the photographs that he had taken of some women he knew," she replied.

"May I see?" he asked.

Noble slowly got to his feet and handed him the first photograph but Clemens noted that he was hoping to look at the list of symbols and names. "Fourteen years ago I was not likely to recognize any by face," he explained as he took the paper from his employer.

Giving it a thorough study, he ran his finger down the names and stopped and then looked at the window and then looked at the paper again before nodding. "This third one I am certain of," he stated definitively. "I know that family and I can not recall what had happened with them, but I do remember they were mentioned in the papers frequently at some time."

"Which one?" Noble asked.

"Nevins," Clemens replied. "They were not in Wanderling but I knew of them from Chatterton where my cousin lived. It's a good two hour drive from here but he is still in that area. I could see if he can get me in touch with them."

With butterflies in her stomach, Genevieve could see excitement in Noble's eyes, but also trepidation, perhaps fearing there was something to actually be discovered about his family. Possibly something that wouldn't shine them in a generous light.

"What would you ask them?" she asked.

Clemens shrugged. "I suppose I would just ask if their daughter, Minerva, is well and whether I can speak to her. After that I would simply ask her if she remembers Valor and see if she mentions anything worth mentioning."

Noble and Genevieve laughed, but it seemed like a valid plan. "We have to start somewhere, Clemens. I think that’s a good place to start. We can't find answers without asking questions."

Chapter Thirteen

Heavy rain pelted sideways against the glass windows of Claremonde loud enough that it sounded like they were under attack. Thunder rushed in from the distance, roaring in like a speeding train and shaking the foundations of the ancient hall.

A flash of lightning quickly followed another and illuminated the surviving ballroom. Simon hunched before rushing over to hide beneath Genevieve's long coat.

While it was not by any means cold outside, thunderstorms gave her a chill but the rumblings deep in the Earth enlivened her. Just the same, she was fatigued from the previous night when she was certain she had seen a shadow.

Having awoken in the dead of night, long after the grandfather clock struck midnight but well before daylight, her ears heard footsteps and her mind awoke unsettled. A light shone in the hall but not from one of the electrical sconces. It was like a lantern light, flickering.

Staring over at the space beneath her locked door, she saw a shadow stop in front of it, blocking most of the light and she froze. There was no reason to think it was Noble and even after the work on his legs she would have known the sound of his walk anywhere.

The maids and other workers couldn't access this side of the house when it was locked but she could hear Simon stirring, sniffing from across the hall. Having lifted her head to stare at the door, she refused to go to it and then after a long two minutes the shadow lifted and the light was unobstructed, and then, complete darkness.

She had never been so tempted to knock on Noble's door and sit in front of his fire, feeling the comfort of his protection, but she didn't. She worried these occurrences were affecting him and while he was genuinely fascinated and spoke openly about his history, she felt there was something he was omitting.

During breakfast he had asked her about the evening and she told him what she experienced and he relayed that he too had noticed. At times in the silence, the space between two sentences, she thought he might offer her to seek him for comfort but she tried not to dwell on it. All too often the heart and its hope were too often distanced from the mind and reality.

Tired as she was, she now sat on a green gilded eighteenth century chair, cushioned but not to the point of pure comfort. Having brushed aside the dust and charred timbers, the chair looked as new as it had been after it was made. In a way she was sitting in time, back in the days when Lady McKinley of yesteryear held court with her many suitors in the ballroom.

Genevieve's auburn colored dress was not so glamorous but it flattered her figure and matched well with her soft gray coat. Her thick brown hair had gotten long over the months and she had little interest in cutting it short like the modern young ladies.

Having waved it each day, she had found Noble always commented on it too, she enjoyed his attention and he came to life under any praise. He knew her to be genuine too and, his mobility, as well as his spirits were better than they had ever been.

Bringing her hair forward over her cooled ears, she knew it wasn't just the draft or the rain that caused the chill to permeate this side of Claremonde. Rain dripped in along the left side where the roof had come up and the wind swirled around the yesteryear dust. But the cold was closer to her because of those that lurked about and Simon was now beneath her chair, calmed by her soothing voice and warm leg that he was pressed against.

Ignoring the discomfort of fear, she refused to let it sway her from learning the truth, from giving Noble peace while releasing Claremonde of its burdens.

Having brought a large cup of coffee with her, she sipped it and then placed it down beside the chair as she opened the next page of Valor's journal. Now thirty, he was more often on this side of the hall for his own pleasures, but she never in her wildest dreams would have expected to read what he had written on that day.

It turned out that Noble's curious nature was well entrenched in his hereditary and his older brother liked to peer into history's dark places and dig up old soil. Having read the first paragraph, she sipped her coffee and stared out at the ballroom. This was the first time she felt it was him that was with her. Perhaps it wasn't always the way but it was simply a strange momentary sensation.

Taking a deep breath, she started at the beginning of the entry and read it thoroughly, being certain of it, not wanting to misunderstand.

The girl is gone, sweet thing, her hair like silk, her skin like milk and she is gone and now I have lunched in the village with old Ormond. He drives slower than I could walk there but he has a story for everything and that which he does not know, he convincingly fabricates.

Let me not delay what I have come upon, and let it be known that I was astonished and dear future. I, he who is not taken aback at any given moment; I am ashamed of the very blood in my veins. Mother is above reproach, but this vile creature that fathered us; I am sickened to my core.

Allow me to digress. I had been in want of mother's attention, there were some dubious papers for her purveyance and I had not wanted the maids to intercept them. There is one attendant in particular that I do not believe is honorable and I have been attempting to find evidence of her misconduct but mother is not easily convinced.

Nevertheless, I went to our old wing, Noble has not visited this past week and it was still. I went into mother's room and looked down from her window only to see her in hearty conversation with Gordon the head gardener. Dear soul he is, I must say, a good man and he watches for her and it heartens me to know it.

But now I will confess to a slight, to a transgression that I can not excuse but I opened the drawer of her desk, her intimate papers kept there. In moments I have found that she has forgotten the most trivial details so I wanted to ensure that she is not robbed by those who may desire her monies.

There was not any damning papers or letters and I went to close the drawer, feeling foolish for having doubted anyone, especially her.

It was then that the most uncanny thing occurred. Do you believe in divine providence? The door of the drawers became stuck, they would not properly close and I began to worry, frantic she would return and accuse me of having ill intentions, which I did not.

Not hearing her, which was fortunate for me as I am not one to take care of matters as hastily as I would like, I was forced to remove the drawer completely to see what obstructed it.

The irony of me writing this here in my journal shall not be lost on you I am certain, but the object in question was a diary, one of her own, my mother's diary.

I looked inside, I read some of it, and that is my sin in this excursion. Of course I should not have rummaged through the papers, but I could have left it there, but I wanted to know. Perhaps I wanted to know if she had thoughts that would not be constituted as proper, and I do believe it was because I would find such a notion hopeful.

In her imperfection I would find reasoning and the excusing of my own shortcomings.

But it was not she, which caused great conflict inside of me, but father, Randolph the tyrant brute. While I jest with childish jibes, I am not at ease; I am in turmoil at my discovery. I am aggrieved utterly. What ails me most is my inability to bring peace to my sister and mother, for certainly the past is gone, unattainable to me for alteration.

I will not relay directly her words but what she was in witness of is a clear account. For myself I can foresee how I might have reacted coming upon such a scene but for her there are many tiers of devastation. She had said, the entry written when we were younger, that Prudence, twelve in age was violated against her will.

It was not that my dear sister had encountered the stable hand that she had so sought the attention of, but this day mother saw who had impregnated my sister.

All along she was aware of the act that led to her pregnancy, but she had sent the stable hand away, likely to divert the attention of us all.

But let it be known, it was <u>father</u>.

I am certain you are unsure of my meaning so allow me to reiterate. My father, Randolph, violated my sister, Prudence.

Mother had seen him just after the vile act was performed and in her diaries she stated that she suspected this was not the only time he had done it. Prudence had been silent on it, as fearful of father as mother was. Mother consoled her and kept her away from father after what she had seen, but she did not approach him about it, fearful he would end her for good and she would not be able to protect her family.

Nevertheless, despite her best efforts, she was too late to prevent the inevitable pregnancy and it is now known to me, only because I wrongfully read my mother's private writings that my sister gave birth to our father's child. Patience is my niece and essentially my sister, it is so, and it is sadly truth.

These years have passed and I now know why Prudence moved away, even with father gone she could not dwell in the memory of the betrayal to her innocence.

But I will not tell mother I know, for it will harm her to see me conflicted by it. She loves us like she is a tree and we are her limbs and I will not further her pain. I am only comforted to know that she had told Mrs. Wilshire, Henny as we call her. Mother had written that Henny was enraged like she had never seen.

I can only speculate that father's departure within a matter of months was a blessing to them both especially.

Genevieve closed the journal and was filled with such a range of emotions that she was uncertain on what to make of it. It was hard to comprehend her first discovery of the bones of Noble's sister, Temperance, who was fathered by Marjorie's father, and now she had to contend with this. This was a greater horror in truth and she knew she would have to tell Noble but was uncertain how he might receive it.

In some ways she wished she had met Valor. Although she was not alike to his goddesses he probably would have flattered her as was his nature, and she imagined him to be talkative and charming.

And yet, with Noble, she had never met a man so polished and wise but so witty and relatable and kind and handsome, he was handsome, she never noticed his scars. She would never leave Claremonde while he was there, not by her choice anyway.

"Miss Belmont!" Clemens ran in, slightly soaked from the outpouring of rain. The thunder and lightning were still strong with quick rumbles one after another but while she was reading she had not noticed any of it.

"You can call me Genevieve," she said with a smile.

Stopping to think about it as he ran a hand through his wet brown hair, he shrugged. "I would but I will forget," he explained. "Once I associate a name with a person I do find it hard to separate them," he added with a chuckle. "I found the girl."

"What girl?" she asked curiously as Simon forgot his fear of storms and ventured to greet his friend with an excessive wagging of his tail.

Approaching her, he suddenly looked around and slowed down. "A little more eerie today," he noted. "Ghosts are about."

"Yes," she agreed quietly. "I am trying not to be startled by it, but I am not succeeding terribly well, Clemens."

Offering her a sympathetic look, she knew he understood, even though he was much more accepting of it than her. "It's not knowing if one is right behind me that scares me most," he admitted, getting closer to her. "I know they used to just be people but I don't understand what they want, why they would stay around? I don't think all of them are good."

"Do you think there is more than one?" she asked almost in a whisper.

Reaching down to pat Simon, he appeared uncertain. "Sometimes yes, but I don't know the difference between a real spirit and the ones that seem to be illusions. Like those times when you can see a bit of the past and they are not actually here."

"Like a movie?"

Nodding, he then looked over his shoulder worried that talking about it would somehow attract their attention. "Claremonde captures them I think. I know someone is here but I don't know why. Just the same, I think you're on the right track with these ladies."

"Oh yes, so *who* are you talking about? What did you discover?" she asked, gesturing for him to sit across from her on a matching chair. "Are you cold?"

"No, I don't feel it so much," he replied with an appreciative smile. "That name I saw on Valor's page of notes, I found her family," he explained. "I knew that name like I said, and I contacted my cousin and was able to drive there and visit with him and they spoke to us. Nice people they were."

Listening, it suddenly struck her that there was something particularly pertinent that he had not mentioned. "And what about her? Her name is Minerva? Were you able to speak to her and ask her about her visit to Claremonde? I suppose it is difficult to know what to ask."

His smile faded immediately and he looked surprised. "No, she was not there," he said. "She was not anywhere."

"What do you mean by it?"

"Her parents have died but her brother said it has been near thirty three years since she vanished. They never heard from her after that time and her friends didn't either, no one had."

Thinking of the ghost of the woman she had seen in the pool, it dawned on her that perhaps it was this young lady. "She might have drowned," she surmised aloud. "In the pool beneath us."

Nodding, his expression was grave. "I thought of that too," he agreed.

"Did they speak to Valor? At the time she was absent I mean."

"Yes," he said, sitting down and removing his black suit jacket and putting it on a wooden crate beside him. "At the time they talked to him *and* Lady McKinley but she did not remember meeting her. Valor said Minerva had visited one afternoon and then left and he had not heard from her after that. He told them he had seen her recently but he could not recall a particular day."

"Did they believe him?"

He shook his head. "They had no reason not to. He gave them no cause for concern and they had known other men and friends they had spoken to that had seen her during that time so they could not know what occurred. She had been living with her sister in another town at the time and the sister worked long hours and they did not often cross paths so she did not even know when she had seen her last either."

"She might have drowned in the pool and he never told anyone," she pondered.

Staring at her, he had clearly given it a lot of thought also. "But she could have fallen down a well or gotten taken by someone," he said. "None of them remember who saw her close to that time so they were uncertain as to where she had been. She had missed three days of working as a housekeeper before her family was contacted."

He was right, it could have happened in so many ways. When someone is not found it could mean a great many things but the journal seemed relevant.

"I just read something Valor had written, perhaps around the same time," she said quietly, her coffee having gotten cold. "He mentioned she was *gone*, his goddess, a girl, but he didn't mention which one. I know that he had taken a lot of photographs of his companions in the creek. That is what makes me wonder if he knows what happened to Minerva. It might have simply been an accident and he did not want to be blamed."

"Gone?" he asked. "That could mean she left also."

"I know," she agreed. "We can not be certain of anything and we would be doing him a great injustice to make assumptions. The only thing I can think of, is to attempt identification of one of the others."

"To see if she was *gone* too?"

She nodded. "I like him, Clemens," she said, wanting to tell him her feelings on it. "I know he has died, but Valor was an interesting man, I do not know what to make of any of this but I can only suppose there are so many variances of reasoning in such cases. Good and bad have a myriad of in-betweens."

Looking at his watch, he sighed and stood, reaching for his damp jacket. "I will see if I can work out who one of the other ladies are," he said. "If you read anything that will give you a clue let me know. But we will work it out, I know we will."

"I'll walk with you," she said, wanting to get away from the eerie atmosphere. "I have something I wish to speak with Noble about," she sighed.

"My mum needs me to pick some items up from Wanderling for her," he said with a sigh of his own. "I hope it's a good afternoon for you, Miss Belmont."

"You as well, Clemens," she said, glad the rain had lessened.

Hurrying back to the servant's quarters with Simon close behind her, she opened the front door but stopped, hearing the sound of laughter. She let Simon in ahead of her but held him and listened before she approached.

"Terrible ruckus!" a familiar female voice bellowed out with a laugh. "I don't know how we ever got through it!"

It was Mrs. Wilshire but there was another person with her and Noble, a younger female voice. "I thought Noble would fall down it!" the younger woman said with a laugh of her own. "I haven't laughed so hard since I don't know when!"

The three laughed together and Genevieve kept Simon with her, uncertain as to what to do. The young woman was clearly someone who had known Noble for some time and called him by his first name as she did. Something halted her in this moment and she couldn't ascertain what upset her.

She had been so lost in their own small world she had forgotten he had a history with so many people and, and he was well loved, justifiably so.

Simon struggled wanting to see his old friend Henny and not wanting to miss out on the merriment, so she reluctantly released her hand from his chest so he could run to them. Drawing in a deep breath she realized she was feeling territorial. Ashamed, well aware of her shortcomings, her state was worsened by her inability to put on a happy face and act like it didn't matter.

While he had said he wanted her to stay there, she knew it to be true but that didn't mean he wouldn't marry someone and keep her on as his employee, and she had no reason to doubt such a thing could occur. Deep down, not wanting to admit it to herself, she felt territorial over *him*.

He had become her safe haven both in vicinity and in her heart. She had fallen under his spell, inadvertently entrusting her thoughts and feelings and ideas to him, enough that she had forgotten her place.

It was too late, her heart had betrayed her mind and now she has little time to rectify her misconceptions.

"Simon, where is your friend?" Noble asked as she could hear him pat him and give him his full attention.

Holding her head up, trying to be neutral and charming, she entered the kitchen and immediately failed. Her smile had faded and she as unable to pick it up again. "Good afternoon, Miss Belmont," he said with a smile. "What adventure have you taken Simon on this day?"

Genevieve nodded at Henny who also appeared happy to see her. She also offered a nod of acknowledgment to the other woman who was wearing a maid's uniform, which flattered her petite figure.

She was in her thirties and quite attractive with dark hair and a genuinely friendly smile. "Oh, well we visited the hall," Genevieve replied lightly. "He enjoys the stairs and likes to run in the old ballroom," she added truthfully while leaving out any further details.

"He does love to run," he agreed, still smiling from his recent exchange. "Miss Miles, please allow me to introduce you to Henny's successor, Miss Belmont. I know I have told you of her, but you had mentioned having not met. She has been here four months gone now and Simon is a fixture at her side."

Henny clapped her hands together and beckoned the dog over. "I have missed you my little friend," she said to him as she bent to kiss his head. "Genevieve, he is a dog of good judgment, and I am glad he is loved by you. A good boy, Master Simon is."

"Thank you, Henny. He has my complete adoration and I am sure he is aware of it."

Henny clasped her hands together and beamed. "Dear boy he is," she agreed.

Genevieve walked over to Ms. Miles and reached out to gently shake the petite beauty's hand. "I am pleased to meet you. Do you work in the adjoining building?"

"Yes," the maid replied with a knowing smile towards Noble as if they shared inner secrets. "I come here for lunch sometimes and I have heard so much about you. I hear Clemens keeps you well occupied."

Concerned that the young woman might think that she had a particular relationship with the driver, she tried to dispel it without seeming overly defensive. "He is a nice young man, and we have made some interesting discoveries as far as the history of Claremonde. I am considering writing a book about it perhaps, with Lord McKinley's permission of course."

"Splendid idea!" Noble enthused. "An apt venture for you," he added with a smile in her direction.

She could tell he was in a good mood and it was hard not to be infected by his charm and laughter but she felt conflicted and was eager to leave.

Thankfully Henny suddenly remembered the purpose of her visit and turned around to retrieve some papers from the table beside the sink. "Miss Belmont," she said quieter, pulling her aside. "These are the worker's wages and I have typed out a detailed explanation of what is needed to ensure they are correctly paid based on their worked hours and pay. If you have any questions there is a telephone at my residence so Noble can reach me there on your behalf."

Nodding, she took them from her, and assured her it would be taken care of. "I will attend to it now," she promised as she turned to see Noble and the maid talking and smiling with each other. "I'm glad to have met you, Miss Miles," she said convincingly, for the young woman seemed genuinely nice. "I have some work to attend to but I hope we will cross paths again."

"Yes, I hope so too," the younger woman said before continuing her thought with Noble and then including Henny.

Genevieve turned to look at Simon who seemed content to stay with his master and she was glad for them all to be diverted enough to have not noticed anything hasty in her departure.

Getting to her room, she closed the door and lay on her bed, looking out at the cloudless sky from her window. She would do the papers and do them vigilantly and diminish the effect of the horrors she had read in Valor's journals and the hurts of her own heart that she couldn't diminish through rational thinking.

Closing her eyes, she made a promise to work harder at not caring so much about everything. Tomorrow she would start anew, brave and fresh and determined.

.

Chapter Fourteen

When the other world stirs it resonates in the subconscious but rarely echoes in the ears.

While the sun hadn't risen, she knew soon the alarm clock that she had brought with her the very first night she arrived at Claremonde, would soon ring out into her cool bedroom. Sitting up, leaning on her elbows she looked around her room, reluctant to see the disturbance that had awoken her, but hoping she would spy a logical cause.

The lamp beside her bed emanated a calming orange hue and she had decorated her room whimsically, filling it with lovely items from Claremonde that Noble had encouraged her to place there so they were appreciated. But now she felt detached to the idea of it becoming a part of her or her belonging there. She had come to depend too much on his smile and approval and attention and now remembered he was sought by many for the same reason.

Feeling sleepy, she considered closing her eyes and falling back into her pillows that were still warm from her face having been pressed against them but the sense of being watched was rising up inside of her. She had not felt that way in her bedroom before and it was potent enough that she wanted to cry out in spite of herself.

That was when she noticed something and she had to concentrate to connect her thoughts, to try and recall if she had done it herself the previous night.

Looking over at the window, the curtains drawn so that not even a slither of the Claremonde landscape could be seen, it was obvious it had not been opened. There was no breeze, no draft along the floor that could have caused it, and her door was locked so no one had come in.

The adrenaline rising in her chest caused her to perspire on her upper lip while her concentration became foggy. Trying to draw in a breath in hopes of getting oxygen into her lungs and sense into her brain, she studied the room intently.

Perhaps she was seeing it incorrectly, so many things could be explained once you drew closer, but she didn't want to leave the bed and part of her wanted to run directly from her room.

Her heart beat so hard inside her chest that she could hear it drum into her ears, the blood pulsing a rhythmic fear. Quietly and slowly, she pushed aside her quilt and two blankets and her partly moist sheet from the summer night's heat.

Suddenly the lamp beside her bed flickered as if the power was interrupted but only for a second. Stopping, letting her bare feet touch the pink rug beside the bed, she stared over at the desk.

She hadn't spent much time in her room of late and she knew in winter the fireplace and the hot bath would soothe and entice her to candlelight and calm. But right now she could not take her eyes from her secretary desk.

She had done all of her typing and paperwork there and was so acquainted with it that she knew immediately something was amiss, something was unnatural.

Stepping quietly, every creak in the floor echoing loud in her large room, she didn't want to disturb what she was in witness of. While she was tempted to call Noble in, she was also trying to deny what she was seeing so she could get through the upcoming day not conscious of it.

The front of the desk was open with the typewriter and handwritten notes in the main section above the closed drawer. Meanwhile, on the very top where she kept an old bronze ink well and quill from Claremonde, was a cup she had left there earlier the day before.

It was a tea cup but she had sipped coffee from it as she looked over Valor's symbols and his photographs. She had discovered more of his work, photos of the pool and the creek bed and the willow trees that he had painstakingly tinted with beautiful old worlde color.

The last remnants of coffee had dried in the bottom of the cup. But what was shocking was the tea cup was now upside down and teetering on the edge of the front of the desk, balancing precariously. She usually would have taken her cup back to the kitchen but hadn't wanted to interrupt Noble and his guests, but she never would have left it upside down like that.

On the other side of the inkwell, she stared at the open journal that she had been currently reading. Standing still, refraining from allowing her breath to disturb it, she stared at the middle, the page to be exact; the page that was sitting upright with no particular thing to bolster it or hold it in place.

Stepping back, she walked backwards, staring at it as she did her best not to trip over her nightgown. Reaching back to unlock her door and turn the doorknob, she was careful not to let the draft fly in as she took two steps to knock on Noble's door.

Fortunately she could hear he was already awake and moving about. "Genevieve?" he asked uncertainly.

"Yes," she whispered in spite of herself. "I wanted you to see something. Are you able to come?"

"A short moment," he said, sounding eager to be there.

Quickly looking at her door, she reached just inside to a small Victorian glove box on a shelf that she kept mints in. Hastily procuring one, she put it in her mouth and sighed, wishing she had put on a dressing gown to keep her warm, but was too afraid to go get it.

Opening his door, he let Simon out who circled her bare feet and sniffed at her long white nightgown. "I'm sorry to disturb you," she whispered, as if someone was listening. "There is something strange in my room and I wanted to show you. I suppose I thought you might be interested and I also thought that perhaps I didn't want to be alone in there just now."

Curiosity grew in his blue eyes while concern was ever present. "Did something frighten you, Genna?" he asked gentle, noticing her shiver a little.

"Yes," she confirmed.

She saw that he had his dressing gown on but nothing else and his hair wasn't combed yet but somehow it was neat anyway. For just a moment, with him getting in front of her to push the door open further, he seemed to have stopped. She lowered her gaze but felt so connected to him, as if she had known him longer than she had known herself.

Perhaps he had felt it because he paused and looked at her a little surprised but then he went into her room with Simon close behind. "What did you see?" he asked, wary to keep his voice low also.

"It is still there on my desk, on the top," she explained.

Staring over at it, he had the same look on his face that she had when she woke. It was a curious thing to see. It was somewhat out of place and yet not obvious until you comprehended the implausibility of it. "*Remarkable*," he said, drawing out his word in pure awe. "Genna, you did not do this?"

"I left the tea cup on my desk," she confirmed. "I don't often do that, but I would never turn it over like that. But the page, I am not certain how it remains up like that, nothing holds it there."

Walking around, they were both staring at it. "It could be a cobweb," he said and she suddenly realized that was quite possible.

But when he placed his hands above it nothing happened and it stayed.

All of a sudden the tea cup crashed to the floor breaking into pieces as the journal's pages simultaneously fell open. They both jumped back startled and she wanted to laugh but she didn't think for a minute that this was a random phenomenon.

"Noble, something is in my room," she said, her voice wavering nervously.

Gazing at her, he couldn't contradict it. "No harm will come to you, Genna, I promise. We are nearing an understanding of the past; perhaps it wishes us not to know."

"*Who* is it?"

Shaking his head, he took her hand and led her out of the room. He took her into his own room, closing the door behind them before lighting the fire. This particular morning had an unseasonably cool chill to it, and the atmosphere was solemn and eerie. "It could be Valor," he whispered.

"But why?" she asked seriously. "Because I am reading his journals?"

He turned his gaze from her and she sensed there was a reason why Valor might be around but he didn't want to say it. Instead he shook his head, trying to work it out.

"You are not the cause," he replied simply and yet emphatically. "Some dead do not rest. I am not certain it is him but I would not doubt it either. If you are afraid in the night come wake me, please I beg of you. I will not have you suffer."

Nodding, she assured him she would, but even now she was not sure how she could return to her room and go about her daily activities sensing someone was beside her unseen. "I should prepare for breakfast," she said.

He straightened his body and looked surprised at her. It was as if all of his thoughts had been consumed in that one moment. But he had other less pertinent things to address, something that had simply been on his mind. "You did not return for dinner last night," he noted.

"Henny told me she made it for you," she replied, getting in front of the fire.

"Did you not wish to join us?"

A hint of hurt was in his voice and she felt he may have felt betrayed or slighted by her lack of attendance. "I thought you were enjoying yourself with Henny and Miss

Miles and I was finishing the papers so didn't want to interrupt you."

"Miss Miles?" he asked confused. "She left only two hours after you saw her," he explained.

"Oh, I was not aware," she said honestly as Simon came to her side and she crouched down to hug him. "I thought you were discussing your many times together. She made it sound as if you had lunched together often. I did not want to be a quiet presence in a room of nostalgia."

Laughing, he seemed genuinely amused by her assumptions. "I thought it very strange she had come seen me during my lunch," he conveyed openly. "She had twice come whilst I was eating it and neither time had I invited her. Yet she would stay ample time, not during her work hours, but I thought it odd that she mentioned it to you."

Sensing his need for guidance, for recognition of his ponderings, she was relieved by what he expressed. "I imagine she is taken with you," she said sincerely. "She is beautiful and you are handsome and you would be a good match. I would think that is how she saw it."

Astonished, he studied her gaze, trying to derive her own feelings on such a statement. "Do you believe so?" he asked genuinely. "My residence and my inheritance might attract her, but to be inclined towards *me*?"

"I could not fault her for that," she said brazenly, afraid he would understand her own inklings with a near admission.

"She is not my match," he dismissed gently. "I do not see that she is overly beautiful and she had once told me that Simon is a dog therefore he needs to be retained in outside quarters."

"*Outside?*" she asked, standing with resistance inside of her. "*Would* you? I will take him in my room. I would not want him to be out in the cold; there are no fireplaces in the carriage houses."

Laughing he reached out for her hands. "I did not like her suggestion nor the lack of compassion behind it," he assured her. "Not only that, but she drinks tea instead of coffee and does not even have sugar in it."

Knowing he was trying to appease her now, she relented and smiled. "Yes well that is a great offense indeed. I can see how she would not be an apt partner for you at all."

Smiling, he gazed into her eyes and she was so caught up in the moment, she considered bringing him closer to her so she could kiss him. But only in a dream would she be so bold.

"Did you make any discoveries at Claremonde earlier in the day?" he asked curiously.

She couldn't possibly tell him about Prudence and his father in this moment, it was not an appropriate time and she had not prepared herself for how she might broach it. "Clemens pointed me to an old chest belonging to you in the study," she said. "I did find something quite delightful, something from when you were young in your early days of schooling."

Now animated and excited, he gazed at her curiously. "Have you kept it near?"

"Oh yes, it is in my room," she said, reluctantly leaving the fireside to cross the hall to her less inviting room. Knowing that realistically whoever or whatever had previously been lurking around there was probably not affixed to the room, she concentrated on the task at hand.

Having only come upon it recently, she knew that it was in the drawer of her desk. Opening it up, she pushed aside a couple of pencils and a garnet brooch she hadn't done anything with yet, to seize the prize.

It was a small notebook, a little frail but sturdy enough to handle and admire. It was leather bound but had many creases in it from where he had leant on it whilst open.

Before leaving her room she was mindful to get her thick burgundy dressing gown from the hook on her bathroom door and put it on, tying it at the waist before returning to him.

"It is from when you were quite young," she explained, walking it over to him before rubbing her hands together in front of the fire. "I do believe it is the sweetest sentiment I've ever read. You must have been an angel child."

Smiling at her, blushing slightly, he opened it to the first page and knew immediately to what she was referring to. "Shall I read it aloud?" he asked coyly.

"I would enjoy that greatly," she encouraged. "How old were you when you wrote it?"

Turning the pages, he finally came upon something that gave him a clue to his age at the time. "Likely six perhaps," he replied, before smiling at her with a laugh and then clearing his throat. "My dog is named, Leon and he is my friend. He sleeps at the bed and snores louder than Valor. I love him and he is not just a dog, he is my love friend. He makes me laugh and he eats all that he sees, even twigs. I hope one day to own many dogs and also cats and horses as well as two swans and a nice tiger. By Noble McKinley."

Laughing, she was impressed by how dear his heart was from such an early age. "I wish you were a child again just so I could adopt you," she said with a smile. "What a lovely little boy you were."

Beaming from her praise and the discovery of his youthful words, he laughed as he clutched it to his chest. "Do you want children?" he asked curiously.

"No," she replied quickly. "But you were special. I suppose if one was able to choose, you would have been the best of all of them."

"Ah, Genna, you make me smile," he stated sincerely, the fire reflecting in his gaze as he studied her. "I suspect you were overlooked sweet girl; you and your big blue eyes staring up at the world for its attention. It is better now for both of us that our worlds have finally collided; most fortunate."

"And you?" she asked, genuinely interested to know.

"Children?" he asked. "Not at all. I had never pined for an heir per se'. My dogs were my underlings and they offered a simpler interaction with the most affection."

Genevieve understood completely. Humans were a complicated species and families were not always bound by love.

Simon, who had quietly gotten to his bedroom door, suddenly let out a loud bark and broke the spell of the moment. "I best let him out before he creates a puddle for you to slip in," she said with a smile.

Soon after she got dressed and took the happy dog outside; starting the morning with a smile that she had not anticipated wearing.

Chapter Fifteen

Henny Wilshire once lived a quiet unassuming life in a nice sized but un-opulent room of Claremonde Hall. Tucked away on the first wing on the second floor, Henny was in a room close to Lillianne and near the last children who grew up there, Noble and Prudence.

Not once had Genevieve noticed the room until Clemens had pointed it out to her, that there was a narrow door beside the last room, the one belonging to Lillianne. It was in the wide wallpapered hallway and not far from Lillianne's bedroom door but it was wallpapered, possibly intentionally hidden because she was considered staff.

But the children had enjoyed her greatly and their mother was exceedingly dependent on her up until her death. Noble said Henny wept for a fortnight after his mother died and Claremonde had grown deathly still during that time.

Now they were all gone and she suddenly felt melancholy knowing that they had each endured so much here when it was such a beautiful place in truth. She was adamant that somehow she would find a way for Noble to have new memories here, happy ones that would start Claremonde afresh.

Clemens hadn't spent a lot of time in their bedrooms but he too had decided that a second look in Valor's room might be warranted. Regardless of what was going on around them, Noble's older mysterious brother had secrets and they did not have to dig deep to find them.

Henny's room was not as grand as the other bedrooms, it was ample for a woman in her service and she was clearly valued and cared for, but she herself, while jovial, was a demure and modest person in her tastes. The wallpaper in the room was pale pink with ivory lines and small floral buds throughout.

Her single bed was brass with a white quilt and a pink cushion while her dressing table had a lace runner and a pale blue vase on it. Other than that, the table had portraits of the three children when they were smaller and one framed photograph of her and Lillianne, a later one probably taken shortly before the fire.

Lady McKinley had aged well and was still a beauty and looking at her in this photograph she wondered if Mr. Atherton on the next property pined for her, both of them being like two lost lovers cursed to be kept apart.

It was simply another tragic sadness in the story of this beautiful hall, but she was gone now, perhaps they had reunited in Heaven, perhaps only the angels would allow them their togetherness.

Entering the room, her yellow cotton dress swishing at her calves, she regretted not bringing a cardigan given the chill. She had decided to keep her hair long and wore a yellow wool hat with a rhinestone hat pin.

Each day she felt more alive and as this was so, she wanted to be all she could be in both presentation and grace. But for now, crossing her arms against the cold, she was focused on learning something or at least eliminating this room from their hunt.

Looking around, the beige rug beside the bed, a small wicker basket with a doll and some linen in it, Genevieve wondered if there was really much to be garnered from this visit. With Henny being alive, she had to tread carefully as to what she looked through, although she was certain the older woman could always return and reclaim any of her old items. Just the same, Genevieve had an inkling about her and while she didn't know what she was looking for, she would know if she found it.

A linen press yielded a basket of threads and needles for embroidery and then a knitting bag of crocheted doilies that she had likely made herself.

After an hour of sifting through some clothing in the dressing table drawer and some scented satchel bags; she noticed a large piece of folded paper. Gently bringing it out, she could see there were a handful of letters and newspaper articles inside.

Bringing them over to Henny's pristine bed, she sat on the edge and laid them out. A couple of them were notices of deaths, both with the surname, Wilshire, so she assumed they had been members of her family. But one newspaper article was very curious; she read it three times over before she could formulate a thought on it.

Essentially it spoke of Henny Wilshire, the widow of a Mr. Daniel Wilshire who had died under mysterious circumstances near his place of work at a factory. By the date of it, Henny would have been in her twenties and had apparently become widowed quite young.

There were some subtle insinuations in the article about him having been murdered although they sited the possibility of a random mugging. Either way, it was said he was bruised and had numerous hits to the head with something heavy.

Presuming them to be a widow's memento of a grief, the report of her husband's passing and part of her history, Genevieve placed it aside. It was only when she read the adjoining letter that her perception of the article became an entirely different scenario.

It was a letter from her sister, apparently her twin, and it had been soon after Henny's husband died, after his strange possible unsolved mugging.

Dearest Henrietta

Please accept my sincerest condolences for your current position and your recent widowhood. Charles, dear man he is, has insisted we send you money to help you along until you can acquire some employment.

You had always said that you prefer to work than be owned by a man, but you and I had a great variance in our marriages. Charles is not my master but my companion and please know, I am well aware that he is a rarity.

But you, my sweet little one; your heart had been taken by Daniel before he dared showed his true being. A savage and a conniving man, I deeply regret I had not seen it and fear I should have interceded.

How does one intercede? Our choices are non existent, our allowances only that in which the men allow us, but the fists he laid on you, dear girl. I curse the day he was born and I ask you forgive me for saying it.

When I tried to string your corset that day and you cried uncontrollably because all those bones beneath your chest were snapped like twigs. I am sincere in my grief for you, my pity for your new position in life, facing poverty.

We will not allow it. Should you not find a comfortable occupation, do seek us and we will send for you. We will not have you in a workhouse, do know that.

Between us only this very breath, these words spoken in complete privacy, my sweet, I am joyful at your liberation. I am consoled by you being free of him. Like a bird whose wings will grow back, you will return to life as if you too were dead.

Rejoice, do not grieve long. I love you dear one.

Margaret

Lillianne's life long assistant had a small window in the corner of the room. Genevieve walked over and parted the curtain, feeling not only the sensation of the oldness of the building, but how it must have been for her living here.

She had lost her husband at a young age but by all appearances had soon after been employed at Claremonde. Perhaps after being beaten by her husband she was reluctant to marry again and this family took her in as their own and allowed her the freedom to be herself.

But the inkling from Lillianne's own diary caused Genevieve to wonder. She tried to remember what Valor had said about his father, Randolph and the night he left Claremonde for good.

He had been seen arguing with someone although the other person was out of sight, standing inside of the building while he was in the clearing.

Looking back at the bed now, she felt she was on the verge of discovery but feared that she should let it enough alone. Henny was still alive and such a secret as this, such an unsubstantiated inclination could be dire.

She would never accuse her and yet, Valor had said that his mother had mentioned how angry Henny was about what had happened to Prudence.

It could have been that after being beaten by her own husband, she had perhaps instigated his early demise. Could Genevieve think such a thing? But even still, if she had her hand in it or not, knowing the way Lillianne was cruelly beaten was likely to have caused Henny a great deal of rage.

Perhaps the violation of Prudence was enough for her to cease his cruelties.

But she should not jump to such conclusions. Randolph's whereabouts had never been established and anything could have taken place with him. But Henny's husband's fate appeared to be disputable at least.

She had to talk to Noble about it; she had to present it to him in a way that she understood they would never allude to it in front of his favored nurse of all those years.

But he had wanted to know everything and perhaps in his knowledge he would be freed of his suspicions. The weight of conjecture could drive a man mad.

Even though the prior occupant of the room was alive and well, there was a presence in the room. She could not be certain if it was simply the sensation of it having been lived in so often; perhaps Henny had spent a lot of time in it.

More than likely though, it was one of Claremonde's visitors, perhaps one that occasionally stopped by to stroll through the halls and reminisce, but likely it was someone intentionally there.

Conscious of her movements, she pondered spirits and whether they contemplated and considered things or if they were bereft of full emotion. Unsatisfied with any definite conclusions, she was not sure if she would relay this particular find to Clemens who was quite fond of the older woman.

It was not Henny that paced the room around her but there was a resonance of something unspoken. Genevieve needed one more thing to substantiate her ponderings, to make her feel justified in what she relayed to Noble when the time came.

Returning to the drawer where she found the newspaper articles, nothing else was noteworthy, but just before she gave up; she pulled the drawer out to see if anything had fallen behind. Pulling out the bottom drawer she was astonished to see something had. It was a small note, handwritten crudely. It was grubby with marks on it and she suspected there might be dried blood on it.

It simply read;

It is done, clean, no suspicion. Leave the bag at the fourth outside privy on Stockholm Street, it is abandoned. Do not be seen. You will not hear from me again. Ask around if you have another deed for my taking up.

A corner of the note had been turned over, and looking at her sister's letter and the article about her husband's death, they each had the same corner turned over as if the three were kept together.

Vague and yet specific, this was an eerie indicator that Henny had indeed coerced her widowhood.

Genevieve was shocked and yet she admired her, a woman who was clearly not of good means and a hard worker, a kindhearted woman who found herself battered and abused, unloved with no prospects. She could not imagine herself taking such a drastic action but what options were there to a woman then, even now it was hard to get away. Where did a woman go?

Her mother didn't escape her father and she ended up dead because of it. Lillianne was stuck for years avoiding her brutish husband.

Standing, she gathered the letters including the small grubby note and knew that it was time for Noble to know. Not for the purpose of taking action but for filling the gaps of knowledge and letting it all out into the open so he could be freed by the entire truth of his past.

She didn't know for sure, but these were all pieces of a puzzle, the kaleidoscope of people who created the story of Claremonde. It was not all bad, it was not all torment and sadness but the fire was still a mystery and she felt Noble too would speak of it.

Suddenly sensing someone behind her, she slowly turned to look at the doorway and found that this time someone was actually standing there. Startled, she jumped back, clutching her hands and papers to her chest as she gasped. "Good heavens, Clemens, I did not hear you coming!"

"I am sorry," he said sincerely, but somewhat subdued as he gently approached her. This day he was not driving so he was wearing a cream knit top with gray trousers. He had mentioned a young woman in Wanderling that he was enamored with so she assumed he intended on seeing her later.

Catching her breath, she studied him, surprised at his solemn demeanor. "What have you seen?" she asked, assuming he had experienced an unsettling presence of his own.

Drawing near to her so he was close enough she had to look up at him a little; he turned to look over his shoulder and kept his voice low. So low that she could barely catch the words but she had heard enough to be certain of the gravity of it.

"I found bones," he whispered with a look of astonishment and fear in his eyes. "It is a whole skeleton, all of it."

Genevieve shivered in spite of herself and he noticed but didn’t say it. "I don’t suppose it was buried in a coffin on purpose?" she asked hopefully.

He shook his head, his movements subtle as if afraid to disturb their onlookers. "I don't suppose so, Miss Belmont, especially not where I found it."

Chapter Sixteen

Reeling from Clemens' admission about finding bones, Genevieve stood in Henny's old room, trying to comprehend it. Remembering something in the drawer she had just opened, she took out a pink floral pillow case and Clemens helped her get the drawer back in. "Did *you* find anything?" he asked as she placed the papers and articles inside the slip, using it as a bag.

"Nothing about the family," she replied truthfully. "I did come upon some interesting little pieces that Noble might enjoy about Henny."

Satisfied with her response, he led her out of the room and she left the door open behind them. "I have to wonder if every one of these rooms held a trove of secrets, Clemens," she said quietly, keeping close behind him.

"We all have them," he replied, musing on it as they walked along the wide ornately decorated second floor wing past Noble's boyhood room. "I think these people lived such complicated lives probably their secrets are more complicated too."

Glancing over her shoulder, wondering if she might see someone standing there, Genevieve sighed and was glad to arrive at the staircase. "I believe that is very likely, Clemens," she agreed. "Where did you find the bones?"

Stopping on the middle step, he turned to look up at her, keeping his voice low even still. "There is a room adjoining the pool area on the underground level."

"I thought they might have kept laundry in there," she surmised as she caught up to him and followed close behind.

"There *is* laundry there and many towels and there are more photographs of Valor's ladies."

"There are more women?" she asked, surprised to hear it.

"I don't think so," he replied truthfully as they got to the main floor and began to exit the hall so they could now enter through the front door on the burned side. "They look alike but you can tell them apart," he explained. "And I think they are the same ones as you have photographs of already, it is just that he took more than one of each of them. They look like they are sleeping."

Entering the burned ballroom, she reached out and turned him around. "Clemens, tell me now, *are* they sleeping? What is your true evaluation?"

His character had him in conflict because he didn't like to make assumptions but he shook his head, doubt in his countenance. "I do believe some of them are. One has a small smile on her face as if she is about to laugh when he takes it, but there are two; I can not tell if they are quite convincing or–,"

She nodded to save him from saying it aloud. "Clemens," she whispered as if the room was alive with all that had dwelled there, walking around them while they studied their private lives. "Why would he take their lives? I am not suggesting he did, but why would he? They were enamored with him. It sounds as if they were compliant in his wants."

Hesitant, he simply shook his head. "We can't know that he did."

She considered he was right. But then there was the matter of his discovery. "Let us just say that he didn't kill any," she whispered. "There is still the question of how the bones are here. Is it possible it is someone other than one of the girls?"

"No," he replied quicker than she expected. "I am certain it is one of them," he said, gesturing for her to follow him.

She was glad Simon hadn't come along on this venture. Noble had given him a special treat to chew on so he had been less interested in leaving it behind.

Entering the side room that adjoined the pool room, there was an instant coldness like the inside of the refrigerator.

The room itself was much larger than she had anticipated. But it was dark without windows, with only the light from the narrow windows in the pool area to illuminate what was in there.

The walls were solid old stone and she could tell these were original walls of the first fifteenth century structure. The wealthy during the fourteen hundreds would build estate houses that resembled castles and this wall proved the decadence intended.

Placing her hand on the right wall, she wished she could stay in there and study it but she couldn't combat the fear, the unsettling sensations that were stronger than her curiosity.

Clemens stared at her hand, his eyes adjusting as he squinted at her. "It's pretty old in here," he said, outwardly observing her thought process.

"I feel like we have stepped into a dungeon, Clemens," she said quietly.

"I know what is in here but I have to wonder if we dig underneath there will be a handful of older skeletons down there."

Instead of laughing, he knew she was in earnest and nodded, somewhat subtly, not wanting to move the tense air around. "I am certain there are some," he stated seriously. "I wonder if he thought so too."

"Who?" she asked, as she realized this room, apart from having a lot of dust and ashes, had remained untouched by time. Large sinks and three linen presses lined the walls.

Regretting his insinuation, he shook his head. "Whoever killed the woman, if she was killed on purpose," he said, trying to rectify his wording. "If say he, if there is a he, was the reason this woman is here, I wonder if he thought there might have been other skeletons here."

"And decided this was a popular spot to bury someone secretly?" she asked quietly but with her particular dry wit.

Laughing he nodded. "Wait there, I have a torch in here somewhere. I left it when I found her," he explained.

She knew all too well what it was like to come upon something scary and feel the immediate need to leave.

Crouching, he ran his hands along the floor and was relieved to find his thick metal torch near a small table. Although it was possible to see in there, it was difficult, and some things were mere shapes rather than discernable objects.

The torch illuminated enough in front of them that she could really grasp the difference in this strange room compared to the others she had seen.

"I imagine Valor spent a lot of time in here," she noted aloud, studying the long velvet runners on some of the tables. "He enjoyed the darkness of the earlier centuries of the house. His journals don't mention this room specifically but he had not spoken much of the photographs either."

He had written in length about his love of the medieval era and the people's wild superstitious ways at the time. His journals spoke of how the eighteen hundreds were so oppressive to grow up in, that a child was immersed in gray and black and covered from head to toe in modesty and etiquette.

Like his mother and younger brother, he was a romantic; he called it an ailment, something he suffered from that was a hereditary trait. But he was passionate about it and loved the imagery of chivalry and scribes and poets and he would joke about having romance in the scullery.

Claremonde had been mostly empty apart from his mother and Henny and a handful of servants when the fire happened. So during those last years of his life, he had the kingdom at his hands but this dungeon like room was most personal to him. She could see that he had spent a lot of time in it.

The photographs were of his mermaid ladies, his dolls as he called them, and they were in heavy ornate silver frames hanging along the ancient walls.

Candles in old bronze candle holders were half melted on an ornate corner table, one he must have brought into this large laundry area close to the pool.

"He must have liked to entertain the women at the pool," she offered. "But this was clearly his favorite room."

"It is like we are surrounded by people," he said quietly, properly looking at the room, now that he had a companion with him. "I feel like we are standing in a crowded room."

"That is an apt way to express it," she agreed. Unsettled by being in there, she was equally enthralled and wanted to get a better study of what was in there. Lord Valor McKinley was a mystery. He spoke so much, he had opened himself up and exposed his inner thoughts and yet he had refrained from expressing what was most important to him.

Plush red rugs were on the floor and old lanterns as well as an old painting of a knight looking up at a castle. The photographs on the walls were of his women and she agreed with Clemens that they were the same six women.

The photos on the wall were beautifully taken and she gestured for him to shine his torch on them so she could see better. These were photographs that the women eagerly posed for, in various romantic poses of love and adoration, looking at the camera, looking at *him*.

But this is not what she had come to see, although perhaps uniquely relevant.

Catching onto her thought, as often Clemens did, he pointed to a very old tall linen press with a mirror on it, and walked her over, opening it and showing more photographs, these ones were in a photograph album.

Opening the first album, she mused that perhaps there was one album per woman; she noticed the first photograph was one with Valor in it. He was quite handsome; and he was with one of the younger women when he was in his early thirties.

He was dressed like his name, Valor, chivalry, flouncy sleeves and vest like a heroic musketeer. The woman clasped her hands looking up at him and Genevieve assumed this was his aim, simply to have fun with this new form of amusement; photography.

He had wanted to capture these moments, bringing the old paintings to life. But going through the next photographs, things had taken a dark turn even then.

The second to last photograph was of the same young woman in the swimming pool, floating on her back, her hair around her. And that was when it all became clear. This was *it*, the moment when Valor became inspired. She could feel it inside of her, his words resonating, his suggestions without saying it aloud.

With Clemens staring at it beside her, she knew him to be curious and contemplative like her, he must have grasped what had taken place. This particular photograph of the first girl with red hair and porcelain skin had initiated his new romantic quest.

Turning the old page, it was thick and creaked a little and this was the photograph, the last one in this album that confirmed what she had suspected. The same woman, young, unblemished, was now in the creek.

He had framed those photographs upstairs in his room where they each lay in the creek looking up at him. Perhaps he hadn't minded if anyone had come upon them. But these he had not wanted anyone to see.

The photograph of her looking up at him upstairs and this last photograph of her with her eyes closed. She studied it intensely, the way the woman's arm was to her side, limp and un-posed. Her face was partially submerged.

Genevieve could see a smooth large rock beside her face which looked like it had been put there to hold her head in position but hadn't quite succeeded.

Her mouth was slightly open, the creek water pressing at her lips and partly resting in one of her nostrils. Valor had mentioned peace often. The words in his journal since his youth echoing the suffering of his mother's cries and his want for peace and serenity.

Whatever his reasoning, or initial motivation, this particular day he had changed indefinitely and had tried to capture these feelings in his photography. "He wanted to capture their peace," she said quietly as she shivered against a chill. "This one doesn't quite express it so he kept trying."

Clemens looked into her eyes, a thousand questions formulating at once in his gaze. "She is dead in this one, isn't she?"

Nodding, she closed the album. "Yes, I believe she is," she confirmed. "Did you find symbols or names in the albums?"

"I didn't look for them yet."

"We will have to take them in with us."

"Are you going to tell Lord McKinley?"

Staring around the room she wanted to spend more time in there, she felt there was so much more to learn and understand. "Yes, Noble needs to know, maybe he has some pieces of the puzzle and isn't even aware of it."

Walking away from her, he pointed to a wall, a thin wall, lightly painted, not part of the original structure. Behind it was a long wooden crate which he had already sifted through. It appeared that perhaps Valor had put this wall in himself and the fire exposed some of what was behind it, what he had been trying to hide.

Behind this makeshift wall in the crate was a top section. Clemens explained it had contained a false bottom, so the top half had mostly towels in it with an assortment of old beachside souvenirs that perhaps Lillianne had collected over the time.

But beneath the false bottom, the wood that was partly rotted now, was the skeleton of one of Valor's women dolls. Her red hair was still there, not fully, but it was faded and yet Genevieve could tell it was one of them.

Her long white silk dress was mostly rotted but fragments remained and she had been intentionally laid to rest with her hands clutched on her chest and a red velvet flower in her hands.

"Look here," he pointed out, beside her head. Following it from her neck, she could see it was a necklace.

Quickly opening the album, she turned pages and stopped at the fourth picture, this particular woman was laughing. It was a candid shot that Valor must have taken by accident as she walked past the pool in a white dress.

But eerily noteworthy was the necklace she was wearing, absent from all of the photographs except for this one, but here it was around this skeleton's neck.

Genevieve held the end of it in her hand to look at it. A simple garnet surrounded by a small black stone. "This is her," she said. "The first one. If she is the only one he killed, assuming he did and she didn't accidentally drown, then that might be why she is here. We are going to have to see if any of the others survived."

"You don't think so though do you?"

Shaking her head, she stood. There was no proof that this girl was killed, not from her understanding, but it all fit and her intuition was telling her that evidence was incidental.

Valor McKinley had a collection of dark secrets and they had to find out for good if there were more of these Porcelain Bones.

Chapter Seventeen

Midnight was considered the witching hour, an infamous bedfellow of those that arose from beyond and haunted those that had yet to die. By some happenstance of fate, the grandfather clock in the hall announced its arrival, and Genevieve's eyes opened, surveying her room with a terrible feeling of something wrong.

Noble had been in a long meeting with the maids, attendants, steward and even Henny the prior day after her and Clemens found the bones. He had asked that she bring him his supper in his room but he had fallen asleep before he could eat it.

Now she wished she had been able to speak to him, especially after she dreamt of the young woman in the photo album, the one who was concealed in a makeshift coffin behind a secret wall.

The dream had started with her laughing as she talked to Valor, who Genevieve could not see in her dream, and then she was in the creek, gasping for breath.

She could not see Valor at all but she felt him there and she couldn't see why the young woman couldn't rise up from the water as only her face was in view.

But Genevieve remembers feeling him close by, feeling him watching the young woman and she believed he was holding her down. He was certainly a presence around Claremonde and perhaps the strongest of all of them. Maybe in his glimpses of clarity he was masterminding the slow revealing of his deeds.

And now she stared into her room, the orange light enough to see everything but muted in its power, keeping it all under a thick haze. Not noticing anything obvious, she got out of her bed, and reached for her thick dressing gown, having observed the early autumn chill had been slowly making its way in the evenings.

Tying it at her waist, she stepped quietly on the floor which creaked beneath her socked feet. She had tossed and turned in the night and explored her hair with her hand, surprised to find the waves still hanging down as if she had remained still.

There was an eerie sense of dread in her, her heart still beating, having partly experienced the struggle of the woman who drowned in the creek.

The woman was so dumbfounded and had been trying to make sense of it whilst, clambering for breath as she fought valiantly to get up and lift her face out of the water. The terror of knowing you were about to die; that horror at the sudden cessation of all of your thoughts and knowing you would never again see your family or eat or laugh.

Inside of this room now was the resonance of her dream, this experience of murder and Genevieve hoped they could do something about it. If only they knew what would suffice for these ominous signs to cease.

Staring at her desk as she approached it, nothing seemed out of place but the energy around her had become more concentrated. It was not as if someone was watching her, rather it was as if they now stood at her back, peering over her shoulder.

Not brave enough to reach back to test her theory; she went into her bathroom and turned the light on at the wall. Immediately the hanging lamp from the old tin ceiling flickered and she turned it off and on again, but it wouldn't stay on.

At least certain that no one, at least no one of the living kind, was actually in her room, she turned her head before she gazed up, and drew in a shallow breath. It was much too early to get up and start the day but she was certainly not going to be able to sleep again.

Just the same, nothing stirred outside her door and the night was still and there was nothing she could do. The nightmare had put her in a poor disposition so she simply had to return to bed, perhaps read one of Valor's journals or a magazine that Clemens had brought her from the village.

On her way, she parted the curtain to look outside at Claremonde. It was beautiful, and sometimes she felt there were not enough hours or days to see its entire splendor. The moon was not very strong and the clouds threatened to send down a cooler rain.

Shivering, she knew her bed was still warm but then she noticed something and she froze. Staring, the window was like a mirror, she wasn't sure if she was seeing anything at all, but it didn't look right to her. It was not outside in the dark of the night or in the ruins of the past, but something in her room behind her.

It was a shadow, nothing particularly dark, but it seemed oddly placed along the wall near the door where the light didn't shine on it too much. Darker like a misty stain, she stared at it, trying to ascertain if she was merely filled with fear and manifesting a dilemma where there wasn't one.

Gazing in the reflection of the window, as if looking at it directly would be much too terrifying, she tried to understand how it was there, and perhaps it *was* a stain. Yet, it looked like it was in front of the wall, the light traveling through and hitting an obstacle that cast this eerie shape.

Minutes passed and she became sleepy and considered that it was explainable and she would now read until she fell asleep again. But then, as if anticipating her disinterest, it moved. It moved!

By its own volition, the shadow of something that was not there in a light that was not cast on it, suddenly moved away from the wall and by all appearances it came towards her.

There was no mistaking that it was real, that it was there and she did not delay to get away from it, running out of her room without a second thought, she reached out ahead of her in the dark cold hall to open Noble's door and she tripped on the hall rug and fell into his semi lit room, hurting her knee.

He shot up, shocked. Simon jumped off his bed to see who was on the floor. Noble looked over and down at her and worry came upon his face immediately. With tears in her eyes she couldn't speak, she had been struck dumb, utterly afraid and now in pain.

In spite of his own limitations, he rushed to her the best he could, reaching down for her.

But she was too afraid, there was a sense of panic as if she was being chased and she ran past him, her knee buckling but still holding together. Arriving at the other side of his bed, she crouched down like a small child but she couldn't curl up small enough to feel safe again.

Coming around to her, with Simon at his side, they both studied her and he was obviously concerned.

"There is nothing wrong with me," she said, fearful that he would consider her mental state weak. "Something, *someone*, is in here, it was in my room moving towards me."

"Genna," he said gently, brushing her hair from her face. "I know. It is true, I doubt nothing about you."

Tears welled in her eyes. She had been genuinely shocked, her heart pounded so much it hurt but she glanced up at his door as he went to close it. "It could come in here, why would they want to be around us?"

"I can not be sure that's their motivation," he stated calmly as he held her shoulders. "Alike to us, perhaps they are merely walking around, unknowing about us."

Looking into his eyes, she wanted to believe that but she knew that something different was taking place here. "It came towards me, Noble. It had intent; it had to have seen me. It anticipated my movements and followed."

Reaching for an unused handkerchief on his bedside, he dabbed at her face where tears had fallen. "I am sorry for that," he stated sincerely. "I do not like to see you suffer."

"*I* am sorry," she interceded. "I should not have run into your room like that. I can barely control my impulses, it frightened me so much."

Noticing her shiver, he gestured for her to stand as he watched her check that his room was free of anyone roaming in their proximity. "My bed is warm," he offered. "Please, you are cold; I will not harm you, get yourself beneath the covers and be warm. I will not send you back to your room."

Genuinely relieved that she didn't have to return to her room, she was not hesitant whatsoever and went into his bed, the warmth of his body where he slept still beneath the covers. "Noble, I didn't get to talk to you yesterday but I have much to tell you. I wish I had not woken you like this."

Sitting on the side of the bed, he studied her face, as if he was seeing it for the first time. "I am glad you did," he said sincerely. "I am aware of your fears; I too observe what dwells around us. It has worsened since your arrival, I am certain because of what you have come to know. I regret I encouraged your discoveries."

"No," she said, noticing that he was crossing his arms against the cold. "I am a curious girl; I would have looked anyway. I do not regret it and you are in no way to blame. I wish I was more courageous."

Smiling, he nodded. "The bravest soul would shudder in the presence of an invisible entity, Genna. Do not be unduly harsh on yourself."

Consoled, she was truly grateful for his kindness but in spite of the possible misinterpretation, she couldn't sit in his warm bed while he sat out cold. "Noble, I mean nothing inappropriate but you look cold. You should get in next to me before you turn into ice. I will leave if you wish me to."

Interest grew in his gaze; he was seemingly surprised that she would suggest leaving when she was so adamant to get away from her room in the first place. "Are your feet cold?"

Laughing, she turned the blankets down beside her. "Not any longer, no."

Getting in beside her, Simon was quick to jump on the bed and lay across their legs, excited at the impromptu gathering. "What was it you had to tell me?" he asked quietly as he leaned back into his pillows, relaxing beside her.

"It is shocking," she warned. "I am not certain I should simply say it in case you are jolted up and no longer repairable."

Laughing, he knew she was lightening the mood but also that she meant what she said. "There is much that I suspect has taken place in my small world, Genevieve. I am ready for you to confront me with whatever might be greatly disturbing."

It was not the right time to tell him about Henny but she did intend to show him the articles and letter so he could come to his own conclusions. For now she could only relay what she had seen for herself. "There is a room branching off the pool area where it appears Valor had spent a lot of time," she began carefully. "Clemens had noticed a wall that had been created much later and behind it was a hidden box with bones in it."

Knowing she would not be overly dramatic about something small, he simply looked at her, his face against the side of his pillow. He was thinking on her words and she could feel the warmth of his body beside her. "Human?"

"Yes," she confirmed. "An entire skeleton, placed in there like a proper burial."

"It could be anyone," he stated justly. "Claremonde has centuries of residents and servants."

Wishing she could tell him that the possibilities were endless, he could see in her expression that she knew better even before she said it. Swallowing hard she explained the appearance of the skeleton with the red hair and the necklace that matched the photograph in Valor's album.

She also went on to explain that there were other photograph albums with pictures that indicated the young women were not necessarily sleeping in the creek. "You had said you wanted me to tell you," she reminded him, filled with remorse.

"I did and I still wish it," he said.

Seeing him truly up close like never before she realized how truly handsome he was; how beautiful his spirit was, the intelligence and valiance of his soul shining through his blue eyes. "You don't seem as surprised as I thought you might be," she said, feeling that he was open to her frankness.

Looking deep into her eyes, she felt they were equal; two similar beings with two greatly differing histories. "I had my suspicions," he whispered, fear in his gaze. "I never wanted to admit it; even now I dare not allow my ears to hear my words. I loved him."

Tears formed in her eyes, she had never felt such pity for another person before. His grief emanated from him and she realized how he must have held it inside of himself for so long. "You were not wrong to love him," she assured him.

"It could have been an accident," he offered. "I would betray him to assume he had done something that is not yet proven."

"Yes," she agreed. Although she felt that everything pointed to Valor having killed her, there was no certainty that he was simply not present for her drowning in some unusual uncontrollable circumstance. "Yes," she said again. "We will have to look into it more. The other women might be sleeping. We only have one dead girl and it may have been an incident that did not occur with the others."

"We have to seek the others," he said, dimmed hope in his voice. "On the day of the fire one of them was there with him at the creek. She went home, I know because I sent her. She may tell us what, if anything, occurred with him."

She felt relieved, not only that she had shared the information with him, but that even though the situation looked grim, he was willing to accept the truth.

Now, exhausted perhaps from being woken and from the daunting conversation, he closed his eyes and sighed.

The room was cold, the chill hung as if it was an invisible fog mid level above the floor. Simon stretched out and she tucked her feet beneath him for warmth.

Staring at the door, she prayed inside of herself that nothing would enter. A wall or a door couldn't stop a spirit but she hoped they could not get anything from her now and would leave them be.

Taking in a deep breath of her own, she glanced at Noble who she was certain was asleep, and she brought the blankets up to her chin, and then up over his hands.

Staring at him, the light low but ample, she considered everything that happened up until now. Not just at Claremonde but with him, her mysterious master. Here she lay at his side, her protector, her friend.

In spite of all things that would dictate that she shouldn't, she gently placed her hand on his chest, just on the side, just to feel close to him. Her heart beat a little faster at the boldness of the movement and she feared it would be considered an unwelcome advance.

Closing her eyes, she thought that perhaps she would move her hand away, but then something happened that she had not anticipated at all. With his eyes still closed, his breathing low and restful, he brought his hand up from under the blanket and placed it on hers and he left it there.

He had not been asleep, perhaps near to it, but not completely, and her heart was lost completely, there beside him with his hand sealing her fate.

In spite of hauntings and feelings and questions in abundance, in just minutes they had both fallen asleep.

Chapter Eighteen

The next morning Genevieve had woken and reluctantly left Noble's warm bed while he still slept. Simon watched her leave and then took her spot where she left her own warmth. Not wanting to return to her room, she did because she had to, but moved quicker than usual, but still with a determined sense of living her life normally. For all she knew, in spite of all that she and Clemens had learned, this might be an ongoing haunting.

Their discoveries did not ensure normality so she had to learn to be more courageous and sensible. If a shadow came at her again in the privacy and protection of her own room, she would at least try to not scream and run. So she had a bath that morning, knowing it would be an hour before Noble's alarm awoke him. Thankfully it was a peaceful uneventful start to the day and she felt better now the daylight was streaming into her room.

The prior night he had placed his hand on hers as they lay sleeping beside each other after the shadow had scared her. She should have been thinking more about the ghost and where it might be now, what it might see if it happened to appear in this moment. But, like the fool she was, the romantic notions that filled her in spite of her senses, all she could think about was his hand and his intention to hold hers.

They did not speak of it over breakfast but his spirits were exceptionally cheerful and there was a feeling between them of belonging and comfort and harmony and she smiled much too much, surely he would have noticed.

Clemens had come early, he talked to Noble a long time about the bones and the photograph albums but mostly Genevieve openly discussed her thoughts on the poor woman that had died.

She must have been afraid and it was sad for her, she felt almost as torn as Noble did about the possibility, the likelihood of it having been his beloved brother. How can a man with such wit and intelligence and skill be the same man who would take the life of an innocent girl?

She did not want to speak too much on it but it had been weighing on her since they discovered the bones. They would soon have to return her home but first they had to learn more so there was no uproar or scandal that affected Noble who was an unwitting party.

After breakfast and a short walk with Simon, she and Clemens went for a drive to a smaller village just outside of Wanderling. There was a thirteenth century stone church that was still used, and its stained glass windows were ornate and beautiful. It wasn't overly large but was situated on a large piece of land, lush green grass and an extensive cemetery behind it surrounded by a low iron fence. "Why are we here at this particular church?" she asked quietly.

"I'm not sure this is the place to start," he confessed. "But I do know Valor liked to come here and who knows, perhaps he talked to someone or they could tell us something about him. I think two of the young women he liked came here also. Being a man of faith maybe we can ask the pastor some questions and trust that he won't repeat them."

Sighing, she wondered if it was going to help or not. "I don't suppose it would hurt. If he knew those women he could tell us where we could find them perhaps."

It was quiet this day, a sunny but cool Thursday morning and the church was not attached to a house or rectory but the open door gave them hope they would have someone to talk to.

Genevieve had taken longer than usual to choose what to wear knowing the task ahead and had finally settled upon a demure gray woolen skirt and matching tight sweater top with half length sleeves. A gray hat and gloves completed the picture of a proper lady and she had somehow gotten her long brown hair into a neat bun.

Clemens remarked that she was a mixture of lovely and intimidating and she laughed, but now they were serious. He parked his car beside the only other one that was there and they closed the doors which were uncomfortably loud, announcing their arrival before she would have liked.

"I don't know what I will say," she admitted quietly as she kept her younger friend, in a black vested suit and hat, close to her side.

"You will think of it when you know what he's like," he noted wisely. "You always have the right words, I know that about you."

Offering him a subtle smile she was grateful for his geniality and the fact that he had observed her enough to make such an apt evaluation of her nature. "Thank you, Clemens. Let us hope he is easy to get information from, or we might have to start grave digging to get answers."

Smirking, they were both surprised when a short older man appeared in the open door way. Rubbing the back of his mostly bald head, he then adjusted his rounded glasses before looking them over. "Are you pair lost?" he asked, genuinely assuming they were.

Waiting until they got closer, Genevieve felt that perhaps he was not the pastor of the church but there was something about him that made her feel he was a permanent fixture there. "Oh no, we are here on behalf of Claremonde Hall," she said congenially but confidently. "We are writing an account of its history for Lord McKinley and were hoping you could tell us anything you know about any of them you may have encountered?"

Feeling proud that she had thought of something convincing so quickly, she could tell that Clemens was also impressed.

The man was immediately receptive and nodded. "Young Valor once attended here, he is the eldest of the McKinley children, but he has passed now."

"Were you acquainted with him personally?" Genevieve asked curiously.

Enjoying the attention of two younger people, the man nodded enthusiastically. "My yes. Any man in the path of Valor was a quick friend. Charming man he was," he informed them gleefully. "Did you know him?" he asked, looking at them both.

Clemens shook his head but allowed Genevieve to do the talking. "Sadly I never made his acquaintance," she replied honestly. "We are both associated with the current Lord McKinley."

"Noble, yes indeed!" he mused with a laugh. "A boy of excellent character; though sure to be well into manhood now. He came here a handful of times with his older brother but did not return after that. Valor was a popular companion of the young ladies, if I must say so," he said with a chuckle. "I mean no harm by it."

Genevieve waved his comment away with a smile. "He was known for his wit and charm," she relayed. "I assume you have worked here a long time?"

Nodding, he looked at Clemens and then back at her as if he was being interviewed for the newspapers. "I've been caretaker forty five years and going on a tad more," he said with a laugh as he rubbed his head again.

Genevieve looked over her shoulder, intentionally making it look like secrecy was important. "Would you mind if we ask some rather frank questions?" she asked, looking him in his intrigued eyes. "I will be honest, the McKinley's would like their story told quite thoroughly and are certainly aware of the intrigues of their predecessors."

"I know there was a fire and they don't live in the old estate house now," he said, quickly willing to offer up whatever he could. "I'd not met the girl, the daughter of Lady McKinley and I'd only once said a brief hello to her. But I'll tell you what I know. There's talk about back then but I can't be certain of none to be sure but you know how talk is."

"Is the pastor here?" Clemens asked, perhaps concerned the man with answers might not speak so freely if heard.

"No," he replied, surprised it should be asked. "He will be back tomorrow."

"What was said back then?" Genevieve pressed carefully. "Was it about Valor?"

Nodding, he peered up into the blue sky as he went back in his memory. "He had been seen with a few of the young ladies from here," he noted, tapping his chin. "Not that anything was seen but it was speculated on that he had a child with one."

Astonished, Genevieve's confident demeanor faltered. "He has a child?!" she asked louder than she hoped.

The man's eyebrows rose and his mouth hung open. "Naw, it was said, but the girl lied about it. She wanted him to marry her. I got it on good authority she couldn't have none of her own, she just wanted him to take her as a wife."

A little relieved she didn't have one more scandal to divulge to poor Noble, she quickly tried to work out how to brooch the subject they came to discuss. "On the subject of hearsay," she began quietly. "I heard about some bones there."

Unexpectedly the man's face turned ashen as if all the blood had drained from his entire body. "You know about the bones?" he asked, his voice faltering somewhat.

"A skeleton," Clemens stated neutrally. "Someone had died."

Wiping the perspiration from his face with a cloth he was already holding, he took in a deep breath and shook his head. "Lady McKinley made me swear not to ever tell about it."

Not expecting to hear Lillianne's name come up, she was quick to place her hand on Clemens' arm discretely. Whatever was going to be said, whether it was about Valor or the girl or not, it was likely something Noble should know. "She died three years ago," she informed him gently as she took in a shallow breath, holding it there to hide her nervousness. "I am certain she would want her son to know the truth."

Closing his eyes and clasping his hands together it looked like he might be praying before he spoke. "The boy should know about it," he agreed, saying it as if he was appeasing the gods that listened. "I was contacted in the dead of night to come take a body from Claremonde," he whispered, gesturing for them to walk away from the church itself.

"When?" Clemens asked.

Shrugging, he shook his head. "Just before the daughter had her child."

"Prudence?" Genevieve clarified.

"Yes," he said. "So, must be thirty eight or so years and I brought my cousin, Raymond with me and we made our way up there with our pony cart. Lady McKinley looked awful distraught and she asked us to take the body away for burial and not to speak about it."

"Who was she?" Genevieve asked quietly as they got to the border of the cemetery.

The man studied her, confused. "Who was she who?"

"The body."

"Oh no," he shook his head. "It was no she, it was the Lord himself. Lady McKinley's husband, the father of Noble and Valor and such."

Genevieve could barely blink; it was completely overwhelming. "*Randolph* McKinley? Noble's father? I don't understand. You took *his* body away?"

Truly worried, he pleaded with them. "You won't be telling anyone?"

"No," she promised. "This is for the family alone. They will utilize what they wish and they have told me to explain that no names will be used or insinuated."

Sufficiently convinced, given that she truly had no intention of getting anyone in trouble, he sighed and relaxed a little. "The Lady said his heart had given out and she wanted us to take him and bury him in the church cemetery and not to mark it with his name or talk about it to anyone."

Clemens, just as confused and shocked as Genevieve, fumbled on his words, not knowing what to ask either.

"Wouldn't they want a proper funeral for him?" he asked justifiably.

The man shook his head and sighed before shaking his head again. "I'd like to say what I think if it's your word that my name isn't being brought up."

"You have my promise," Genevieve assured him.

Looking out at the tombstones, perhaps at where Randolph was at this very time, he sighed again. "She said too many people would be after them for money and wanting to take advantage of them without a proper man heading the household. She says to protect her and her children from thievery and savagery, she asked we take him quietly away and bury him."

Genevieve assumed he and his cousin were paid quite well for their secrecy but it looked like it had weighed on him. "You suspected otherwise?" she asked careful not to appear judgmental.

Looking into her eyes, he nodded subtly. "My cousin, Ray, he's worked with corpses for a long time, even back then. He said he knew the signs of poison all too well. He said it was obvious, no doubting it."

Feeling that Clemens was about to defend Lady McKinley, someone he had often spoken about highly, Genevieve decided to draw back a little. After a handful of further questions, not much else was derived other than general gossip about Valor.

Thankfully Prudence was not raised at all so her particular dilemma must have been a closely held secret with only a couple of people knowing. The man then spent a short time asking them when their book would be in print and where he could get a copy and will his photograph be in it.

Genevieve reminded him that he begged them not to use his name and he then laughed and agreed with her but asked that they let him know when their research would be completed.

The drive home was mostly quiet as Clemens and Genevieve were both thinking to themselves, confused that they went for one thing and instead returned with another in its place.

"We didn't find anything out about the girl," he noted with a sigh.

"I know," she said. "But we will, Clemens. Obviously you chose to take me somewhere that we might find answers and we did, so truly the quest was a successful one."

Glancing at her as he turned the car onto the long road back to Claremonde, he sounded a little consoled by her statement but something was bothering him. "I cared a great deal for Lady McKinley," he said with a lump in his throat. "I don't know what to feel now. I feel sorry I went."

Rubbing his arm, she felt bad for him but she also knew better. Trying her best to refrain from too much divulgence, she kept it simple. "Clemens, I have discovered some things over the time and I am quite certain Lady McKinley did not have a hand in her husband's death."

Shocked, he looked at her three times before questioning her. "She called them to come get him," he reminded her. "She knew about it."

"Yes," she agreed. "But I believe she was told about it after it happened. I honestly do not believe she committed the offense."

"Poison?"

"Correct," she said firmly. "I don't believe she poisoned him, she was likely hiding the actual culprit. She did not want them exposed so she was protecting them."

He glanced at her with a question on his lips, but he did not ask it. She was quite certain he assumed it was Valor that killed his father. After all, he was already suspected of murder and she had read his journals so she might have known something Clemens didn't.

If he asked if it was Valor she would have to deny it, but thankfully he looked relieved and she could tell that the assumption would remain with him. He was just glad it was not Lady McKinley and she was glad she didn't have to detail her own suspicions.

When they drove past Claremonde, it felt like there was a resurgence of the past and all of the pieces of the puzzle were swimming around, waiting to be connected.

Slowing the car in the clearing, she could see the tension in his brow and worried for him. "I will tell him," she stated emphatically.

Looking at her, he looked defeated. "I shouldn't let you take it all onto your shoulders, Miss Belmont."

Shaking her head, she knew he would receive it better from her. He would want to be able to express his feelings openly and would be guarded for the sake of Clemens if his young friend was there. "I know some things that he might not want anyone else to know," she said carefully. "I will make him his favorite meal."

Smiling, gratitude was in his eyes. "Our world has changed since you arrived in it."

"Yes, well I feel responsible for that," she confessed truthfully. "Perhaps I have created the chaos and I'm more to blame than to thank."

His smile faded as he shook his head. "You are stronger than anyone I've ever known," he said seriously. "You are like a knight without armor."

Laughing, she opened the car door, ready to get the next conversation over with. "Yes, well iron clothing is much out of fashion nowadays, Clemens. Do not trouble yourself this evening with anxiousness. It will be well, Noble will be well, as will I. We will reveal what must be discovered to end these otherworldly interferences and then we will have lunch outside in the sun."

Smiling, he offered her a wave. It was clear they still had a long way to go, but she did believe that the light would triumph over the dark eventually; it had to.

A light breeze wafted up past the ancient building and she shivered, wishing she had taken a light coat with her. With autumn soon approaching, fear would be harder to escape when the sun was not around as much to distract them.

As soon as she opened the front door, Simon ran to greet her, and she bent to hold him and kiss him, listening to the sound of familiar voices. Walking down the long hall, Noble called out for her and she stopped in the doorway, Simon stopping beside her and licking her hand.

The maid was there, the one that indiscreetly favored Noble. Glancing at the table, Genevieve could see she had baked him a cake. "Hello, Miss Miles," she said calmly, clasping her hands together. "I am glad to see you again."

"Good day to you, Miss Belmont," she replied with a genuine smile. "I hope you are well."

Genevieve nodded politely while Noble reacted to her countenance. "Were you and Clemens successful in your endeavors?" he asked evenly. "Did you discover anything?"

Not being able to hide the gravity from her expression, she nodded. "We did," she confirmed.

Sensing the seriousness, he offered the pretty dark haired maid a polite smile. "Thank you again for your visit, Miss Miles. I will need to have a meeting with Miss Belmont at this time. She has been doing some research work for me."

While disappointment was in her eyes, she nodded at both of them and turned to smile at him. "I hope you enjoy the cake, it was my mother's recipe."

"I know I will," he confirmed genuinely. "You have a natural talent for baking, thank you."

She left the kitchen without an acknowledgment in Simon's direction, and Genevieve felt sorry for her, although she pitied herself more so in this moment.

Once the front door was heard to close, Noble was quick to question her. "Clemens said he took you to a rectory beyond the village. Was the priest able to enlighten you?"

"We spoke with the caretaker," she said, standing where she was instead of sitting. "We were careful how we questioned him and he confirmed he knew of some bones."

"Did he know who the girl was?"

"He did not."

Studying her curiously, he approached her and drew close enough as if he could derive the details from his vicinity. "Then the bones, of what identity did they possess? Did he know?"

"Noble," she said, having prepared herself in her mind on the way home but now at a loss for proper words. "I want you to understand that once I tell you something there is nothing I can do to rid you of the knowledge."

"We have discussed this before, Genna," he said, even more intrigued than before. "I would rather be aware of the entirety of what has happened than imagine worse."

"This is worse than I would think you could imagine," she said. "It is not what I expected to hear. I am burdened on your behalf just knowing it and I feel conflicted on whether I want to be the one to tell you."

"You must," he said, more pleadingly than assertively.

"I know," she said with a sigh, as she pat Simon's head, stroking his soft fur. "But you will always remember me for it; you will always think of my face as I tell you this tragic news and then when you see me you will be repelled."

Laughing in spite of the situation, he seized her arms and then grabbed her hands and held them to his chest. "When I see you, all I think of is your courage, your beauty, your foolish wit and your sharp mind. What you tell me is not what represents you. I am ready. Please."

Lowering her head, she once again had to face being the one to reveal his family secrets, but this one was darker than a lost child and an affair. "Valor wrote in his journals of the night he last saw your father. He said your father was arguing with someone unseen and after that night he was gone, and then never heard from again."

"Yes, it took some months before we were certain he would not return as he traveled often."

"How old were you?"

"Thirteen."

Nodding, she knew he had witnessed his father's violence to his mother but they had not discussed him any further than that. "Were you close to him?"

Frowning, he shook his head. "He barely acknowledged me. He only spoke to Valor because he was the elder male and only for the purpose of grooming him to be his successor. I avoided him when I could. Why do you ask it?"

Drawing in a deep breath, she looked into his eyes. "When we spoke to the man about bones and Claremonde all he knew was that he was asked thirty eight years ago, to come and retrieve a deceased person from here and bury them in an unmarked grave in that church cemetery."

"Who asked him to come?"

"Your mother," she replied honestly.

Studying her face, reluctant but insistent, he frowned again before asking. "And who was he dispatched to retrieve?"

"Randolph McKinley," she replied staidly. "He came for the body of your father."

Chapter Nineteen

Truth had a way of settling in the stomach and fading into the back of our minds until the tragedies and woes were a resonance rather than a scream. After all of this time, Noble had learned what became of his father all those years ago.

In a small space of time he discovered his mother had given birth to a sister to her true love, Giles Atherton. He was also conflicted by the resurfacing of old suspicions about his brother and his porcelain lovers who seemingly never returned home to their families.

But there was more to divulge, more to tell him and she felt that perhaps there was more he could tell her. For now it would unfold as it did, gradually so that they could combat one realization at a time and be respectful of each unique situation.

Without telling his workers why, Noble had asked his steward and the gardener to bring in a gold metal daybed from an empty room in the other side of the quarters. He had them set it in his room against the wall and close to the fire and that is where she slept that night. It is also where he insisted she sleep if she felt too scared to go into her own room from now on.

There was no rationale to their assumptions but they felt these ghostly wanderings inside of Claremonde and the servant's quarters would be a temporary affliction. Given that there was a great increase in these appearances since she started investigating their past, it seemed plausible there would be a heightening in reaction from them.

Either way, her master had gone to the same church with Clemens to see the caretaker and somehow coerce him into exhuming the body he had buried when he was younger. They had to convince him that it was a secretive exercise and that no blame would befall him and no consequences would come of it.

He had gone early and left her and Simon alone to have breakfast and take a quick walk outside before lighting the fire in her bedroom.

The chill was no longer an infrequent imposition now but rather it was more definite and the seasons had somehow changed seemingly overnight. She only had two winter outfits and would eventually have to go into Wanderling to get more.

Although Noble was glad to compensate her for any garments, she did not like to take advantage of his generous nature and preferred to wait for when things were necessary to acquire.

For now, as she busied herself in the kitchen, she had on a brown long sleeve knit top and longer skirt as well as stockings and socks to keep her feet warm with her low heeled shoes. She also wore a tan scarf to keep her neck warm and took to wearing gloves in the house.

Keeping Noble's food inside of the oven, she cleaned around the kitchen knowing the maid tidied there rather than polished too much. Restless, she considered putting a record on the gramophone but wanted to hear any noises in the house, especially any creaking on the floor behind her.

The daytime was a reprieve from the gravity of the night, but it was still frightening to see something and not be forewarned of its approach. This is how life was now, her senses heightened as her ears and eyes and feelings were acutely attuned to unseen movements.

Finally the car pulled up in the clearing and she could hear him getting out, and knew that he took longer than Clemens, even though his leg and hip had improved. When the door opened she only heard one set of footsteps, his and his cane, and Simon was quick to greet him as she went to the stove to take out his breakfast.

"Are you hungry?" she called out once she heard him in the doorway.

"I *am* rather famished," he admitted. "I know that such ventures should have me lose my appetite but I am uncertain as to how I feel. I am conflicted purely because I am not reacting as one should under these circumstances."

"Your circumstances are not so straight forward," she reminded him.

She watched him walk over to the table and take his favorite seat. He wore a gray suit with vest and hat to match, a tailored suit that a gentleman with money might own, and he looked handsome and elegant in it.

While she knew he was resistant to being seen in public since he had been scarred and disfigured by his burns, she could tell this wasn't on his mind this day.

"You are quite a striking figure, Noble," she said aloud, forgetting herself in the moment. "You remind me of a man in the movies walking down the street while others turn to watch."

Taking the warm plate of eggs and sausages and potatoes from her, he laughed loudly. "You say the strangest things at the oddest times, Genna. You have completely thrown me off my guard and flattered me while bewildering me. Do you really think it?"

"Yes, of course I do," she insisted as she sat across from him. "On the occasion when I speak before I think, I am apt only to say precisely what is on my mind without having watered it down with etiquette and propriety."

Laughing again, he poised his fork and knife and cut his sausages and scooped some potato on his fork along with it. "And let us just say that I was walking down the street in such a movie, would *you* also turn to look at me?"

"Not only that, but I would stop to ask for your autograph."

Laughing with his head tilted back, he swallowed his food and nodded. "Silly girl, how can I live without you now? How could I spend one day and not hear your silly words and be delighted by you?"

Smiling at him, she poured his coffee and then one for herself, while keeping a piece of toast and jam for her and

Simon. "I can not answer that," she stated neutrally. "You would be in a poor way if forced into such a position."

Smiling as he ate, they allowed the joyful moment to settle and she sipped her coffee while Simon lay at her feet with a groan. "Noble–,"

"It *was* him," he said, finishing his mouthful before looking at her. "It was my father, just as the man had said it would be."

Studying his face as he ate, she couldn't imagine how he felt in that moment. She had not really loved her father all that much, especially after he killed her mother. But there were moments in her childhood where she saw his vulnerability and intermittent kindnesses. Love was inexplicable by nature. At times it could not be justified, nor could it be feigned, it was as it was in its utter purity. "How can you be certain?"

"I recognized the suit and his right arm, which had been broken during polo, had healed as well as the pocket watch my grandfather had given him. I have no doubts of it, nor do I believe the caretaker to be insincere."

"I believed him to be truthful," she agreed. "What do you feel about it? What will you do with his body? I suppose you thought that perhaps up until now he could have been alive all this time."

Nodding, he looked past her at the window, the cooled sun streaming through as the morning awoke. "As a child I did, and when I thought of it I mostly feared it. He had never been pleased to return to us and we were merrier without him. But in my young manhood, I would look at my mother and realized she did not appear worried or anxious. I never thought that she was aware of his fate, but I felt she believed he would not return."

"But that night he never left, not alive anyway."

Nodding, he did not seem pained, rather he was pensive. "I considered having him buried near Claremonde in our cemetery here."

'There is a cemetery here?" she asked curiously.

Laughing, he nodded and then sipped his coffee, the one he had added breakfast cocoa to. "Yes, it is down that first turn closer to the entrance, you can't see it for the trees but it is down there."

"Oh, I should like to see it."

"Yes, I should have thought to tell you about it before, I'm sure you would enjoy it," he said with a smile. "Just the same, I did not feel it appropriate. While I am fully aware that my mother is not out there, she has gone to heaven and is not likely to be lurking around her body for any reason. But I did not want to show any disrespect by placing his body there, not after what he had done to her. Claremonde was in her family, he did not belong in its soil."

Sighing, she thought it wise to leave it be but she could tell by the look in his eyes that there was more. "Where will he go?"

"I have arranged a discrete burial in the cemetery where his parents are buried. A gravestone will be made for him with no particular death date so as to not elicit curiosity. That will put an end to that particular crisis so we can again concentrate on other more pertinent issues," he said, mulling it over as he finished his breakfast. "My only concern is my mother. I can not properly rest knowing the secret she had harbored. To have become so conflicted she would take his life, I can not imagine how it must have eaten at her."

Taking the empty plate and cutlery from him, she stood but did not immediately go to the sink. "There is something you should know regarding that," she said, knowing this had to be the time she told him, not only about Henny but about why.

Leaving the kitchen with Simon following her, she ignored the concentrated sensation in the hallway and went directly to her room. There had been a small pile she had kept for this particular moment and she gathered the items together to bring to him, lowering her gaze at the feeling someone was in the doorway.

Noble had walked over to look at a bird outside of the window and turned to gaze at her curiously whilst also giving her a head to toe study. "It is about my father?"

Laying it all out on the kitchen table in front of where he had just been sitting, she drew in a deep breath knowing this was going to be some hard news to accept. "It is about who likely caused his death and particularly why."

"You have known for a while?" he asked seriously.

Nodding, she did not want to admit it, but it had been for him that she had not divulged it all at once. "I was not certain how I was going to tell you. I do not know how this will affect you at all, but it is a dreadful reality, Noble. I do not want you to know it, but I know that you wish it."

Hesitant, his gaze was mixed with interest and reluctance but he approached the table and stood beside her, looking at what she had lay out for him to see. Simon positioned himself at their feet as the morning birdsong echoed around the quiet quarters.

"First I wanted you to see this," she said, handing him the newspaper article about Henny and then the letter from her cousin. Once he was done reading them both, he was about to comment but she gestured that he needed to see the small note, the one about her having paid someone for a particular *deed.*

"Henny?" he asked quietly, rereading parts of it. "She was married," he said aloud, surprised at having not known it before. "He harmed her also."

Genevieve nodded, but still wanted him to come to his own conclusions. "Genevieve, you derive from this that she had him murdered?"

Looking into his eyes, she wondered what he wanted to hear, but she knew all too well that he only wanted to hear what she thought. He had a similar way of thinking but he was certain to tell her if he thought differently.

"I do believe that," she said quietly, shivering. "And I do not want you to worry; I have no intention of speaking to her about it or telling anyone else about it either. I have not told Clemens and I intend to keep it that way."

"I will not speak of it either," he said, almost looking at her for approval. "I am not certain how I will behave around her now," he admitted further.

"I know," she said regretfully. "That is why I refrained from telling you straight away, but I can not have you think your mother had held a guilt that she did not possess."

Frowning, he looked at the article and then at her again. "This does not suggest she had her hand in the death of my father."

Walking behind him, she took Valor's journal from the table, a piece of yarn inside holding where she wanted him to read. "Your brother mentioned that Henny was particularly upset by the way your father treated your mother," she said before drawing in a deep breath. "She wanted to protect your mother *and* Prudence."

Shaking his head, he looked at her troubled, as if he thought she had made a large leap in assumption. "He was violent with my mother, not Prudence."

Looking at his face, wondering if he could ever see the world the same again after this revelation, she reluctantly handed him the journal. "You are correct," she said. "He did not hit her."

Watching him open it up, she pointed to where she wanted him to read. She watched as he came to understand what his father had done to his sister, how Prudence was impregnated by him. He also read that his mother had told Henny and she reacted with wild fury.

Given that she had more than likely arranged the death of her first husband, a poisoning of someone she reviled would not be an implausible act. Reading it quietly three times, his finger running along it as thoughts raced through his head, she knew he had come to the same conclusion.

Closing the journal, he now appeared saddened and somewhat disgusted. He shook his head and held his hand to his mouth, sickened and also angry. "I denounce him as my blood and as my father," he spat.

"I am sorry," she said truthfully.

Sitting down, he stared at her, but his thoughts were elsewhere. "Patience, my niece," he stated simply.

Nodding, she knew he was trying to make sense of facts before he could grasp the connotations. "She is also your half sister," she explained.

"Does she know?" he pondered aloud.

"I wouldn't think so, Noble," she consoled. "I couldn't imagine Prudence telling her and I do not believe she would want *you* to know, or even Valor. He made it sound like he would never tell her or your mother that he was aware of it, especially because he read it in your mother's private writings."

"That is why she has kept away from here," he sighed. "The memory of father, Claremonde must be a bitter sight to her."

"I imagine so," she agreed. "I wish I hadn't told you. I hate to see you this way. I wanted so much to make you smile and hope again. If I hadn't looked into anything, I would never have found any of this out."

Reaching for her hands, she had never seen him so sad, but he still managed to radiate a sense of warmth when he looked at her. "I knew my father was not a good man, Genna. This only tells me how evil he was. I am sorry most for my beloved mother who had held this in her silence. But dear Prudence;. I had often thought she had become quiet and reclusive when we were children and now I know why. He was a thief, robbing from her the vivacity that she once possessed, the innocence of a young girl."

"He is no longer here," she reminded him. "Not in presence but also not in resonance. The only way you can override his deeds is to maintain your goodness. Your legacy must be one of kindness and gentility."

Standing now, without warning, he took her into his arms and nothing had felt more natural to her. She had held him so often in her mind and heart that his arms already felt a part of her. The warmth of his body, pressed against hers, mixed sensations of amorousness and pain.

Pulling back only slightly, he placed his warm scarred hand on her face and stared into her and she placed her hand on his, knowing she could never escape how she felt for him. Leaning forward, his face so close to hers, the sound of the front door echoed out into the hall and Simon quickly went to greet whoever it was.

Not wanting to let go of the moment, she reached up and placed her hand on his face, quickly smiling at him and he laughed a little.

"*You* make me happy," he whispered. "*You* give me hope, Genna."

They stood apart just in time for Clemens to enter the kitchen and thankfully he did not notice any strange sensation although Genevieve felt love was written all over her face.

The younger man was still reserved around his master because they had just returned from seeing his father's bones; just the same, he was wide eyed and eager to speak.

"What is it, Clemens?" Noble asked, fully alert to his driver's sudden shock.

"I could be mistaken, but I don't believe I am," he said, his lower lip trembling a little as he tucked his shaking hands under his arms. "I saw your brother," he said quietly, perhaps worried he had been followed. "I saw Valor down by the creek and he saw me too."

Chapter Twenty

Clemens, emanating a mixture of excitement and fright, could barely contain himself as he explained how he had seen the ghost of Noble's brother, Valor. "I know what he looks like from the photographs and portraits. He looked like he did when he was younger, maybe thirty or so but I hardly saw through him, he almost looked real."

Noble didn't doubt him whatsoever, instead he glanced at the window and an expression of determination came upon his face. "Did he speak to you?"

Shaking his head, he glanced at Genevieve who was as enthralled as he was, but Noble was more personally invested. "Where was he?"

"Near the carousel," he replied, placing his hands out to gesture for him to not get his hopes up. "He didn't say anything but he was standing at the creek looking down and I thought I was just watching the past but then he turned and looked at me. I swear it, he saw me; I know he did."

"Did he disappear?" she pressed him for more information.

"No, *I* did!" he replied. "It scared me so much I turned heels and came right here to tell you!"

Noble had taken in a lot of information at once but she assumed there was a part of him that wanted to speak to his brother, if it was possible. "Do you know where the chair is?"

"It's under the seat of my car," Clemens said quickly, racing out to get it.

Even though Noble was walking better, he was in a hurry to get to the creek and this would be the best way. Before they knew it, the three of them, with Simon joyfully running behind, made their way to the carousel.

It was not a warm day and Genevieve regretted not having brought a jacket along, but time was of the essence.

Arriving at the edge of the carousel as the clouds began to forebodingly race across the sky, Noble got out of the wheelchair.

Clasping his cane, he used Genevieve's shoulder and bolstered himself up and started to weave through the old grandly painted horses. "Valor!" he yelled out, not concerned that his companions would think him foolish. "Please, if you are here, speak to me! Show yourself!"

Glancing back at the creek, Genevieve felt that if Valor had been roaming around here, he was probably not there now. It was too hard to say whether he was there intentionally or merely passing through, but Clemens said that he looked directly at him.

"Have you found anything else out?" she asked the younger man quietly as Noble made his way around the other side of the ornately decorated carousel center.

"Yes," he divulged much to her surprise. "There was a woman here on the day of the fire."

Believing Noble had mentioned it, she could not recollect with certainty. "How do you know?"

"*He* told me about her," he said, gesturing to where Noble had just been. "He said Valor had brought her here that day, just like the others, but because of the fire she was sent home."

"Have you found where she is?"

"Yes," he relayed quickly. "She lives in Wanderling even still, much older now though," he explained. "She became real quiet when I brought him up but I told her that I wouldn't tell anyone; only that it's for the records, like you had said."

"Did she suggest he did anything to her?" she asked, glancing over at the carousel and seeing Noble sitting on the small row boat, dejected.

"He asked her to go in the water and she said it was hot that day," he began. "He was charming and told her she was the most beautiful woman he had seen. He wanted to photograph her like she was an angel in the water, so she got in and let him take the photographs."

"I read his journals," she said as Simon approached them wagging his tail. "It sounds like Lillianne had really passed on a sense of eloquence and wit in all of her children. I think he had an easy following of young women even as he got older."

Clemens nodded. "He was fifty one when he died but I saw a photograph somewhere and he barely looked forty," he agreed. "Just the same, she did say that he made her lay certain ways and then he held her down."

"Under the water?"

Nodding, they both looked at Noble. He would learn of it no doubt, but his thoughts were intensely occupied and she wanted to soothe him but decided to give him a little longer. "Did she nearly drown?"

"No," he whispered, straightening his hat and crossing his arms against a light wind. "She said he held her down and told her that he just wanted to get the photograph right, that she would be under the water, still and peaceful so she allowed it. But then he held her too long and she got scared."

"Did she think she was going to be drowned?"

He shook his head. "She didn't like to say much about it at all," he explained. "After all this time she doubts herself. Just the same, she said at the time, he held her down and she was struggling and she could hear him saying that she needed to be at peace. Something like, her spirit was not at rest until it was over and the waves were calm."

"Clemens," she said quietly. "I wonder if he said that to the other women too?"

"That's what I thought," he agreed.

"He mentioned often how the violence towards his mother disturbed him and he needed peace. He must have tried to make it happen in these women."

Placing his hands in his trouser pockets he sighed. "Even so, he must have suffered from some kind of delusion or obsession perhaps."

"Yes, and it is a shame. It seems their father has left quite a trail of burden behind him," she said before looking up at something moving. "Noble!" she screamed out and began to walk towards him.

Clemens saw it too, saw *him* too. It *was* Valor and he did look like a young man. He was not looking at them, but he was just walking around to the other side of the carousel.

Noble got up, and rushed the best he could to the other side. "Valor!"

His brother, who they could all still see, turned a little but not completely, as if he could hear a distant voice; past overlapping the present. "Valor!" he called again, getting closer to him. "Please hear me, speak to me! I'm sorry!"

Genevieve stood back a little, she couldn't believe her eyes, but Clemens was on the cusp of fear and voracious curiosity. "He looks so real," he said to her.

"He is," she reminded him. "To Noble he is not a ghost; he is his brother as he remembers him. It is astonishing we can see him."

Noble had tears streaming down his face now, overwhelmed with grief. "Please brother, I love you, I'm sorry. Valor?"

Surprising them all; the thirty-something Valor turned his gaze towards Noble and astonishment formed in his eyes and then a smile formed on his lips. He didn't seem aware that he was dead, he was just happy to see his brother. Reaching out, his smile faded and he looked concerned as he touched the scars on Noble's face.

"I'm sorry," Noble said again and Valor did not look angry. Whatever had happened between them, it was forgiven, but Valor's ability to see him was soon gone and suddenly the carousel came to life, scaring them all.

The music started up slow and the merry go round creaked on its very old wheels and mechanisms and the music sounded distorted, pushing through its long period of inactivity. Genevieve rushed to the carousel and jumped up, rushing to Noble and grabbing onto him so he didn't lose his balance. She then walked him over to one of the horses and he held onto it while she looked at Clemens.

A sense of bewilderment rose up, it was frightening and they didn't know what was going to happen next, so the younger man got up onto it and made his way over to them, hovering beside them protectively.

"He will not harm us," Noble said.

In spite of herself, Genevieve instinctively wiped the tears from his face. Getting a little faster, the music sounded normal and circus like while the storm clouds gathered to conspire above them.

"Where did he go?" Clemens asked quietly.

"He went around to the other side and I believe he is gone," Noble replied. Genevieve could see relief in his eyes but he was also shaken by the experience.

Worried that another spirit would appear out of nowhere, she clung to them both when all of a sudden a loud smash echoed out just a short distance from them.

With her heart pounding, she stayed until it was clear that the merry go round was coming to a distinct slow and the music stopped again.

After a few minutes of stunned silence, the three remained where they were. Finally Genevieve was brave enough to walk over to the shattered glass, a mirror that had broken off the center ornamentation, and she stared at it and then at the treasure inside.

Being careful not to hurt herself, she gently reached into the exposed area behind where the mirror had been. It was likely the mirror had only barely been hanging there and the hole inside looked smoothed off so whoever put their hands in it was not hurt by sharp edges.

Genuinely feeling Valor was not going to come up behind her, she peered in and pulled out a handful of photographs.

"What is it, Genna?" Noble asked, not entirely certain he wanted to see it straight away.

"Wait," she replied. "Let me see, it looks like there was a hidden place behind this mirror for things Valor didn't want anyone to see."

And a quick perusal of the photographs confirmed it. This was a secret hiding place for his most prized work. The photographs were of all of his lady friends and they were all either at the creek or pool and mostly naked.

While the women were very much alive in these photographs, she didn't want to show them to Noble and Clemens and blushed just by having inadvertently seen them herself.

"Some very personal photographs that you don't need to see," she called back, knowing Noble would understand what that meant. "But wait," she called back, not believing her own eyes. "But wait, look at this."

Walking back around to them, she turned the other photographs downwards so they couldn't see, but showed them the one she just noticed. "Look," she said, handing it to Noble.

The two men stared at it, and there was not mistaking what it was. It was not a photograph taken with intention because Valor was quite meticulous about his setting, but it gave them a highly significant clue.

One of the women was lying under the water. She was clearly not breathing and her head was contorted where she had been struggling to get out from under his grip. Valor's hand was on her chest where he had been holding her down and he was looking back at the camera, his arms and legs wet, his face full of perspiration.

It was not tinted but black and white. There was a small blurred area where the camera may have been falling over and the grass looked blurry in the distance. But there was no mistaking; he had literally just been in the act of killing one of the girls, one of his porcelain dolls.

While they stared at the photograph, she shuffled through some more until she found one she could not work out at first. "Look at this," she said, giving it directly to Noble. "What *is* that?"

"It's the family mausoleum at the Claremonde Cemetery," he said. "See here, this is the face of it, the entrance where they have many of the older graves from our sixteenth century ancestors.

Staring at it, she could see now what he meant, but something else stood out. "There are these little illuminated crosses here."

"He probably added them in by hand in his studio," he surmised. "He enjoyed coloring the photographs but was apt to other additions as well."

Looking at them both and then back at the creek, the rain started to come down and they huddled beneath the shelter of the carousel top. "Six crosses he drew on here," she noted again. "Perhaps one for each of the women."

Noble stared out into the distance, his brow furled and his heart heavy. "Yes, that is precisely it, Genna," he stated decisively. "Those crosses are for the girls and the cemetery is where we will find them."

Chapter Twenty One

Sleepily staring down at her hand, Genevieve could not understand why it looked different and why she was standing, winding a clock in a familiar hall that she also didn't recognize.

It was said so often that history never repeats; it was frequently proven that it does more often than not. While the faces and names and places are changed, human nature continued the same hopes and conflicts with each generation fumbling the same way.

Yet, on occasion, it was not just the echoes of the past that trod the same path, but in glimpses, it overlapped the present and the eyes would see what the mind obscured.

And somehow Claremonde had raised the dead to life and suppressed the living to mere observers, for in this moment it was clear she was elsewhere. She was in Claremonde Hall, as it was in its former glory, as it was when Noble was a child; somehow she stood in a past moment.

Every movement of her arm, of her long dress, of the shoe of her toe against the hard floor, was crisp, everything else was silent and still. It was as if she was in a doll house, real but not real, only experiencing small things around her, the rest not quite complete.

Unlike a dream, it was more a sense of waking up after an illness, the hazy lack of comprehension and elongated pauses as one tried to regain their bearings.

This was the wide ornate hallway she had come to know well, the wing where the last McKinley children had lived. The clock in front of her had been moved as it wasn't there in present time, and the hand that wound it was not hers, but whoever it was, was now gone, out of sight.

While she remembered falling asleep on the day bed in Noble's room, she knew it had taken a long time, but had no idea how this was happening. She couldn't feel anything like cold or hunger or anything at all. Her body was weightless, she could see and hear and she was finally able to look down and see her own body in her nightgown, but it was a strange sense of not being able to control it.

Turning her head slowly, as it was difficult to move fast, a sound of laughter rung out from one of the rooms and surprised her. Unafraid, she was suddenly accosted by two children, perhaps close to ten or so in age as they ran out in front of her. The boy was chasing the girl and she was laughing as he, dressed in old fashioned musketeer like clothes, was using a ruler as a sword.

She, with her long dark hair, was in a princess style dress and was pretending to be frightened but could not remain in character while she held her hands to her face in feigned terror.

"You are not very convincing, Prudence," the boy protested.

Genevieve stared at her, yes of course it was her, the poor little girl who was violated by her father, but it hadn't happened yet, and now she was as vivacious and playful as any young girl should be.

She wished she could stop any of it from happening, so much suffering and horror to come, but she knew that everyone had their burdens to bear and in many ways it was what created who they became.

Noble became strong, Prudence became weak and Valor became delusional, no one could have anticipated it back then.

"Mother! Noble insists I be the damsel, but I want to be the hero!" she called out loudly with her arms crossed.

"You can not expect your brother to be a princess now can you, dear?" Lillianne's voice called out from her own bedroom where the door was open. "Noble, let her have the sword for a little while. She can wear one of your shirts and knickers after you have rescued her."

Prudence laughed and Noble, the handsome boy, perhaps eleven or twelve, frowned, but was quickly coerced into smiling by his sister.

Relenting, he held his sword up to make a declaration, before doing a gentlemanly bow. That was when he was interrupted by a friendly face behind him, a scruffy tall terrier who was curious to join the commotion.

Noble, who was in the middle of his bow, turned his head to look at him and pointed his ruler at him. "Hark! My valiant steed has arrived and we will ride together!"

"Where's *my* steed?" Prudence protested. "Why is it that the dog is always *your* steed?"

"Martin is *my* dog," he explained rightly. "But if the princess shall like it, he will lick thine royal hand!"

Prudence, one of the prettiest girls Genevieve had ever seen with youthful rouged skin and big blue eyes scrunched her face up in disgust. "You will tell your valiant Martin to keep his tongue away from thy royal hand!"

Lillianne laughed from her bedroom and Noble sighed but he didn't look completely angry.

Genevieve couldn't take her eyes off of them, especially him. Before the fire and the scarring, here he was, his brown hair tied back in a ponytail, his blue eyes alive with youth and vigor. She couldn't believe she got to see him here and he was remarkable, so kind and gentle and delightful in all sincerity.

A stream of sunlight shone through Lillianne's window and the house was calm and the atmosphere was welcoming. Genevieve felt like she stood there for a couple of hours, watching them, listening to them talk and watching Noble with his dog.

Valor was probably away, being grown at this time, but when the door opened downstairs, she knew immediately who it was. Even Martin the friendly dog, did not go out to greet him.

Noble's smile faded immediately as he looked at Prudence who ran into her room and gently and quietly closed the door so as not to make a sound.

Lillianne suddenly popped her head out into the hall, checking on her young and looked at Noble, who knew that he had to run into his room as well. But he didn't close his door, he left it open a little to listen.

Their mother, a dark haired beauty who would have easily turned the head of any man who may have seen her, clasped her hands together in front of her. Genevieve could feel fear off of her, looking around frantically, searching for anything she should fix in case it would upset him; *him* being Randolph.

And then another familiar face came out. While she was significantly younger like all of them, this young woman looked determined. It was Henny coming out from her room at the end of the long hall.

She looked at Lillianne who slunk back in her room, holding a finger to her lips.

Henny, who was only slightly less plump than she was now, did not look afraid. The look in her gaze showed that she was a woman who was waiting for one more reason to end the tyrant's reign. Unfortunately for Prudence she waited too long and no doubt Lillianne would suffer the beatings for a number of years yet.

Suddenly someone tapped her on the shoulder and she spun around, terrified. It was Valor and he was looking right at her!

While she knew Randolph was slowly coming up the wide staircase, his heavy shoes echoing in the shuddering silence, she couldn't see him. The hall, the stairs, the wallpaper, the bedroom doors and the children were all gone from her sight.

She was in the swimming pool room and Valor was with her. Crossing her arms, she could feel that her body was different, she felt more petite and taller in some ways. It was not a dream or a reality but she was here in this woman's body and Valor was there looking at her.

Here he was in his forties, the age she was now, quite handsome and he was smirking as he beckoned her with a finger to come closer to him. She could see how these women might be captivated by him; he was seductive in his nature, dressed romantically, perhaps in his ancestor's clothes.

"Why do you look at me this way?" he whispered to her, drawing close.

Trying not to give away her true identity, she didn't want him to kiss her. While she had made no promises to anyone else and this wasn't really happening, she was not going to be stuck with the memory of it. "Where are you taking me?"

His step ceased and she inadvertently got closer to him. He was slightly taller than Noble and she could see the resemblance. She didn't feel fear in this moment; like it had been robbed of her along with many other senses. Just the same, she felt endangered, because she was in the body of one of his girls.

"I will take you to heaven and you will be the torch that lights the hearth," he whispered, bringing his face close to hers.

Stepping back, but not too abruptly, she tried to think fast. "Then you lead and I will follow," she stated simply.

"You bewitch me," he said, suddenly excited by her seemingly playful resistance to him. "Remove your gown my dear, I will take you into the water and bring you new life. I will resurrect your skin and hasten your heart."

Glancing down, she couldn't tilt her head easily but felt she might only be wearing a dressing gown and nothing else. She was, however, able to look at the pool on her right and it had no water in it. "The pool is empty," she said, her words coming out like vapor in the air.

"It is not there," he said, and then curiously his tone changed, confused by her statement. "We are gone from there, now lay here on the rocks, and cast your hair out like flames in the blue water sky."

"I don't want to lie in the water," she said, speaking her thoughts aloud. The fear that had somehow been withheld from her before was no longer subdued. A severe panic went through her as she felt the creek water rising up the sides of her face and her body.

The sun was in her eyes and she could see him standing over her, his feet bare and his trousers folded at his calves. He was taking photographs and his gaze had changed. It was a mixture of lust and detachment, of both desire and destruction.

No matter his words, what he used as an excuse for silencing these women, there was something in him, in his eyes that showed he was bereft of empathy. He loved his family but these women were a means to an end. He relied on their obedience so he could carry out his objective. Compliant or not, they all died, because that was his intent.

He lured them here to the creek on the pretence of love and romance and ended their lives for the hunger a natural man shouldn't possess. And when she tried to push herself up out of the water, anger formed in his eyes, this was not an acceptable action to him.

"You must be still so I can take the photographs," he insisted, barely disguising the fury in his face. "You will ruin them if you move. You will be at peace; you will show me the tranquility like an angel."

"I am not at peace," she insisted, still struggling to move, and realizing that one of his feet had pressed lightly on her stomach.

Angered by her rebellion, he crouched down and looked into her eyes. "You are not her," he seethed quietly. "She was the only one that denied me. You will not. You are not fit to fill her shoes."

She was about to die in a horrifying way, but no matter what she went through, she needed to learn what she could. Just the same, she wanted him to know she would not go lightly. "I am not your flame haired Marjorie," she said. "Nor am I the complacent Lillianne or poor little Prudence."

Gasping as if she had stabbed him, he was completely taken aback at what she had said. She knew he could not comprehend how she could make such a statement. In his eyes he could not see Genevieve; he was looking at one of his obedient red headed admirers and as far as he was aware, none of them knew anything about his family.

This was too much for him, he could not bear it, and she thought he might have a heart attack as he gasped again. "Who are you, devil?!"

"*You* are the devil, Valor McKinley! To kill these poor girls when you had their love!"

"*Marjorie*," he replied, doubled over and whimpering, but then he couldn't hear her and she couldn't hear him and it was as if she, Genevieve, had spoken to his ghost. And she had come to know him through his journals and she felt such great pity for him in this moment, this poor conflicted man.

But then it was lost, it was as if the conversation never happened, a momentary lapse in the illusion. Now he was focused again on the girl. His obsession was with Marjorie and these girls were poor copies. He began to press hard on her neck with both of his hands.

She had never felt so panicked, doing all she could to push up and hold her breath beneath the water. He was pressing so hard she thought her neck might break and she couldn't see as the water was coming over her eyes.

She was trying to call out for him to stop, to say something to halt him in his step, but the water was echoing in her ears. Finally she had to open her mouth for one final attempt at air and it her mouth filled with water. It tasted disgusting, swamp like and it rose up through her mouth and into her throat and in through her nostrils.

Her lungs were filling up; her heart pounded while it tried to keep her alive, but the rest of her was giving up the fight. The need to breathe was suffocating, relentless, without mercy and it was horrifying as she reached up, her arm too weak to lift.

No longer could she hear her own gasping and the pain in her throat was overwhelming but then a voice formed in her ears, sounding like it was coming from a long distance.

"Genna!"

It was so faint and she wondered if she was dying and the last hope of her heart was to see Noble again.

"No!" the voice screamed. "Be gone! Get away from her!"

Simon barked in the background, he also sounded distant.

Genevieve was afraid to open her eyes into the water but felt the pressure release from her neck and tried to lift her head but couldn't. Finally she looked up to see Valor but now she was in the hallway just outside of her bedroom.

He was fading, but he was confused. He was killing the girl but at the same time partly cognizant of his brother there. He glanced at her and then at Noble.

"Please don't harm her, she belongs here," Noble begged with tears in her eyes. "I beg you not to take her from me."

Valor, reached out for Noble, but then looked down at her and she knew, if only for seconds at once, he actually saw her, Genevieve, not one of his victims. His mouth opened, he was confused, but then he looked at Noble again and stepped back and he disappeared.

It was not like in ghost stories where someone vanished from the spot. It was almost as if in that very instant one was left questioning if they were ever there to begin with.

But she knew it had happened because Noble was still there, standing over her as Simon rushed over to sniff her, pushing his cold snout under her limp hand. "Genna, no, please don't leave me," Noble said, tears in his eyes, cradling her head as he stroked her face. "Stay always."

Leaning her head into his lap, she could hardly feel the fabric of his pajamas. She felt as if she was fading away, every part of her skin and bones and muscles falling into the ground beneath them. This had to be what death was like, the body lifting into the ethers while the mind was the last to leave.

This might be her last breath and she didn't know if she could even push out the words, but she had to. "I love you more than I could imagine myself capable of," she said, her words raspy and hoarse. "You are literally life to me."

A heavy darkness weighed over her eyes and her body and she assumed she was dead. She prayed to feel his touch; her only wish was for his voice to be the last thing she heard.

Chapter Twenty Two

Her ears picked up the sound of a crackling fire and Simon was licking her right hand. She was lying down and just before she forced her eyes opened, she caught a glimpse in her mind of Lillianne standing over her.

Like a protective mother, the age she was when her children were smaller, her long dark hair hung down as she stared at Genevieve. She smiled at her and then she was gone. Perhaps she was wrong, but in that moment she thought maybe she had returned Genevieve back to her dear son.

"Genevieve?" his familiar voice questioned from somewhere close to her.

Opening her mouth, she was severely fatigued and had difficulty getting the words out.

"I will bring you water," he said, as he walked away and quickly returned, gently kneeling beside her and holding the glass to her mouth. She didn't enjoy the taste of it but it did help sooth some of the soreness in her throat.

The house was still and without looking she could tell it was still night, or in the very early morning hours before the sun rose. The birds came early to Claremonde and there wasn't any singing just yet.

Opening her heavy eyes, it made her dizzy to look at him, but a strange peace came over her. Moving her hands she was able to feel that he had put a lot of his bedding, and her blankets and pillows on the floor beneath her because he wasn't strong enough to get her into a bed.

But he too had pillows behind him and a blanket, having felt the need to sit and watch her, ensure she was well enough. She wondered if he had heard her when she last spoke or even if she had spoken the words aloud, nothing seemed clear now.

"I saw Valor," she said, intentionally offering a vague statement to see if anything had actually occurred or not.

"As did I," he said; his face grave and troubled. "I am aware of your experience, Genna, you had not dreamt it."

Drawing in a shallow breath, she swallowed hard and managed to prop herself up slightly, staring at him. "I don't think he knew it was me," she explained. "I think I was inside of one of his girls, in a vision I suppose, but I could feel what she was feeling in her body when she died."

"When he killed her."

Nodding, she still pitied him, not just Noble but Valor himself. What a troubled mind would allow such an act to be done without empathy and yet he had such a capacity to care for his family. "Noble, I think he enjoyed killing them. I do not believe it was a mere effect of his youth. I think he perhaps realized it was something he liked to do."

Not flinching at all, he simply nodded. "I believe that is a fair evaluation."

Sensing he was conflicted, she studied him as discretely as possible, his pale blue pajama top nearly unbuttoned all the way. He was leaning against a velvet footstool, his legs to the side; she had never seen him so serious. "You asked him to leave me alone," she said, mostly to see if all of it had occurred.

"Yes, I asked that he do you no harm. I had not seen him this close, his ghost so vividly. All of your discoveries have awakened him, Genna."

"I thought I was dying," she said. Finally sitting up a little, she slowly brought her legs up so they were bent and she could hold them. "I thought those were my final minutes alive."

Studying her, particularly her eyes, where most people conjectured that the soul could be seen, he shook his head at a thought that was never spoken. "I heard your final words even if they were not your last," he said.

By the way he had expressed it, she did not know if she should feel ashamed or embarrassed or not ever bring it up again, but there was more to it that she couldn't work out. Her lips opened but she couldn't think of what to say.

"I do not wish you to be misled," he said seriously as he reached out for Simon who was pacing in the room. "It would be unfair for you to express those words if you were not in possession of the entire truth."

Suddenly concerned that he was going to shock her with some admission equal to the acts of his brother's, she allowed him to speak instead of questioning it.

Glancing over at his door, likely hoping no ghost would enter as they spoke, he looked at her again, now with a hint of regret and concern in his gaze. "I am responsible for Valor's death," he said.

Blinking, once then twice, she did not know if he meant directly or not. "Did you kill him?"

A smirk came on his face, the upward turn of the good side of his face and he shook his head. "It was not my intent. I did not take a knife to him, if that is what you are indicating?"

Smiling as well, she sighed. "I can not make assumptions about anything," she confessed. "I did not think you capable of intentionally harming someone."

"You are correct," he confirmed. "I am not of my brother's ilk or persuasion but I caused it inadvertently and the fact alone haunts me more than he does."

"The fire?" she asked carefully.

"I started it," he said, a single tear falling down his cheek.

Her mind went wild, in many directions, her thoughts unable to connect. He was perhaps forty at the time of the fire, it hadn’t been a childhood accident. "But why, Noble?" she asked, genuinely confused, knowing he had to have had a reason.

Lowering his gaze, concentrating on his beloved dog, he shook his head. "I wanted to stop him, it was my only objective. I could not think of anything else in the moment. I didn't foresee the consequences."

Thinking of all they had seen and read and experienced, she remembered Clemens had talked to one of the women. She hadn't wanted to speak of it, but she was there the day of the fire. "You told her to leave," she said, mulling it over. "The woman that was with Valor, you told her to leave. But you told Valor that Claremonde was ablaze, it had already been lit."

"Yes, I did not know it would spread so hastily, I assured the safety of my mother and sister and Henny but I wanted him to put it out. I was hoping he had the wiles to know how."

"You wanted him to leave her," she said, realizing it as she spoke it. "You started the fire so you could save her. Noble, you started the fire to save the woman that was with him, was that what you were intending?"

"Mother said he had taken a girl to the carousel. She suspected what I did, but we never would have discussed it aloud," he said quietly. "I knew inside of me that those poor girls were not leaving here," he confessed with deep regret in his eyes. "I could not admit it to myself. If I went there to see him, to intervene then it would be that I would be partly responsible for the girls I did not rescue."

"None of us can be certain of the actions of others, even with valid assumption, Noble," she asserted. "You did not commit these acts; this is not meant for your conscious."

Shaking his head, she knew he agreed, he must have thought it over many times in his own mind. He was wise, not one to fall into despair at the first sign of distress, but it was a great concern. "I could not have another die at his hands," he said. "I did not know, not with certainty, but it had seized me long enough that I was compelled to intervene."

"But how did he die?" she asked gently.

Sadness was in his expression but she also saw relief in his eyes now that he finally had the opportunity to unburden the weight he had carried all these years.

"I started a small fire in the ballroom and ensured it was alight enough to cause concern but I hoped that was all. I emptied Claremonde of the people and then hastily made my way to the creek. Valor had the girl in the lake and she appeared shaken. I knew of his photography, of his creative pursuit of it, but he was angry that I dared interrupt. When I told him of the fire, his demeanor changed and he ran to the aid of our mother."

"But you had gotten her out."

"I did not think to say it, I hoped it would end quickly and I would send the girl away."

"But he went into the house."

Nodding, he sighed and leaned back and she was glad she was physically feeling better, even her throat. "I wonder if he was attempting to salvage some of his photographs and keepsakes," she pondered.

"I suspect this too," he agreed. "And when I arrived, I knew he was in his side, where I had started the fire. It was already burning well out of control having barely touched the stairs where it began, but it had engulfed the upper floor. He saw me when I entered Claremonde and he asked about mother."

"She was safe?"

"Yes, and I believe he knew that, but then he was attempting to run upstairs. I can only suppose there was something there, personal to him that he wished to retrieve. A large ceiling rafter came down in front of him and he was unable to come down."

Enraptured by a tale she never anticipated hearing, she leaned forward, making sure he knew he had her full attention. "He went into the fire above him?"

"Yes. I can not tell you how it was done but I managed to lift myself over the rafter and I followed him up to the first floor. He was searching drawers and I told him we had to leave. I was coughing, we could barely breathe and it became dark. And that is when I heard another beam come down and I knew we could not return to the ballroom."

"How did you survive?" she asked, although the real question was, how did Valor *not* survive.?

Swallowing hard, she could see he had a lump in his throat as tears welled in his eyes. "He asked about the girl," he replied, frustrated. "Because he asked about *her*. That is why he is dead. He asked me if I left her there and I told him I instructed her to leave."

"Was he angry?"

Nodding, he then sighed. "I was certain he would lash out even as the timbers fell around us, but then he looked at me and he knew why."

"Why you told her to leave?"

"Yes," he confirmed. "He looked in my eyes and his countenance altered and I knew then that I had saved her life. I knew what I suspected had to have been true and more tellingly, he was aware of my conclusion. His temperament was even when he told me that we must go up to his library where the window opens."

Returning to her normal physicality, she moved around to him, wanting to comfort him. She was hesitant, not certain he would welcome her attention but when she crawled over in her nightgown, he moved over so they could rest against the same pile of pillows. "That is how you hurt your leg?" she asked.

Nodding, he confirmed it. "He told me he loved me and I tried to argue with him but eventually I told him I loved him also, because what if I did not have the chance to say it again? Another beam came down, the hall beside us was destroyed and the fire seized my foot and rushed up my side. The pain was not immediate. I was too panicked to notice. He assisted me in putting it out but my clothes were either missing or affixed to my burned flesh."

"I am sorry such a thing happened to you Noble. It must have taken a long time to heal," she said, saddened by his ordeal.

"The scars were my fragility but my loss of him was a greater wound," he stated sorrowfully. "He helped me out of the window and I was scared. I still believed then that he would follow. I told him I would get some blankets from the other side so he could jump out. When I jumped out, my leg broke, I believe in two places. But I would have crawled to the ends of the Earth for him."

"Was he too afraid to jump?" she asked.

Studying her face, this had been something that he had kept secret for so long, he probably never told his mother about having caused the fire, a guilt that could befall any good man.

"He knew why I sent the girl away and he was ashamed. He did not express directly what he had done but he decided to end his own destruction."

"Oh no, Noble, he stayed in the house? He was not injured?"

Shaking his head, he closed his eyes, a truly painful memory overcoming him. "He said he was a disgrace to the family and to tell mother that he loved her and to tell Marjorie that he was sorry. I begged him to jump. I pleaded with him that he was loved and we would seek help for him that we would not let him endure his shortcomings alone, but he was determined. He said he was an abomination and then he stepped back into the dark and the fire rushed upward and he was gone, not a sound."

Tears fell from her eyes as she took him in her arms. "You did not kill him, Noble. He chose to end it all. He was suffering too, please know that. He chose to end his suffering as well as prevent the loss of more girls. He wasn't strong enough to control his impulses. You are not to blame."

"I set the fire, Genna," he said, his face pressed into her neck as he sobbed and they clung to each other.

"You set the fire to *save* a life not end one," she asserted. "Your act was heroic, your intent purely good. Valor sacrificed his life because he learned from you. You are a good man, he knows that."

The tears fell for minutes and she cried with him and for him.

Comforted, and tired, they held each other a while. "He would not have killed you," he finally said quietly. "I do not believe it possible. He did not know it was you."

"I know," she said. "I believe I experienced what they did but I would not have truly gone through it to the point of death, but I honestly do not want to go through it again."

"No," he said. "No, the dust has been kicked up and time has been confused around us but now it will be ended. We will find those girls and return them home and he will not remain. He will not be lost or have any to remain for. His penance will cease and he will have that peace he strove for, we all will."

"We need to go to the cemetery."

"Yes," he agreed quietly. "We will go as soon as Clemens arrives, he will come early. Let us sleep now; no harm will come to you."

"Here?" she asked, although she was extremely tired and the fire was warming her face and her hands.

"Yes," he replied placing his hand on her face and gazing into her eyes, studying her reaction to him. "Genevieve, do you now have second thoughts about your final declarations?"

"No," she quickly insisted. "Your admissions have only strengthened my want of you and my protectiveness of you. Do you welcome it?"

Considering her seriously, he brought his thumb over and lightly placed it on her bottom lip, openly studying her face, every detail. "If you commit your heart to me I will not be able to remove myself from you, Genna. I would have your words as a vow and promise; I could not untangle myself from you."

"Then so it shall be, Lord McKinley," she said. "We will be the lovers that all dreamers wish to emulate."

Smiling, he pulled her closer to him and ran his hand through her hair as she melted into his body and kiss. His lips were warm and his scent inviting, his hands upon her like strength and invitation.

And in that one moment, in their fatigue and fear and sadness and hope, the world ceased and expanded simultaneously. Lying back, she kissed him again, voraciously full of love and adoration. And life in its essence suddenly became clear, for he was her world, and nothing was more real than that one epiphany.

Chapter Twenty Three

The three stood quietly at the ancient iron fence, staring across at the lush grass littered with century old tombstones and angelic statues.

It was a breathtaking sight and Genevieve knew she would return here many times after this day. But today their mission was a grim one and not a word was spoken as a light fog hovered above the sacred ground.

Centered between the two men, there was a sense of obligation to remain respectful and still on their approach. Clemens was on her right in a gray suit and hat as well as a coat.

Noble was on her left, his cream knit top and tan trousers partially hidden beneath his own brown coat and hat. The prior night they had fallen asleep in each others arms, having been so tired from their encounter with Valor's ghost.

Her heart was filled with him and the astonishment of at least an admittance of their feelings still echoed inside her ears. The taste of his kiss still on her lips, his warmth, and his body pressed against hers, his security and yet it was not over. There were some big hurdles to face and the dead were walking in their midst.

For the task ahead she also decided on some black dress trousers and a gray knit top. Her burgundy coat had a fur collar but she had wished she had worn a scarf. Even Simon was quiet, keeping at Noble's feet, perhaps confused by the strange atmosphere that seemed exclusive to this land.

Death in itself was not mysterious. It was the departure of one world for another, a complex journey but a simple transference. But for those that remained behind, it must have been confusing and disorientating.

She knew what it was like to be murdered by Valor's hands but the physical effects were impermanent even if the memory was forever ingrained in her mind. He was still here with them, unaware of his in between world and intermittent appearances. In moments he saw them, the true them and it was shocking for him.

She could only hope that when the women were discovered that perhaps he would have nothing to stay for, no one to oversee. Pulling her coat over the bare space on her neck, she had not seen such a gloomy morning since she arrived there. If they were not searching for dead women's bones there would be something beautiful in the eeriness.

The gate had an ornate seal that bore a coat of arms with two griffons and the name, McKinley at the center. Clemens pushed it forward and it creaked loudly into the fog laden haze.

There was a long stone path leading from the gate to the distant mausoleum. It was a small old brick structure like a house for children but tall enough for an adult to enter.

Quietly walking together, Simon was the only one who got ahead of them, sniffing every bush and headstone he could find. Some of the century old statues and gravestones were taller than them. Genevieve was trying to keep her head up and not be intimidated by the sense of their every move being observed.

Catching a glimpse out of the corner of her eye, she noticed a beautiful stone angel. Her sorrowful face was so detailed, her eyes cast down at the grave she hung over.

Genevieve thought she might simply turn around and look at her, lift her head and stare right at her. That was the kind of place this was. Claremonde possessed a reality different to any other and the boundaries had dissipated leaving the dead to pass through unhindered. "They are watching us," she whispered to Clemens.

Her wide eyed friend nodded. "It is not like anything I've ever felt before," he agreed. "It has to be them, the porcelain girls."

He was right, she deduced. While many considered cemeteries to be the most haunted places, she assumed them to be the least. After all, it was rare that anyone actually died there, only their bodies were here. But in this case, these women were unsettled, perhaps disorientated after having their lives taken so dramatically and horrifically.

Noble leaned close to her ear. "Stay close, Genna."

"I intend to remain a centimeter from you at most," she replied quietly. "But if anything jumps out at us I may have to run from it."

Smirking, he placed his hand on her back. "Will you take me with you?"

"If Clemens can help me lift you, we should be able to run together," she replied dryly.

Laughing, but low, he nodded. "This is the end of the road, do you believe it?"

Knowing he was serious, her smile faded.
"I *do* believe it," she said, looking at him. "This was your life journey, Noble. This was your story and now it's at a pinnacle. I only hope this will improve things now, your life and the life of those that are so conflicted."

"You awoke them Genna. This is your story also. We are bonded by it, my past and our future; do not discount your significance. These women have sought your assistance and we will do what we can for them."

"What if we can't find them?" she asked solemnly as they approached the small building, a scent of history in its midst.

"We will," he assured her. "Destiny has conspired for you to be the hero of the tale. You will save us, the women and then me."

Smiling, she watched him give Clemens the keys and the younger man went in front of them to open the thick hinged door.

Stepping back a little she, pulled Noble aside for the briefest of moments. "I love you," she whispered, feeling it pertinent to say it because she could no longer hold it in.

Clemens finally got the door open and turned to look at them before pulling out his favored torch and switching it on, illuminating the stale air inside.

Noble stared at her, uncharacteristically shocked, his mouth hung open at her declaration. Perhaps he hadn't heard it from a woman so openly before and yet she had been unable to withhold it from herself because it had been such a strong emotion.

Glancing at his hand which she was sure was going to touch her, he went to speak but Clemens rushed out, pale and unsettled. "I saw something in there, something moved and I don't believe it was an animal."

The air was thick from many years of confinement. The last time someone had been there it had likely been Valor if he had in fact buried the women here. But immediately there was an ominous sense of dread and the hairs pricked up over Genevieve's body and she shivered wildly.

Daylight streamed in enough for them to be able to see close to the entrance and it wasn't an overly large building but long enough that the torch was necessary. A narrow walkway of cold cement bridged the two sides where various displays of coffins were set up. The difference in eras was obvious because of the differences in coffin, ornamentation and grandeur. Some were raised on platforms behind ornate iron fronts while others were surrounded by gold and velvet and jewels.

In spite of their situation, she allowed some time to look over them while she had someone with her. The unnerving feeling of being surrounded was overwhelming and the silence was deafening with every tiny sound an echo causing them to flinch.

The first coffin closest to the door and the last available place, belonged to Lillianne. Genevieve stopped to look at it and was conscious of Noble standing over her shoulder. The wall was marbled with a glass front and she could peer inside at a whimsically medieval style sarcophagus.

Instead of a coffin it was in the shape of a woman with her hands poised in prayer, much like the way the kings and queens were buried a thousand years ago. But it was Lillianne's youthful face, serene with her eyes closed, carefully and accurately sculptured to preserve history. "She must be truly proud of you," she said to Noble, whose eyes were glistening with sentiment.

"I still remember her face like yesterday. They brought her body in from the outer doors, I have not been in here since," he noted. "She would have enjoyed you, Genevieve."

Simon suddenly came running towards them, panting and then running back, past Clemens again, anxious and whining.

"Come to me, Simon," Noble ordered gently, reaching his hand out.

Simon glanced back but obeyed his master, rushing to him and pressing his face into his trousers.

"That does not encourage me to go in any further," Genevieve stated straightly.

Clemens chuckled, but she could tell he was nervous too.

"What did you see?" Noble asked him.

He shook his head. "It was a shadow, which usually I can ignore in Claremonde, but there aren't any windows here and it was much taller than an animal."

"Keep your torch by us, will you, Clemens?" Noble requested, although certainly he wanted to have him nearby for protection also. "Whatever we see, we must not abandon our intentions. If they lay here then we will find them and the journey will be ended."

"I agree," Genevieve said, her fists clenched beneath her arms, having crossed them for warmth. "I do not wish to return here for a second time. But it is beautiful," she added, stopping at one coffin site. It was a small heavy wooden coffin for a child.

It read, *James Samuel McKinley, age 4, 1797.* The coffin itself, which was within the second crevice inside the wall, was affronted with iron fencing and painted with cherubs and angels. "We will all perish," she whispered aloud. "We can not resist or prevent it."

Coming close enough to her that she could feel the warmth of his body; Noble peered in and stared at the old print on the stone plaque below the small coffin. "But it is us who decides what we do with the time, Genna."

Turning to face him, feeling Clemens stop, it was profound in this moment as they searched for the bones of the poor women who were murdered. Valor's delusional plight and yet his love for his family and all that had brought them here.

But he was right. It was not only momentous that they would all die, every single person that ever lived here. But more significantly, it was the power of how they used their time while they had it. "I intend to be good," she insisted.

He smiled in spite of their situation, "You are already good."

"I will be better," she added.

The two men smiled but she could see they too were inspired to make the best of their time. Being surrounded by those who came before them, who were once so full of life and hope and desires of their own, they understood how little time they truly had.

Clemens was about to speak but was interrupted by a low growl emanating from Simon whose fur began to stand up defensively. He was glaring at the end of the small walkway which turned into another area on the right.

"We intend you no harm!" Noble called out, his voice startling her in the way it broke into the silence. "If you need our assistance, we are here to seek you so we can return you to peace. Permit us our intrusions!"

Simon barked low and then growled again before sniffing the ground and settling. Genevieve drew in a shallow breath, having held it in since they entered, and she was not calmed yet.

Determined to get the task done, she stepped ahead only slightly and urged Simon to come beside her. Getting to the corner where it turned, she noticed a plain wooden coffin belonging to an elderly McKinley. Looking back at it for a moment, she entered the next walkway and suddenly came face to face with a woman.

Screaming, she stepped right back into Clemens, who gasped as they both watched a woman quickly dash away, forming into a ball of light before disappearing into the wall at the end.

Reaching back for Noble, she clutched his hands, hers was shaking and Simon ran after the ghost, barking loudly as he made his way to the end wall where he continued his protest.

This was a shorter walkway, very dark and Clemens' torch was only illuminating small areas, but the coffins were older as they came around, probably sixteenth century, more simple but still with touches of wealth and care.

Nevertheless, nothing untoward was immediately apparent and there was nothing left of the mausoleum to explore. Looking back at Noble, she could tell he was thinking the same thing; that perhaps they had not quite stepped into the answers so readily.

But she pondered the ghost, apart from being terrified by it, the girl who she only saw a glimpse of, had to have been one of Valor's victims. She must have been there for a reason.

"Look at the wall better," she instructed with the slightest hope left inside of her.

Clemens walked over and they kept close to him, not quite being able to stand side by side in the dank narrow area.

The cool was worse here and the dreariness outside permeated tenfold at the back of this ancient stone.

Clemens shook his head. "I don't see anything," he sighed before crouching down to study the wall with his fingers. And then he glanced over to his left at the last coffin closest to the floor, likely the oldest and completely cemented into the ground, barely raised in old stone.

"What is that?" he asked, reaching out for it.

Genevieve crouched down beside him to look and noticed it too. It was a small slot, not old looking but almost like a brass handle. Throwing caution to the wind, she reached out and pulled on it and a loud shifting noise erupted.

The three of them stepped back and watched as part of the floor opened, a spring set door which opened only a small way but enough to get one's hand in and pull it back. It was not cement like the rest of the floor but painted to look like it was.

"Ingenious," Noble marveled. "Who is first down?"

"I recommend Simon for the task," Clemens said.

Noble laughed. "I don't think he will tell us much I'm afraid."

At this stage, while she was filled with trepidation, she was also eager to have it all over with, so without a word, she pulled back two wooden painted slates and stepped down a small ladder.

Clemens came in behind her, hunching because the ceiling was not high enough for them to fully stand.

Shining his torch around, here he found a light switch and turned it on, surprisingly it worked, and even though the hanging lantern was not overly bright, it illuminated the whole room.

A cement floor with wooden panel walls, this was what they had come for. Each side had very wide drawers, four along each wall.

"Did you find anything?" Noble called down, unable to get down the steps. "Is that a light down there?"

"Yes," Genevieve confirmed quietly. "Wait, I will tell you."

Looking at Clemens, who appeared as reluctant as her, she could hear Simon sniffing above them as she approached the first drawer along the right wall.

Grabbing onto the simple bronze handle, she pulled it but it didn't respond so she had to pull a little harder and bringing it towards her, it all became clear.

It was a skeleton, most of the white dress intact but deteriorated and a lot of the long red hair still remaining in the cool air that preserved it. Each drawer had been apparently made large enough to have a full sized body placed on it, but now they were skeletons.

Clemens pulled one out opposite her and nodded, seeing the same thing. "Look," he said, pointing to a symbol painted in black in the corner beside her head. "I bet they all have them."

Opening each drawer now, she sensed the girls would not bother them too much now; they had simply been leading them there. With less hesitation, the pair quietly opened each drawer verifying the six women. One drawer was empty without anything in it, but on her side, the top drawer held an ominous clue. "Look," she whispered.

Clemens came over and his eyes widened as he peered in. This drawer was lined with white satin and a symbol was drawn on it but no skeleton had been placed there. "It was the girl the day of the fire," she said. "This was intended for her."

"What do you see?" Noble called down curiously.

"We see that you saved someone!" she called back. "There is a place here for the girl that you told to leave the day of the fire."

Not replying immediately, she was certain he had a lot to think about. "Are they down there?"

"Yes!" Clemens called up. "They are all here, six of them!"

But there was something else that caught Genevieve's eye and she went over to what seemed like an altar, the light not quite capturing it. She gestured for Clemens to shine his torch there and together they crouched and stared down.

It was a long cement platform with dried rose stems and perfume bottles and small tokens of love like brooches and small porcelain dolls.

Genevieve realized he had been looking for his missing doll, the one he had wanted to keep, perhaps if she had stayed with him these women wouldn't have died. "We have to talk to her!" she called up. "She is the missing piece!"

"Who?" he asked as realization formed in Clemens' eyes.

"Marjorie Atherton!" she called back. "The one he loved."

Chapter Twenty Four

The Atherton estate house was equally as majestic as Claremonde but more simplistic in its ornamentation. While the McKinley lords and ladies had a penchant for grandeur and gothic details, the Atherton's were less fantastical.

Having to leave Simon behind, it was a quiet journey to the illustrious grounds on the next property to them.

While waiting for the door to be answered, Genevieve thought about the house itself. She pondered how the father of Marjorie had once taken Lillianne into his arms and how they had loved each other and had been forced to keep it secret.

And now this was the next chapter of the story of both families, but little did any of them suspect the revelations that would soon occur. The three of them had spent a great deal of time trying to find out what they could about the women's families and were in the beginnings of compiling their information.

Soon the police would have to be involved and they would have to present Valor's journals but one day it would all return to normal. For now, they would have to sacrifice their time and comfort to assist the girl's families. The remaining members now mostly consisted of siblings or cousins.

There would be enquiries and questions and investigations but Noble assured her that he had sound legal representation and that Claremonde would not be disturbed. Just the same, it would kick up a lot of dust and would take a year or two to settle.

For now there was one loose end that needed tying and even though neither she nor Noble knew what they would say, they felt it necessary to talk to Marjorie. It was not the easiest thing raising the subject of those that communicated from beyond, but they had to try.

The doorman finally answered, an older gentleman that Noble recognized, but had said he hadn't seen him for a very long time. "We are here to see Lady Atherton," he said.

"I apologize but she is unable to accept visitors, Lord McKinley," he said sincerely. "I will retrieve her son for you."

With a subtle bow, the older man in gray suit, turned from them and Noble's polite smile quickly vanished and he looked at Genevieve as she questioned him. "Did you know she had a son?"

He shook his head. "She had not been married, I am certain her attendants are sworn to secrecy," he whispered back. "I had never heard it."

Genevieve glanced back at Clemens who was looking at them curiously from the car. The door now opened inward and they could see an expansive greeting area with glossy tiled floor and three sets of staircases.

The instant the man came into their view, Noble gasped and Genevieve was lost for words. He appeared to be around his early to mid thirties, he was tall and handsome and most of all curious.

But what struck them both immediately was his uncanny likeness to Valor.

Genevieve wanted to discretely nudge Noble not to say anything but thankfully he had the mind not to voice his astonishment. "You are Marjorie's son," he marveled openly. "I am sorry I have not made your acquaintance earlier."

The son nodded, although he was probably guarded because he did not likely know the identity of his father and his mother had kept him a secret from the outside world.

Just the same, he seemed strained but pleasant and the way his eyes moved and his expressions were reminiscent of Valor himself. "My name is Jonathon and I am sorry, mother is ill and can not take visitors," he said straightly. "May I enquire upon your intent?"

"I am Lord Noble McKinley and this is my betrothed, Miss Belmont," he replied without hesitance. "I am saddened to hear of her poor state of health, but will you please enquire as to whether she will see us for a short time? It is of utmost importance."

"My mother speaks highly of your family," he said, staring at the scars on Noble's face. "Please step in and Mr. Barnes will attend to you whilst I approach her."

The doorman led them to a sitting room branching off a small hall, a large room with many occasional chairs and lamps on small tables but it was orderly and not as colorful as Genevieve was used to.

Sitting close to each other on modern armchairs, the doorman left the room with assurances they would be attended to soon. During their wait, all that could be heard was the echo of a grandfather clock in the lobby.

There was a foreboding sense of imminent death and looking at Noble she felt he might have noticed it too. "Valor," she whispered.

Nodding, he agreed. "It has to be his son," he agreed. "Had he alluded to it in any of his journals?"

Shaking her head, she listened out for footsteps. "No, I can only assume he didn't know," she said quietly. "I do not believe Jonathon should be told," she added with hesitance.

Glancing at the doorway, he nodded and leaned over a small marble table to keep their conversation completely confident. "He will not hear it from us. It is clear Marjorie had kept this from him. Soon my brother's deeds will come to light and such knowledge would only harm this young man's reputation by association."

"The resemblance between them is remarkable," she noted, astonished.

Noble sighed; he appeared fatigued by all that had occurred, not just this day but all leading up to it. "Indeed," he confirmed. "It is my brother's face and I miss him still. I can not separate my heart from the man in spite of his sin."

"You do not have to excuse his behavior to love him," she said seriously. "Love him as you remember him, you can not be faulted for that."

The sound of squeaking wheels echoed out in the quiet greeting area. Genevieve quickly shot one more look at Noble. "You called me your betrothed."

Smirking, he appeared amused by her delayed observation. "Ah, you noticed that."

"It seems presumptive," she said, leaning back with an intentional frown on her face.

Smiling wide, he shook his head. "You will not have me die an unmarried man, will you Genna?"

Scoffing, she crossed her arms. "Oh, that is your reasoning, is it?"

Hearing the footsteps and wheels approach, he quickly did away with his smile as did she. "If you do marry me, Genna, it should be for love," he hurriedly whispered. "But I do think you will see the good sense in it because I will not be happy until you give your heart to me."

Not able to give a response, they watched as Marjorie entered, pushed along in a wheeled chair by her son, she was weak; her long red hair faded and tied back, her porcelain skin gaunt and sunken. "Noble," she said, her voice barely audible. "I am pleased to see you here."

"How long have you been ill, Marjorie?"

Regret was in her eyes, dark rings beneath them as she was withering away each moment. "Months," she replied. "It has come on hastily and the doctor has assured me I am near the end. He does his best for me and for us, we are indebted to him."

She then reached her hand up for her son without looking back at him. "John, please leave us a moment, I wish to speak to them alone."

Surprised, he nodded, but glanced back at her, perhaps wondering if at any time he might return to a room and not find her alive any longer. He closed the door behind him and Noble went over to wheel her closer to where they were sitting.

"I have not told you of my son," she began.

"There is nothing to say, Marjorie," he assured her, coming around to return to his seat and keep her close to them. "He has his face, there is no question, but I assume he is unaware."

"I had my reasons for not telling Valor," she said. "I loved my son the first moment I held him and so I raised him quietly and kept him from the judgment of others, but soon he will be alone."

"I will not tell him," he assured her and relief formed in her gaze. "We are here about Valor."

"I came upon his journals in Claremonde," Genevieve explained.

"Does he mention Jonathon?" she asked worriedly.

"No," Genevieve replied. "I am quite certain he did not know of him, but there are some troubling things we must tell you. We were hoping you could help us with any information you have."

Staring at them both, it appeared she had her own things to divulge. "I have seen him," she said, looking directly at Noble for his reaction.

"Where?" Noble asked.

"He stands outside and sometimes I see him outside my bedroom door, he looks at me and he is lost, like an aimless child."

"He comes *here*?" Noble asked again.

"He is dead," she replied simply. "Perhaps I am losing my mind with the illness."

"No," Noble assured her. "We have seen him too. That is why we are here."

Looking at Genevieve now, Marjorie studied her face. "Did he mention me in his journals?"

"Often," she replied quietly. "You were the only one he loved. He sought you in others but they were never sufficient."

A tear fell down her cheek and she shivered. "I loved him dearly but he had wants that were not–," she stopped, worried about saying too much in front of his brother. "I suffered for leaving him but I had to."

"We know of his particular fixations," he said carefully. "We know why you would turn from him."

"I believe he understood why you left," Genevieve said. "I believe he was conflicted inside between love and unnatural desire. He was restless."

Marjorie nodded a little, the words resonant with her understanding of it. "Restless, yes, he spoke of peace and tranquility but he was unable to find it."

"He was looking for it in the girls, even in you," Genevieve explained, remembering all that she had read, all of his thoughts and musings. "He never realized that he was the one who had to bring the change within him. He was the one lacking peace."

"I saw some of the girls back then," she noted, her voice breaking in moments. "They looked like me, I did notice."

Noble brought his chair in closer to her and hunched a little to whisper as low as he could. "They are dead."

Marjorie looked at Genevieve but she did not flinch, there was no deceit. "The girls?"

Noble nodded. "There are seven, all dead. Soon they will be investigating Claremonde where one was discovered and our cemetery where the remainder were placed."

"They died by his hand?" she asked.

"Yes."

Drawing in a breath the best she could, she was surprised but not entirely. "Did he drown them?"

Genevieve, knowing that it was imperative that no one outside of the room would hear what they were saying, also leaned forward. "There is enough proof to point to that being the case," she confirmed. "Is that what he tried to do to you?"

As if years of secrets washed off of her, she nodded, glad that she could tell someone. "I honestly do not believe it was his intention to harm me. But there was a time when I was frightened, he held me beneath the water. He released me but I knew I had to leave for my protection. He was not in control of himself when he got a certain way. I could not help him. I am sorry these poor women suffered and yet I pity him, and I loved him."

Genevieve looked at Noble who was burdened with the same guilt of loving someone who had committed great atrocities.

"How can I help you?" Marjorie asked feebly. "I am not here long; I have days at best. Did you come to tell me what he did?"

"We were not certain we would tell you, but we also don't know how you can help us," Genevieve admitted. "His ghost or spirit is becoming wild and dangerous and we feel it is because we discovered the girls and what he had done."

"But we also believe he wanted us to know," Noble stated fairly. "We hoped you had an answer but we do not know the question, Marjorie. You were the one he attempted to emulate with those girls. You were the only one he cared about."

Looking at them both, Genevieve was surprised to see a determination in the dying woman's eyes. "Take me to him," she said. "Take me to Claremonde."

Marjorie's son was reluctant to allow his mother to go with them but she assured him it was necessary and that they were good people. Clemens had questions in his eyes but they would have to speak to him later. For now the four quietly rode back to Claremonde which did not take long but was quite a distance for two houses beside each other.

Clemens and Genevieve helped Marjorie into her wheelchair which had been a difficult fit in the back of the car because it did not fold. Within minutes, all four of them entered Claremonde into the ruins of the old ballroom.

Marjorie, in spite of her feeble body, was in awe and expressed how magical it was to be there, how impressed she was by this side and how much Valor had loved it there.

They had spent many nights dancing there and singing and laughing. Some of her happiest memories had been there.

Tears suddenly streamed down her face at not having seen it since the fire. "It reminds me of our love," she stated openly to them. "We, like Claremonde Hall, were alive with love and the future and then we parted and it became ruins."

Noble's eyes filled with tears too and they all stood there listening to the birds outside and studying the burned ceiling tiles and timbers around them.

Genevieve was about to say how much she found it beautiful still, for truly she did, but then they all heard something and simultaneously turned their attention towards the bottom of the stairs.

There was no question as to what it was, they all knew now and it seemed that more than ever they had to hurry. Not only was Valor's spirit gaining strength but Marjorie's illness was taking hold. "Leave me here," she said.

Noble looked at her, wanting to protest but she gave him an adamant look and he knew to allow her what she wanted. "Jonathon knows my wishes for after my death," she explained. "But I am the one Valor is looking for so I will be the one to speak with him. If it is your only chance then I am willing to take it."

"You have my deepest respect, Marjorie," Noble stated sincerely.
"I can not be sorrier for what has become of you and what he had put you through."

Smiling lightly, she reached for his hand. "He would be proud of you, Noble. He cared for you greatly. Do not be concerned. He is confused, but as always, he needs to be put in his place."

Noble smiled and gestured for Clemens to come with him. Genevieve looked over at the room when Marjorie motioned for her to come to her. When the men were out of earshot, Marjorie quickly questioned her. "He has asked you to marry him?" she asked, her voice broken again.

Genevieve nodded. "It has been alluded to," she replied honestly.

"Do you love him?" she asked in a motherly way.

"More than life itself," she answered quietly.

Marjorie appeared relieved, perhaps feeling responsible for Noble, having known him as the young man who lost his brother and his house and was scarred for life in more ways than one. "Be happy, Genevieve. May both of you have the joy that you are deserving of."

"Thank you," she said genuinely, moving aside a long strand of hair that clung to the sick woman's perspiring face. "I hope soon you will be energetic and hopeful again, Marjorie. I think Valor might want to apologize to you."

Nodding, she agreed. "He will have his chance," she promised.

Genevieve nodded and walked away, an eerie sense was in the room, darkness and hope intermingled but the feeling of someone right behind her was startling.

Getting outside, the rain was beginning to drizzle down and the clouds were conspiring to dampen the air further. It was cold and it was uncomfortable and a light wind picked up a little harder and swept across the gardens until it penetrated their small gathering while they huddled outside the door.

"How long will we leave her there?" Clemens asked. "Should we go back to the car?"

Noble seemed distracted and although cold, he was staring at the door, pondering his response. "Not long, Clemens, only long enough. We can only hope this is our remedy. Marjorie is brave to face it on our behalf."

But they each knew that she had to. If anyone was going to cease this situation it had to be her because she was the one Valor wanted. It was hard to say if he was fully aware of his surroundings now, perhaps in and out of the past and the present. But she was his constant, his thoughts and his feelings.

She was the missing doll from his collection.

The rain was a little heavier now and they were able to press themselves against a front wall where a small stone overhang kept them dry. "There was a place for her body too down there at the cemetery," Clemens said, thinking it over.

Noble shook his head. "Genevieve said it was more like an altar, perhaps he was not intending it for her but imagining her there."

Genevieve didn't know either. How could you know the mind of a man mad with his passions and unique perceptions? But Clemens had her thinking. If she was the porcelain goddess that was absent from his collection, then perhaps that is the very reason he never moved into Heaven. His will was too obstinate and determined.

"What if he did not intend to hurt her," she began. "But once he began to enjoy murdering them, he wanted to have that feeling with her?"

The men both stared at her, Noble particularly mulling her words over hastily in his mind. "We best return to her."

"She does not have long," Clemens reminded them. "She said so herself. If she can stop him, we should let her."

Conflicted, Noble, looked at Genevieve. "Even if she has minutes, we can not allow him to have that victory. If he wishes to kill her then that should not be how she spends her last minutes."

"But you said he couldn't truly kill," she said, recalling how he had attacked her in that partly physical vision.

Seizing her arms, worry was in his eyes. "Not us, Genna. But if she is at death's door he could take her the rest of the way through."

Not wanting to discuss it any further, she went for the door and pushed it inward only to see Marjorie's frail body slumped sideways on the wheelchair. Her arm was hanging, her hand nearly touching the dusty ballroom floor.

But that was not all. She saw something that struck her dumb, froze her to where she stood as she saw the ghost of Valor, as clear as day, young and handsome and dressed in his romantic sixteenth century clothes. He was walking towards Marjorie with outstretched arms.

And she, her spirit, a youthful, pristinely beautiful young woman with striking red hair and pale skin, awkwardly lifted herself up out of the chair and stepped out of her old useless body so she could reach for his hands.

"Don't kill her!" Genevieve shouted. "Don't do that to her!"

But then he got onto his knees and pressed his forehead on her hands and sobbed. The walls echoed with his cries so they could all hear it and Noble and Clemens rushed in to see the sorrowful sight.

Marjorie in a long white flowing dress like she was an ancient Grecian goddess bowed her head and kissed the top of his. She was forgiving him and he was pleading for her to do so. In this one moment of clarity for both of their souls, they were permitted this time to clearly see each other and offer love from one to another.

No matter what happened next, who he would have to answer to for his actions, *she* had shown him clemency and forgiven him with love. His love for her had been sincere and his remorse offered in earnest.

Genevieve took Noble's hand in hers and Valor looked over at him, his immortal blue eyes looking upon his younger brother gently.

"I love you," Noble whispered and Valor brought his hand to his lips and extended his hand out, showing the feeling was reciprocated. He then looked at Genevieve and smiled at her. Perhaps he knew what she had been through and what she had learned of him. But more than anything she felt he was happy that she was taking care of his brother and she smiled back at him.

And in an instant the light was gone and the dust swept up where their spirits had just been standing. Marjorie's body was still slumped in the chair and somehow it was beautifully fitting, for she was the last ruin of Claremonde.

Chapter Twenty Five

The winter was a cold one and two months after Marjorie Atherton died and the bodies of Valor's girls had been taken from Claremonde, stillness settled on the frosted grounds.

Sitting on the bed in Noble's childhood bedroom, the feeling in the centuries old mansion was one of joy and revival since Valor's ghost had concluded his reign.

Genevieve was wearing a beautiful blue dress, fitted at the waist with a cross over bodice and flared chiffon skirting. But she held a blue knit shawl around her cool arms even though the fireplace had been lit, the first time in fourteen years.

Simon rested at her feet and her and Noble had just finished breakfast there, having spent considerable time the prior day with one of the maids trying to work out how to use the oversized stove in another wing's kitchen.

There was so much yet to explore and now, without so many eyes watching, it was something she looked forward to even more. But now Noble wanted to come with her more, to learn more about his own history piece by piece.

She had read the remainder of Valor's journals. While he never admitted completely that he killed the women, he spoke of some deep regrets. He said he did things that his mother and siblings would be ashamed of and he was not able to understand why he was the way he was.

He wanted to change, he wanted to start again and re-begin his history having not harmed anyone, but he did not trust himself to refrain long. And so it was the day of the fire, his last entry mentioned a porcelain girl.

She awaits me and I will bathe her and awaken her and she will be still. Her pale skin will glisten in the water and her flame hair will alight the blue. Her soft youthful lips will quietly allow her breathe to escape and there they will remain open, not a word spoken.

Her serenity will be my ecstasy and in white satin she will be wrapped and red roses will complete her portrait.

But for me, there is no peace. When shall I have my last breathe and what will I see and feel? If God awaits what will he do with me? I will be too late for redemption but still brilliant enough to salvage.

Let this day bring hope, for all, for me.

He died that day in the fire, choosing to stay in Claremonde as the ancient timbers fell. His last act was one of courage and sacrifice and so, perhaps there was hope for him, they wouldn't know until they themselves died one day.

A steady rain began to fall and she could hear it echo out downstairs in the main waiting area. But she was dressed beautifully, her hair was done in thick ringlets, her smile unwavering and she felt like royalty.

It wasn't the house or the grandeur or the gold leaf on everything she touched; it was contentment and hope and love that made her feel that way. Walking over to the window, she parted the curtains and could just make out the edge of the cemetery from behind a large cluster of trees.

The girl's bodies had been removed but the police still returned on occasion, looking for clues, searching for answers. They had finally come to tell them that they believed Valor wholly responsible for the women's deaths and after looking through Claremonde, which took a week, they were satisfied they had accounted for all of his victims.

Most of the girl's parents were deceased but a couple of their siblings wanted to talk to Noble. They had questions, he thought they might want compensation too, but he employed legal representation and slowly but surely the scandal lost wind.

Marjorie's funeral, by her own request, had been an intimate affair and she had ensured that John would inherit the entirety of the Atherton estate. He had visited twice already, opening up to the world and wanting to know more about life in general. Noble had warmed to him, especially seeing his brother's face in the young man and knowing this was like a second chance in a way.

While it was a long road ahead, it never looked sunnier for either of them. Hope painted everything in the hue of the sun and daylight was greeted with exuberance and want again.

Sensing someone's eyes on her, she turned to see Noble standing in the doorway, leaning up against it. They had decided to dress fancily this day, the first day of the rest of their lives.

He wore a tailored Victorian suit with a blue flower in his vest pocket to match her dress. They were going into Wanderling for lunch and while he was hesitant about the reactions of others to his scars, he was genuinely unconcerned.

"Clemens tells me they have left Claremonde cemetery and will not return there," he said, talking about the investigators.

"You should have asked them to stay," she said straightly. "They could help me clean downstairs."

Laughing, he glanced back at where the open space below the wide staircase was. Yesterday they held a special celebration there with Henny and Clemens and John and all of the Claremonde staff. But it had left a lot for her to reorganize, even though she was more than happy for the task.

"What will you do now, Lord McKinley?" she asked as he walked over to her.

Simon jumped off of the bed and sniffed at him and then followed him over to her as they stood looking out of the window.

Drawing in close to her, his hand on her face, he sighed as he breathed her in. "I have decided I will spend this fortnight with my wife. We will make love and eat breakfast all day and we will gaze at each other in mutual adoration."

Smirking, she placed her hand on his as it was warm, pressed against her face. "Who is this wife of yours?"

"Lady McKinley," he replied straightly as she laughed. "I have somehow convinced her to marry me and never leave. I do believe she has been the losing party in the gamble, but for now she is appeased."

Smiling, she had never wanted to look into someone's eyes so often. It was as if the warmth emanated from him in such a way she wanted to dive into him, heart and soul. "I am glad we held the wedding here," she said quietly. "I feel your mother was here. I feel your ancestors and perhaps even Valor had been allowed the time to see us."

Studying her face, occasionally she saw doubt in his eyes, the old belief that the scars robbed him of all he had to offer, but it happened less now. "Are you happy, Genna?"

"Only on Mondays," she replied plainly. "And then for the remainder of the week I am merely content."

Laughing, he brought her hand up to kiss it and then moved in to kiss her on her lips, forceful with passion.

Lingering in his embrace, she sighed as he held his lips there and finally he pulled away to question her. "Are you afraid to be happy?" he asked genuinely. "Tell me, does it frighten you?"

Thinking about it, she loved that he searched her like a book, reading every line twice. He wanted to know her thoughts and feelings and he had a way of lifting them up from her.

"Yes," she replied honestly. "Happiness is a great responsibility. When you are too high in the clouds you risk the greater fall. But you give me courage to try it. You make me feel that perhaps I am not in jeopardy."

"You are not, Genevieve," he assured her, moving closer as he placed both his hands on her face. "I have never known my heart better than when you revived it. I love you in a way that I depend on your approval and your opinion and your wisdom and your laughter. You are not at risk, for I will love you always. And should I die, then I will continue to love you after then."

Having seen all she had in her life, she never thought that such a love could truly exist but in this moment she could not see that it was impossible at all. She could love him now and beyond mortality, strolling through the old halls of Claremonde when they were ghosts together, youthful and eternal.

"I henceforth promise to share my cloud with you."

Bringing her into his embrace, he kissed the side of her head and then again, fervently on her lips. "Yes, always Genevieve McKinley, my bride, my immortal beloved. And it will be wildly amusing and blissfully adventurous."

Laughing she thought of when she saw him in his youth and that playful nature had returned in him and it echoed her own nature. "Then I shall be happy on Tuesdays also. But what will we do after our fortnight in each others arms, pray tell?"

Staring out of the window at the gloomy cold skies, all they could feel was the inviting hearth of the fire and the sensation of good memories in the making. "We will become older and we will plant flowers and raise Clemens together."

Laughing loudly, she brought his scarred hand up to her lips and kissed it. "And so it shall be."

Suddenly the sound of footsteps ran up the staircase and down the hall, stopping just before approaching the doorway. "May I enter?" Clemens asked, perhaps worried about their modesty.

"Please do, Clemens," Noble called back. "You will sit with us on our lunch will you not?" he offered the younger man as he came into sight.

Worry was in his face, he too was dressed in a nice fitting black suit and matching hat, but he appeared to have encountered something. "Yes, I would be pleased to," he replied sincerely. "But I know there is some time before then. If there was something I was concerned about that I believe you should be aware of, would you prefer that I withheld it from you so you can enjoy being married a while?"

Laughing, Noble, placed his hand on Genevieve's shoulder as he bent to pat Simon's head. "I will always enjoy being married, Clemens. If there is a conflict you would like to make me aware of, that will not detract from my happiness; I assure you."

Smiling, the genial driver nodded, but then he sighed. "There was a room on the upper floor, the one above here that was used for the display of Claremonde's history, particularly that of your ancestors and especially their marriage commemorations and such. I had a special gift for you both and placed it up there for you to find."

"You did?" Genevieve asked. "What is it? Clemens you always make me smile."

He nodded but seemed distracted. "I will show you, but when I was up there I heard someone walking and I thought it was one of you so I went looking for whoever it was in Lord McKinley's room."

"My father?" Noble asked seriously.

"Yes," Clemens confirmed as Simon went towards him with a wagging tail. "And I did not see directly but when I went to speak to you, you were not there. No one was, but I heard more walking in the hall and I rushed out into the hall to look."

"I don't think I could be so brave," Genevieve admitted. "You are getting better at the fearlessness."

He smiled, flattered but shaking his head. "Will you come up?"

They readily agreed and the three of them, with Simon rushing up ahead of them, ascended the polished carpeted staircase to the top floor, one that Genevieve had not really investigated yet.

He took them into the room he spoke of and she noticed that he had gotten a painted portrait done of them both, her and Noble, standing in the gardens and smiling with Simon at their side.

They were both extremely grateful and Genevieve could not imagine a better gift. It was a sign, it was a confirmation that she was now truly a part of Claremonde's history, and this solidified the notion and brought it life.

But then Clemens pointed at where he had followed the footsteps into the hall. He said for a brief glimpse he saw the back of a man and when the man turned, he only noticed a medallion of some kind on his coat.

He had been wearing old fashioned clothing centuries old he believed and he only had the faintest glimpse of him, leaving him to doubt he saw him at all, but then when he returned to the room, he noticed the medallion on the table not far from the portrait.

He gave it to Noble, and they followed him into his father's room as he sifted through the drawers of his tall old desk. Pulling out some papers, he took it to them.

Instead of being deterred, he was enthusiastic, expressing that the three of them would soon have more to look into.

"The medallion belonged to my father's father, Foster McKinley," he explained. "He wore it when they executed him. He was accused of treason for his political beliefs but it was thought afterwards that he had been falsely accused. There was talk that his sister had wanted him out of her way and it has remained a talking point in our family."

Genevieve stared at the bed Randolph, the tyrant father and poison victim, had once slept in. The world kept turning, history kept churning over new stories, unique and similar and yet without cessation.

While it scared her greatly, she could not help but be infected by the curious glee in her husband's eyes and the ideas that Clemens was quick to offer.

"I suppose there are more spirits here that need resolution," she said, taking Noble's hand in hers. "Perhaps it is up to us to help as many as we can."

Clemens clapped his hands together and began to leave the room. "We should go see his grave before we go to lunch!" he stated exuberantly as he entered the old hall.

They walked out laughing as Simon licked her hand and jumped on Noble before rushing to catch up with their inquisitive driver.

"You impress me beyond words, Genna," Noble said, wrapping his arms around her and sighing. "Your willingness to battle the dark halls so you can bring peace to another lost spirit. You have resurrected me, utterly."

Holding him close, she closed her eyes and thanked God for every blessing inside of her. She could never have imagined things would end this way but she was glad that by some strange hand of fate, she was sent here.

"I simply pulled you from the ruins, Lord McKinley," she said, placing her hands on his face and sighing the kind of sigh one does when all of their wishes become reality. "In the end, we saved each other."

Made in the USA
Columbia, SC
18 March 2021

34211847R00164